# I CHOOSE YOU

Natalie Wilson

**KDP**

Copyright © 2024 Natalie Wilson

All rights reserved

The characters and events portrayed in this book are fictitious. Any similarity to real persons, living or dead, is coincidental and not intended by the author.

No part of this book may be reproduced, or stored in a retrieval system, or transmitted in any form or by any means, electronic, mechanical, photocopying, recording, or otherwise, without express written permission of the publisher.

ISBN:9798329347494

Cover design by: Darren Baldwin
Printed in the United Kingdom

# CONTENTS

Title Page
Copyright
Prologue
Monday   1
Tuesday   45
Wednesday   65
Thursday   104
Friday   145
Saturday   175
Sunday   208
Monday   230
Tuesday   248

# PROLOGUE

A wise man once said, "Life is like a box of chocolates, you never know what you're gonna get." Boy, did he hit the proverbial nail on the head with that one. I wonder if he knew then what a sickly sweet and accurate analogy that was? Take my life for example, one minute everything was great, some might say it was coming up Roses (excuse the chocolatey pun). It was a delightful combination of soft centre caramels and milk chocolate ganache. Work was good, my love life was blossoming and the BMI calculator on my phone assured me that I was not in any mortal danger from 'lifestyle diseases', a miracle given my penchant for anything deep fried and covered in sugar. And then one day – BOOM! Just when I was confident enough not to need to refer to the little contents card stuck to the lid of the box, I was blindsided by a heinous Turkish Delight masquerading as a benign Walnut Whip.

I guess life is like that though. It lulls you into a false sense of security. It gives you enough of the good stuff so that you fail to see the crap hurtling towards you (or in this case, being stuffed into your mouth). It distracts you with a heady mix of unctuous milk chocolate and crunchy praline, so that you forget that you are only ever one unpalatable strawberry cream away from disaster. One day you are skipping through fields of golden honeycomb, one of life's winners, the next, you are rolling around on the floor, clutching at your throat, trying to expel the pink, perfumed gloop you mistakenly ingested. From hero to zero in one fell swoop.

And just when you think life cannot get any worse, it manages to pull off a feat even Satan would be proud of. Whilst sitting back and laughing sadistically at your discomfort, it orchestrates a scenario far worse than anything you could imagine; far worse than death and even more deplorable than forcing you to consume a whole bar of 100% dark chocolate. But what could be that bad? What could possibly be worse than the intense, bitter, almost acrid taste of pure cacao? I'll tell you what. Having to choose between the last two chocolates in the box, both of which you have deciphered are varying types of toffee, and therefore, both of which you love. How on God's earth are you supposed to choose between two things that although technically different, are so remarkably similar? Which one do you snaffle up yourself and which one do you politely offer to your friend? The one which you have eaten multiple times before and therefore know its flavour profile and just how comforting it can be, or the one that somehow, you missed until now, but its look, and description alludes to something divine, something truly mouth-watering. Which one should be the winner, the safe, familiar option or the riskier, unknown quantity? "Go on sucker, choose. You can't have both so which one's it gonna be?" taunts life from its vantage point nearby.

Is there a lesson lurking somewhere in all of this, a hidden message perhaps? And if so, what is it? Is it the universe's cruel way of teaching us mere mortals that with chocolates, as in life, there is always a choice to make, that bad things happen to good people (blah blah blah), or is it something far more basic, like always read the label? Twenty-nine and a half years and about the same number of chocolates in, and I'll be damned if I know the answer.

# MONDAY

The shrill, incessant beep of the alarm sounded at 5.30am sharp, dragging me kicking and screaming from my glorious slumber and dumping me unceremoniously into an already sticky and unseasonably muggy June Monday morning. With my eyes half welded together, and my brain not yet fully engaged, I hauled myself from my sweaty pit, cackhandedly threw on my running gear and made my way downstairs. One day, I would fail to navigate this treacherous alley littered with clothes, bike wheels and other bits and pieces found commonly in a skip and would end up headfirst in the wash basket which sat patiently on the bottom step, waiting for me to take it back to my room. Luckily for me though, today was not that day, and I glided past every obstacle and potential threat to life with the grace and elegance of a gazelle (or that of a newborn foal, it was hard to tell given that I was still half asleep). I veered briefly off course to grab my earbuds and water bottle and then headed straight for the front door and out into the waiting world beyond.

Now one might assume, as I had naively done before moving to London, that at 5.40am on a Monday morning, the streets would be calm and people-free. But as Julia Roberts in Pretty Woman once proclaimed, "Big mistake. Big. Huge!" because in our newly discovered, post pandemic world, every Londoner and their dog was embracing (or at least pretending to embrace) a new, healthier lifestyle. This meant that days started earlier – much earlier. The fact that we were now four years down the line, and Covid was nothing but a blip in our rear-view mirror had done nothing to alleviate Average Joe's fear of being judged by this relatively new brand of superfood eating human. I am loathed to admit it, but I too had found myself falling victim to the odd toxic green looking juice and succumbing to at least one vegan chicken salad (do not even get me started on my general stance on vegan meat alternatives!).

Call me old fashioned, but I was raised to believe that a little bit of what you fancy will not hurt you. If you want a chocolate bar, knock yourself out. Fancy a bottle of wine? Er…hello, let me open that for you! Craving a chicken nugget? DO NOT. I REPEAT, DO NOT invite Linda McCartney to the party! (I mean, honestly, how many birds did she really think she was saving, everyone knows that meat-free chicken nuggets contain only a fraction less chicken than the real McCoy).

No. In general, I am proud to say that I am the kind of girl that if given the choice between a large portion of fries with my Big Mac, or a bag of carrot sticks, the latter would have about as much chance of being ordered as a block of flax seed encrusted tofu (which is absolutely no chance at all, just in case I need to clarify). Do not however, let my love of a chocolate covered biscuit or tendency to 'go large' at a drive-thru fool you. I am not unhealthy (per se). In fact, because of my love of running, and due to the excessive number of times I walk to and from the loo at work (to check Facebook and Instagram away from prying eyes, rather than due to a nasty urinary infection or weak bladder), my average daily step count is impressive. I am therefore extremely comfortable with my weekly carb intake and my inability to turn down a glazed doughnut or six at the office on a Friday.

I believe that as with anything in life, it is all about balance and moderation. It is okay to indulge in diabetic inducing treats (unless of course you already suffer from diabetes, then it is probably not advisable) so long as you counteract that with doing something which is good for you. My something good is running. For me, going for a run is about more than avoiding heart failure and cankles, it is a form of therapy. It makes me happy, and I have embraced my early morning jogs around the city wholeheartedly since moving from Oxfordshire five years ago. They help me to clear my mind and focus me for the day ahead. Most of all though, running gives me a sense of peace. Peace to accept whatever has happened and whatever will be. No amount of clean eating or juice detoxing can guarantee the same benefits. Plus, it is far cheaper than a David Lloyd membership, which I was dangerously close to getting after indulging in a particularly bountiful Chinese take away one evening. I had to remind myself that putting on a full face of makeup just to go and sweat it off again in a room hot enough to give Satan's armpit a run for its money, surrounded by scantily clad strangers, there on the pretence of getting fit, but who ultimately saw the gym as an extension of their Tinder app, was a hard no.

Instead, I choose to revel in the solitude that running outside provides, and the sense of freedom it gives. Knowing that even if only for a fleeting moment each day, I am the master of my own destiny, the one in control of the direction my life takes, the captain of my ship, the CEO of my choices. I have always found it utterly amazing that even as I am bounding down a bustling street full of noise and distractions, the sense of calm and purpose which floods my body drowns out the surrounding chaos. It is just me and the rhythmical pounding of my feet against the pavement which reverberates around my body like the steady beat of a drum – or at least that is what Google suggested I imagine when I looked up 'How to regulate your breathing whilst running'.

Today, in the stifling early morning heat, the only place I wanted to run to was the park, where I knew the trees would still be gently swaying, where the residual moisture in the freshly cut grass would dampen the fabric of my trainers and seep through to my toes, and where if I was lucky, I would pass the family of swans who had recently taken up residence on the boating lake.

I pulled the door quietly to on my house, being careful not to wake my housemates, and set off along the road in search of some calm.

Today, more than ever I needed a clear head. It was imperative that I was focused and could block out unwanted distractions. But as I passed other running enthusiasts (or potential imposters, it was so hard to distinguish between the two these days), I could not help but wonder what they might be running to or from. What was their reason for being out here? Were they just getting their steps in, or were they preparing for a big week ahead like me? Everyone had their own agenda, but as per the unspoken rules of engagement, everyone kept their gaze focused on an unidentified fixed point in the distance, seemingly blind to the people around them. Curious but unperturbed, I bounded onwards, focusing on the metaphor that was Google's beating drum.

As a marketing manager at Taylor Marketing Ltd., I had spent the past few months devising a huge campaign for a property investment corporation who were looking to launch a new product. If we pulled it off, it was the kind of contract that would mean a huge payday for our company and was sure to get everyone involved some well-deserved recognition for their efforts. I had taken the lead on countless projects, but the level of pressure surrounding this pitch was unlike anything I had experienced before. I guessed it was due to the potential revenue associated with it, but that did not help quell the sicky feeling that resided deep in my stomach. It had been months in the making, and the whole team had devoted many man-hours to get it to where it was. It had been a real collective effort, everyone playing a vital and equal role. This was the week that we were finally going to be presenting our ideas to the board of directors at LJT Investment Ltd., and the feeling of impending doom was almost suffocating. I knew that the next few days were going to be nothing short of hell. For a brief second, I contemplated doing a Forest Gump, continuing on my run indefinitely, ending up in Land's End or John O'Groats (depending on which route I took) blistered and sunburnt, with leg hair long enough to plait and an inexcusably angry looking monobrow, an army of followers jogging silently behind me keen to know my back story. It was only the fear of not keeping up with my pension and NI contributions which persuaded me to head back in the direction of home and a regular pay cheque. Sometimes, all that was needed to pull myself out of a funk, was a stern talking to, a few good slaps around the face and the threat of no wine for a week, and I was good. This time was different. I could not shake the nagging feeling of doubt which threatened to overrun everything. The fact of the matter was it was crap. Not the part about us all being equal and valued (we all know that is just a line pedalled by HR departments to help with employee morale), but the part about LJT's product. It was a steaming pile of excrement.

In a nutshell, they had developed a new property portal app (the word 'new' giving the incorrect impression that it was somehow ground-breaking and innovative). The app allowed a person to advertise a house, apartment or commercial outlet, and then enabled others to enter an online bidding system whereby they could then purchase those properties. The aim was to have the entire buying and selling process contained within one central location, eliminating the need for external third parties such as estate agents, solicitors, and financial advisor. The idea was simple, but in reality, it was a GDPR nightmare waiting to happen (and dare I say it, a bit of a rip-off of another online bidding platform already in existence). Despite all its shortcomings and my overwhelming lack of enthusiasm for it, it was my job to suck it up and sell our ideas to LJT, giving them and every other sucker on the planet the impression that we whole heartedly believed in their shitty app. Why was it so important to do this? Why was I willing to go against my instincts and better judgement? Why was I prepared to put my principles aside? Money of course. So that we could make the bigwigs of both company's inordinate sums of money. So that they and their shareholders could continue to lavish their mistresses with unnecessarily expensive gifts, keep their spoilt, ungrateful children in private education, and keep their wives quiet. It was as clear as day that I was guilty of facilitating this abhorrent world full of greed, excess, debauchery, and wrongdoing, but what else could I do? A girl's gotta eat right?

I was yanked from my daydream by a portly, middle-aged man on a bike, yelling at me to wake up and pay attention because I had nearly caused an accident by running out in front of him. That was followed by something that sounded faintly like did I have a fucking death wish, which I found slightly ironic, given that it was him who was bombing around the streets of London on a flimsy pedal bike, and not me. Nevertheless, I smiled my best shit eating grin and swiftly raised my middle finger in his direction before carrying on my way home. No man clad head to toe in fluorescent pink Lycra, looking like an engorged penis was going to drag me down today. I needed to be focused; a laser guided missile. I, Jemma Lucas was a badass bitch who was going to nail this week at work and change the world in the process. Or at least make it through to Friday alive, and ideally without my P45 in hand.

I reached the faded and peeling front door of home in nearly record time *(yay me!)*. The others were chatting animatedly in the kitchen, but as I was already running behind schedule, I offered my apologies, bypassed them, and headed straight upstairs to the bathroom, leaving my water bottle next to my wash basket. "I'll move it later" I promised myself. Turning on the decades old shower, I let the lukewarm water cascade down over my body, cooling my muscles, whilst grabbing the bottle of inexcusably expensive shower gel a client had given me a few months back. The luxurious ablution was on its last legs, and I was in two minds whether to save it for a special occasion or use it and try and tap them up for another bottle. I decided instantly to go for the latter and surreptitiously squeezed the remaining contents into my palms, rubbing them together vigorously to lather up a pillowy foam. Utter bliss. It gave the sensation of my legs being as soft as satin (despite my five-day old stubble having made an appearance). It was true what they said, sometimes, buying expensive things (or accepting expensive gifts) was justifiable.

Once showered, I donned my pretty floral blouse, tucking it into a high wasted camel pencil skirt, which I paired with my faithful nude KG heels, loosely tied my hair in a bun, added a bit of blush, mascara and some of my new pink Chanel lip gloss, sprayed some perfume with gay abandon and then made my way back down the stairs through the gauntlet of death, whilst ordering an Uber. The nearest one was ten minutes away, plenty of time to get the first coffee of the day under my belt. Sarah, Claire, and Ben had vacated the kitchen already, leaving behind in their wake a litany of dirty dishes and debris. I adored my friends and would never want to live anywhere else, with anyone else, but my god they were feral. I had been saying for months now that we needed to invest in a dishwasher, but they all agreed that it was not necessary, that they would much rather spend the money on takeaways or eating out which would in turn help reduce the number of dirty dishes we created. I could see some logic in what they said but not enough to think it was a plausible idea. Needless to say, we had now spent the equivalent cost of a dishwasher on take aways, and the dishes were once again stacked high on every inch of the wooden counter. I filled the kettle, found my Thermos coffee mug in one of the cupboards, and managed to gingerly nudge a pile of cereal bowls a couple of inches to the right so that I could make my drink. One heaped teaspoon of coffee granules, three sugars and a large glug of semi skimmed milk later, and I was stood there stirring the heavenly mixture, savouring the aroma that wafted up from the silver vessel. I tightened the lid, grabbed a biscuit from the jar on the windowsill and headed outside to wait for my cab.

Mum said my Ubers were an unnecessary luxury, and that my generation was solely responsible for the destruction of the country's public transport network. "If more people used it, perhaps the government would invest more money in it" she barked down the phone one day when she had been left high and dry at a random station, miles from home due to cancellations. The truth was, I had always detested public transport. I could never understand the inherent need in people to make polite, inane conversation with total strangers. Not even headphones were enough to deter the most determined conversationalist. As I did this morning, I would much rather jump in the back of a cab, throw the driver a look that said, "Don't you dare try and talk to me," and wind my way through the roads to work in silence.

As the car pulled up outside the office, I was met by the usual hum of people chatting and drinking their obligatory spiced chai latte whilst walking purposefully to their destinations. Much like death and taxes, the early morning shop bought coffee was a thing of certainty around here, a rite of passage. Throwing open the door, I thanked Igor for not speaking to me during our journey and stepped out to join them, holding my Thermos aloft for all to see – I was a rebel in more ways than one!

Like most commercial buildings in the city these days, our office was ultra-modern, sparce and quite indistinguishable from all the others surrounding it. It rose from the ground like a grey monolith, clambering skywards trying desperately to reach the piercing blue above. Inside, it was just as stark. I yearned for a bit of wood panelling or the odd high back leather armchair, some warmth and respite from the cold monochrome colour scheme, a nod to the history of the company, an acknowledgement that it was born in an era pre-dating facial recognition and carbon neutral heating systems. *Hey-ho, it is what it is*, I mused as I flashed my pass over the electronic turnstile and headed across the foyer to the lift, following in the path of hundreds of other mindless lemmings who had made the same fateful journey that morning. Surprisingly, one was waiting for me (a lift that is, not a lemming). I hit the button for the twenty second floor and then as per the lift etiquette handbook, stared blankly at the ground a few feet in front of me, ignoring the handful of other people around me doing the same, as we made our way methodically through the floors, stopping periodically to let people out. After a while, the little green light on the number twenty-two button illuminated, accompanied by the sound of a joyful ping, and the doors sprung back energetically to welcome me back to my second home. As if responding to a war cry, I gathered my thoughts, held my head high and strode into battle, weaving through the masses until I reached my desk. So well-rehearsed was I in this morning routine, that I was able to do it completely automatically and without thinking. I placed my bag neatly under my desk, switched on the monitor (whilst taking another swig from my coffee), checked the phone for messages and then nonchalantly tapped in my eight-digit password to log in. All the while, scrolling through the emails on my mobile just in case I had received any in the last five seconds which I might have missed. The word monotonous did not even cover it.

My screen came to life and an email sent with 'high importance' flashed up. It was from my new boss Jake.

**From: Jake Bales**
**To: Jemma Lucas**
**Subject: LJT Investment Ltd – Thursday's pitch**
**Sent: Today at 8.33am**

**Morning Jemma,**

**Please can we make some time to sit down and run through the pitch before Thursday? Let me know what works best for you and I'll check my diary.**

**Jake**

My stomach lurched at the sight of it and beads of sweat sprang from every orifice. *Is it normal for ears to sweat?* It was the same reaction I had whenever I received an email from him, or there was any interaction between the two of us, come to think of it. My stomach would churn, my legs would turn to jelly, and my mouth would go as dry as one of Ghandhi's flipflops and do all sorts of inexplicably embarrassing things. Last Wednesday for example, when grabbing lunch orders, I had casually asked him if he would prefer tuna, cheese or me in a sandwich. Obviously, I was not intending to offer myself up to him between two slices of bread, but the way his eyes held me intently as I reeled off the options, had me feeling all discombobulated. *What would it be like to be eaten by him? Stop it! Stop it!* Luckily for me, he very politely went for the tuna option, sparing me any further blushes (and damp underwear). I did not know whether my inability to act normally around him was due to the way he looked (insanely gorgeous), because of his personality (which I found incredibly intimidating in a charming sort of way), or both.

Today was no different. I could not say how long I sat there staring at him, all I know is that when I spotted him leaving his office out the corner of my eye, my coffee was still piping hot, and I only had three unanswered emails in my inbox. By the time I had been pulled up on my stalkerish tendencies, the coffee was on the cold side of lukewarm and my inbox had grown exponentially to fifty-three, not to mention the fact that the red flashing light on my answer phone was screaming angrily at me, meaning that somehow, I had also failed to notice the phone ringing.

He had only been here two months, but already Jake Bales had caused a stir in the office. Brought in because of his reputation for being a ruthless negotiator and general hard ball when it came to high profile, high value contracts, he had been offered the role of Chief Executive over and above others older and arguably more experienced at the company who had seen the job as theirs. Regardless of this, he prowled the office in his trademark, predatory, alpha male way, overseeing proceedings with a confidence and charisma unmatched by anyone. He knew he was the man for the job, and now, it seemed, so did everyone else. Despite his enviable credentials (professional and dare I say physical), productivity levels within the office had fallen off the edge of a cliff (I can confirm that no lemmings were hurt in the process). No woman, or man come to think of it was oblivious to his presence and charm. I too was not impervious to his masculinity and beautiful face (clearly, given that my email count was now nearing seventy). In the short space of time that he had been with us, what negative impact he had had on work rate, he had more than made up for with his impact on the physical appearance of the workforce.

It may have been my imagination, but the office now smelt more like a bowl of my nan's potpourri than an active place of work. The idea that a bit of roll-on deodorant was sufficient to keep the stench of hard graft from our artificially air-conditioned office had gone straight out the window. Suddenly, everyone was all Dior this and Gucci that. If I carried on spraying at my current rate, my fresh and fruity Chloe eau de parfum would be all out by the end of the week, and I would be smelling all kinds of fruity, and not particularly fresh. Not only did everyone smell like they were going on a night out, but they dressed like it too. Gone were the sensible office flats, and the 'please take me seriously' below the knee skirt and jacket combos. Now, everyone was rocking a pair of six-inch killer heels and a dress that they would need to be physically cut out of once they got home. Anything that might help to catch his eye and take home the prize. Even the men were guilty of making too much of an effort. Never, had I seen so many slim fitting shirts and ankle grazing trousers in one room, and I was sure that expenditure on male grooming products had gone through the roof since his arrival. The Jake Bales effect was immense. As a marketing company, if we could have bottled it, we would have made a fortune. You either wanted to be him or be with him. There was no middle ground.

Helene was the only exception to this rule, the only human in the office who seemed completely indifferent towards him. We had accused her of being crazy, of not being 'normal' but instead, she had cited the menopause, and her resulting dry vagina and involuntary mood swings for not wanting to 'bump uglies' with anyone – not Jake, and certainly not her long-suffering husband Richard. The self-proclaimed 'mother' of the group had a way with words that was most unbefitting of her role, something which I was convinced she revelled in. Helene's shock and awe tactics were most definitely the reason nobody in the office dared approach her, hence she was able to go about her work unbothered and unchecked – unlike the rest of us. I envied her. When I grew up, I wanted to be just like her (minus the dry vagina, obviously).

"How can one man be so damn beautiful?" I sighed. It was a rhetorical question; I was not really expecting anyone to be able to give me an explanation for his god like appearance. He was a heavenly mixture of a younger version of Hugh Jackman from The Greatest Showman (his eye and hair colouring), Thor, the God of Thunder (his rippling muscles) and a little bit of Hugh Grant (his 'Britishness'). He had impeccable manners though, so maybe the Hugh from Notting Hill rather than Bridget Jones, who let's face it, was a bit of an arse, even if still worthy of a 'shag' (his terminology not mine).

"Oh, please! I thought you had more about you than the rest of the airheads in this place" Helene scolded, whipping round in her chair so that she could chastise me face to face. "Women have spent how many decades fighting for the right to vote, for the right to be equals, and you sit there fawning over some man like a simpering wench who would give it all up for five overrated minutes in a dark store cupboard with him." She looked utterly disappointed in me. "Do not confuse beauty with worth, Jemma, it will be the undoing of you, mark my words. I can assure you that Jake Bales is entirely human, and if Debbie from accounting is right, he is currently dealing with a very nasty case of genital warts courtesy of his most recent dalliance with a very pretty, but very stupid young girl from HR." Clearly, she was not suffering fools gladly this morning – much like every other morning. I made a mental note not to do anything to piss her off this week. I needed her as an ally, not a foe.

"I'm not confusing beauty with worth, and I'm very thankful to have the vote actually!" I said defensively, instantly recalling how I had failed to vote in the last general election because I had chosen to attend a last-minute nail appointment instead. "I just think we should all be able to appreciate a good-looking man … or woman when we see one. You can't deny that the man is a walking, talking Greek God!" I continued undeterred.

She shook her head in defeat, her grey hair swishing from side to side. "Well don't come to me for a lift to the sexual health clinic when he's finished with you and all that's left of your sordid encounter are some angry warts on your flaps!" she warned with a dire expression. "Greek God or not, an STI is an STI whatever the nationality of the person giving it to you. The warts aren't any prettier just because they're European."

"Oh jeez, I'd forgotten how crass you could be! You're supposed to be the more sophisticated one out of all of us!" I joked, almost choking on a mouthful of cold coffee.

"You mean I'm old" she fired back in an instant.

"No, that's not what I meant at all, although I'm not sure if at fifty-four you should be brandishing the word 'flaps' around willy nilly!"

"Don't be such a prude Jemma, a dick's a dick, there's no need to blush over it." I had no comeback, other than that I strongly disagreed that all dicks were the same. I had not seen a lot, but I had seen enough to know that they were not all cast the same. I instantly wondered what Jake's willy looked like. I imagined it was well proportioned, straight as a die and quite attractive - as attractive as those things could be. I also envisaged it being exceptionally clean which was a huge thing in my book – although the warts were obviously not ideal. But there was cream for that right?

"Did somebody say Adonis?" Effie dragged herself painstakingly across the floor on her wheelie chair. Her towering stilettoes and bodycon dress made the six-foot journey look more like a treacherous voyage across the Antarctic than a quick scoot between desks. If it were a crime to be too young, too pretty and too stupid, she would be guilty as charged and banged to rights on all counts, but she was also extremely sweet, inoffensive, and quite frankly the source of much of our daily entertainment. In that respect, she was a very valued member of the team. Her father also happened to be on the board of directors here, so there was no chance of her leaving anytime soon. Nepotism ran rife at Taylor Marketing.

She looked at Helene seriously. "Adonis, he's the Spanish looking guy from Love Island, right? He's so fit, plus he has nearly one million followers on Instagram, he's absolutely smashing it since leaving the villa!" Helene looked skyward as if beaconing someone to come down and slap some common sense into our nineteen-year-old trainee.

"I wouldn't know" she said exasperated. "I've never watched a single episode of that trash in my life and have absolutely zero intention of ever doing so in the future. Maybe you'd be better off watching something on National Geographic occasionally rather than obsessing over a bunch of braindead, bikini-clad Barbie dolls and their even thicker Ken doll counterparts" she suggested in a tone which was quite literally oozing sarcasm and contempt. Effie, stared blankly at the back of her head, unappreciative of just how cutting the remark was. Now was not the time to admit that I had become quite addicted to the series over recent years and was heavily invested in the potential futures of several of the couples outside the villa. I physically wept when Millie and Liam won in 2021. Admittedly, I had not been as keen on Ekin-Su and Davide, there was a limit to just how good looking a couple should be.

Effie had already switched off and had turned her attention to the next distraction, poking her way around a Graze box which sat at the edge of my desk. A client had sent it in as a gift. A kind gesture, agreed, but I could honestly say that I had not so much as even looked at it since the day it arrived, choosing instead to rely on the coffee shop downstairs for my mid-morning snacks. It was not that nuts, seeds and unidentifiable yoghurt covered dried fruits were not for me, on the contrary, there was a time and place for everything, but when at work, I required caffeine, carbs and sugar in equal measure, and a stale piece of dried banana did not hit the spot like a cream cheese laden bagel or an unctuous triple choc chip muffin did.

"One double shot, full fat latte with caramel syrup and a cinnamon bun." Claire threw a brown paper bag in my direction which I caught deftly in one hand, whilst the other one halted the paper cup which was being slid perilously close to the edge of the table.

"You're an angel. You read my mind, thank you darling, how much do I owe you?"

"Nothing, you can buy me a drink tonight!" she said with an

excited grin on her face. I looked at her uncomprehending. "You haven't forgotten that I've manged to get us a table at Sancho's, have you?" she asked, noticing the blank expression on my face.

Shit. In all honesty, I had completely forgotten, which was odd because I had been wanting to go since it opened. Sancho's launched about six months ago. Billed as a trendy Cuban wine bar and eatery, it was just off Kensington High Street, was ridiculously overpriced, and staffed with the most pretentious, self-important waiters. It was therefore exactly the type of place that every B and C list celebrity in London wanted to be seen at. Claire, bless her, had spent the best part of a week on hold trying to get a reservation, only to be told that there was currently a six-month waiting list for the 'general public'. Grudgingly, she had accepted her social status and booked a table for four on the 18th of June – today. I had been so wrapped up in work the past few weeks that it had completely slipped my mind.

"Oh Jem, you've forgotten, haven't you? Well, tough shit, Sarah and Ben are looking forward to it so you've got to come!"

"Of course, I'll come; I wouldn't miss it for the world! I'll be there with bells and whistles on, or at least my new Sophia Webster sandals!" I grinned, thinking of my beautiful new shoes sitting in their box back at home.

Claire slumped down in her chair, "Ooh, I'm so jealous! They're so pretty!" Her voice was all high pitched and girlie. "Which ones did you go for in the end?" There was a distinct look of envy and desire in her eyes – quite understandably, the shoes were majestic! Just the right amount of glamour and femininity without being too ostentatious or gaudy. They were worth every damn penny I spent on them (although I still could not bring myself to say the figure aloud for fear of my bank manager overhearing and demanding I return them to clear my overdraft).

"I went for the black and purple ones. I thought they'd be more...

practical" I sang excitedly. Practical, huh! Who was I kidding? Who bought bewitching high heeled strappy sandals adorned with delicate butterfly wings to be practical? That was just a thinly veiled attempt at justifying the price tag. If they were practical, I would get frequent use of them, which reduced the cost per usage, making them a sound investment rather than an extravagant luxury I could not really afford. My mind wondered absently to the potential outfits I had in my wardrobe which would show the little beauties off to their fullest.

"Good morning ladies... Jemma, how are we today?" His voice was as smooth as silk and dripping with a self-assurance that only those either in a position of power, extremely beautiful, or both could own. My head snapped round a little too sharply, and I instinctively raised my hand to my neck to stem the shooting pain that was now surging through it. How did he do that? He was like some kind of silent ninja creeping around the office, popping up in the middle of people's conversations unannounced.

"Morning Jake" I stuttered, silently pleading with myself not to say anything stupid. *God you're gorgeous! Do you want to come out with me tonight?*

"Are you ok?" he asked, looking concerned, noticing the vice like grip with which I was holding my neck.

"Umm... yeah, I think I just pulled something in my sleep" I lied, trying to unfurl my fingers from where they clung.

A look of amusement crossed his face. "Looks painful. If you need to have someone look at it, I know a great sports physio who might be able to help you out."

*Yeah right. The last time I did any form of sports was twenty years ago in PE.* I tried to make my voice light and breezy, as if the pain that was threatening to make me black out was nothing more than a twinge. "Thanks, but I think it will be fine. I just need to stretch it out" I smiled, grabbing my head in both hands, and pulling it from side to side like an athlete warming up for a race.

My little routine seemed to humour him. "Okay, but if you change your mind just let me know." His eyes lingered a little longer on me than was necessary, and for a fleeting moment, it looked like he wanted to say something more but then changed his mind. My cheeks flamed. Everyone else seemed to revel in Jake's attention, but with me, it had the innate ability to make me come across like a complete buffoon. Remember the days as a socially awkward teenager, when every interaction with the opposite sex left you sweating, or wishing the earth would swallow you up? Well, here I am, over a decade later, still stuck in that phase. He went to walk off but then stopped. "Did you get my email about catching up at some point about the presentation?" Was that a trick question? Was he trying to catch me out? How should I respond? Did I profess to not seeing the email yet, or admit to seeing it but being too pathetic to know how to reply? Surely, as a manager, I could not openly confess to being so pitiful? How could he trust me to do my job properly if I went to pieces whenever he sent me a fricking email?

"Er, yes, sorry. I was about to come back to you. I can do whenever, so just let me know what time suits you best."

"Okay, I'll go and check my diary now and come back to you. Is everything on track?" Up close, he was mesmerising. He was proof that physical perfection was attainable, even if it was reserved for the few. His chiselled cheek bones and square jaw line made him look authoritative, the light scruff across his chin and cheeks gave a hint of something more playful, whilst his glossy hair and St. Tropez tan (which no doubt came from the place itself rather than the bottle), gave the impression that he had just stepped off a plane (probably a private jet, accompanied by a bevy of European supermodels). And then of course, there was his physique. Six foot two at least, not an ounce of fat, his body looked like it had been sculpted from marble. Even his pale blue shirt could not mask the contour of his beautiful, muscular torso underneath.

"Err……." My brain had temporarily turned to mush. *Stop staring at his chest, stop staring at his beautiful chest. Oh God, those muscles! How do you even get muscles like those?* I managed to prize my eyes away before it became too awkward (but only just). My mouth felt like it was full of cotton wool, my lips were unable to move as normal, my pupils were dilated. I was suffering from complete facial paralysis. *Do I have allergies? Did they put something different in the bun?* "Yep, of course, it's all under control" I mumbled incoherently, my tongue lapping at the side of my mouth like some kind of slobbering dog. "Claire and I were just saying how everything was coming together nicely on this. Isn't that right?" I looked pointedly over at her, begging for her input, hoping she would distract Jake so that he would not notice the shit show that was unfolding before him.

"Umm…. yes, absolutely. It's going to be great Jake. Jemma's presentation makes a compelling case for them to sign with us," she said casually wiping away the cappuccino moustache which had sat resplendently over her top lip. Clearly, she had not been prepared to participate in this conversation, but she took it all in her stride. No amount of milky froth could hold her down.

A flash of amusement darted across his face. "Great. There's a lot riding on this one. Geoff, the CEO of LJT is golf buddies with Mr Taylor, so it's imperative we land this contract, or he'll use my balls to tee off with the next time he's out on the course." *If only you knew what I would like to do with your balls.* I took a swig of my coffee and nearly choked on the thought.

"You can trust us Jake, your balls are in safe hands!" replied Claire automatically. The words left her mouth before she realised what she was saying or who she was saying them to. At least I hoped that was the case. She was often guilty of saying the first thing that came into her head, regardless of who she was speaking to.

"Thank you, that's very... reassuring!" he replied with a wry smile. "Speak to you later Jemma" he said more quietly. I looked up at his handsome face, noticing the way his lips appeared so full and soft. *I wonder what it's like to kiss him?* He turned and sauntered casually back towards his office, stopping briefly to make conversation with one of his many admirers.

I spun back round to face Claire, who was now a beetroot shade of red. "Your balls are in safe hands! What the hell was that? Who even says that? What was I thinking?" she cried.

"I'm just glad it was you that said it and not me!" I burst out laughing unsympathetically, the feeling having returned to my face now that he had left the vicinity.

"Great bloody friend you are" she moaned half-heartedly throwing her paper napkin at me and returning her head to her hands. "And are we not going to acknowledge the serious fuck me eyes he was giving you just then?" she mumbled from behind closed fingers as if that might divert some of the unwanted attention away from herself.

"Don't be daft, that's how he looks at everyone with a pair of boobs! He just sees me as the girl who is incapable of stringing a sentence together" I replied, dismissively.

"He's never looked at me like that before, and I've got a very impressive rack" Frank whined as he paused by our desks on his way back from the loo.

"Perhaps you aren't showing them off properly" Claire suggested seriously.

"Darling, I couldn't wear a smaller shirt if I tried. Any tighter and these buttons are going to throw in the towel, and I can't afford to be hit with another indecent exposure charge. Not that the last one wasn't a complete misunderstanding and a total miscarriage of justice, you understand" he added, holding his hand over his heart, as if he were testifying in court. "The guy wasn't even that hot, and who goes into a men's cubicle at a club and doesn't lock the door after himself?" Claire and I looked at each other, wondering how exactly you expose yourself by accident, but then thought it was best not to ask.

"Never mind Frank, there's a guy out there for you somewhere."

"Tell me honestly girls, what do you think my chances are with Jake, do you think he's ripe for turning?"

"I reckon you've got as much chance as any of us!" I chuckled.

Frank looked contemplative. "Maybe I could try one size smaller" he said with a twinkle in his eye, running his hands seductively over the tightly stretched fabric of his shirt. I admired the self-belief of those poor buttons; they really were putting in one hell of a shift. "See you in a while girlfriend, don't go making your move until I've had one last shot!"

"He's all yours Frank, go get him!" shouted Claire as he sashayed away like he was working the catwalk on America's Next Top Model.

"What I wouldn't give for some of his sass" I mused.

"What are you talking about? You've got way more sass and you're just as fabulous as Frank – actually, fuck that shit, you're way more fabulous than him! Plus, you don't have a criminal record which goes a long way in my book." I smiled at her appreciatively.

Claire and I had been friends since primary school, and we had done everything from ballet classes to army cadets together (the latter only lasting two weeks until we realised that following orders was not really our cup of tea). As a result of our friendship, our families had become friends. We had partied and holidayed together as if we were one big happy family. Being an only child, Claire had always been like the sister I never had and always yearned for. We were family, and that is why, when she was made redundant during the pandemic, I did all that I could to get her a job here. In fairness to her, she really did not need my help. With her master's degree in digital marketing and her accomplished resume, the role of digital marketing manager was a huge step down from her previous role as assistant marketing director, but she accepted it gratefully, and now we lived and worked together!

I returned to my computer screen in time to see another email come through sent with high importance.

**From: Jake Bales**

**To: Jemma Lucas**

**Subject: Catch up on LJT pitch**

**Sent: Today at 10.55am**

**Hi Jemma,**

**I have a few appointments already today but could do tomorrow about 11. I'll send you a diary invitation in a bit.**

**P.S The shoes sound great. Very … practical!**

**Jake**

Oh, dear God, how long had he been standing there listening to us? What exactly had he heard? "Shit!"

"What's the matter?" Claire mumbled from inside her cocoon.

"Oh, nothing. Just turns out I'm an even bigger cretin than you, that's all" I replied.

"That makes me feel a little bit better" she beamed brightly, straightening herself up and returning to her work as if her earlier blooper had never happened. How did she find it so easy to pick herself up off the floor?

Now, what was the correct way to reply to this email? Clearly, I needed to accept the time for tomorrow's catch up and acknowledge the comment about the shoes, but I could not let on that I was mortified he had overheard our conversation, or apologise for it, otherwise it would imply I had done something wrong, which I most definitely had not. Confident and resolute, that would be my response.

**From: Jemma Lucas**

**To: Jake Bales**

**Subject: Catch up on LJT pitch**

**Sent: Today at 10.58am**

**Hi Jake,**

**11am works for me. I'll make sure I have everything ready. Practical is my middle name!**

**Jemma**

Send.

**From: Jake Bales**

**To: Jemma Lucas**

**Subject: Catch up on LJT pitch**

**Sent: Today at 10.59am**

**I thought it was Louise?**

**Jake**

How the hell did he know my middle name? *Perhaps he needs it for my P45.*

**From: Jemma Lucas**

**To: Jake Bales**

**Subject: Catch up on LJT pitch**

**Sent: Today at 10.59am**

May I ask how you know my middle name?

**Jemma**

The wait for a response seemed to go on forever.

**From: Jake Bales**

**To: Jemma Lucas**

**Subject: Catch up on LJT pitch**

**Sent: Today at 11.02am**

I make a habit of running background checks on all my staff when I start a new company just in case there's any surprises!

Just kidding. I had to authorise everyone's payslips for payroll this morning. They have your full names on them.

**Jake**

Was he joking with me? I let out a relieved little chuckle. Okay, so I still had a job – for the moment at least.

The rest of the day passed uneventfully. Jake left the office for meetings in the afternoon which enabled everyone to knuckle down and get on with their work without distraction – a rarity these days, and I spent what seemed like an eternity trying to find solutions to the obvious pitfalls of LJT's app. It astounded me how so many people became millionaires off the back of such mediocre ideas. Find me someone who could create a biscuit that you could dunk without it disintegrating, and I would wholeheartedly agree that they deserved their seven or eight figure bank balance. But unlike an unsinkable Digestive, I could not see how this app was going to change lives. I wondered who had been responsible for checking whether the idea worked practically. As far as I could see, the plan raised far more questions than it answered. For example, what happened if more than one person were to bid on a property? How would the system distinguish which offer was best? Anyone could imply they were a cash buyer, but without someone to physically verify their status, how could they be certain? Sometimes, the best purchaser was not always the most obvious one, what safeguards would there be to stop the wrong person 'winning' the bid. Not to mention the question about how they intended to store people's sensitive information. Had they made inroads into developing a CRM system or were they going to use an off the shelf one? GDPR was such a huge thing these days, that the risk of losing or incorrectly storing people's data was a potential lawsuit waiting to happen. These were just a few basic questions which I had thought of. I had to keep reminding myself that it was not really my problem. At the end of the day, it was my job to package and promote the product, not worry about the legal ramifications or to determine if it had any worth. That would be the job of some other poor sod in LJT's legal and finance department to answer later down the line.

By 6pm I had finished the pitch. Somehow, I managed to suppress my personal feelings, and devised a strategy that with any luck (and I would definitely be needing some of that) would land us the deal. All I was waiting on was some data to come through on click rates and enquiry numbers for other property portals which I could then add into my PowerPoint in the morning. Now, I had a date with a Mojito or ten, and a taco. *Hang on, that's Mexican food, not Cuban. What do Cuban's eat? Please tell me they still have Mojito's?*

Claire had left early as she needed to pick up a dress from the dry cleaners for this evening, so I gathered up my bag, switched off my computer and headed off towards the lift. The office was quiet now, only a few of the most hardened, career focused individuals remained – and me. I casually hit the down button and started rooting through my bag to find my phone, my mouth watering at the thought of an ice-cold Mojito. The doors parted unexpectedly and Jake, looking as fresh as he had done at 8am this morning stepped out.

"Sorry" I said flustered, sidestepping him so as not to impede his exit and get in his way, but managing to do both simultaneously, throwing him off-guard and making us perform a crazy line dance around each other. I closed my eyes and sent up a silent prayer to the gods to make this stop. *Give me a break!*

"No need to apologise" he smiled, finishing his Cotton Eye Joe impression and coming to a standstill. "How did it go today? You all finished?"

The scent of pine trees on a winters day hung in the air. My eyes closed automatically and I breathed it in, allowing the gorgeous smell to wash over me. *Why do you have to smell so good?* He cleared his throat, and my eyes shot open. "Yep. I think it's done!" I said flustered, remembering where I was.

"Good. Well, we can run through everything in the morning, but if you need help with anything before then, just give me a shout." *Pardon?* Was he under the false impression that I went home and carried on working? A novel concept I admit, but not one I was willing to try out anytime soon. *Wait, are there actually people out there who do that? Should I be doing that? Oh God.*

"Thanks Jake, I will do. Have a good evening." I escaped into the waiting elevator and hit the ground floor button, praying the doors would close quickly so that I could finally take a breath.

"Night Jemma. Have a great time tonight. I hear the food is amazing!"

I stared at him blankly. How did he know about tonight? The look of confusion on my face must have given me away.

"I heard you talking about Sanchos earlier" he offered apologetically. A glimpse of something softer, less confident, flashed across his face, but it was so fleeting it was gone before I could fully register it. Was Jake Bales attempting to have a non-work-related conversation with me? Of course, he was not. I needed to stop fantasising about him because I would be imagining all sorts at this rate; marriage, children, a four-bed detached house in the suburbs ... *Stop it!*

"Oh, right, yes of course, thanks!" I muddled, trying to focus my mind on the present – on reality. The doors laboured shut and I began my descent to the foyer. I was exhausted. *Damn that sexy man and my traitorous lady-bits.*

❖ ❖ ❖

By the time I staggered in through the front door, the others were at least a bottle and a half of wine in. Claire greeted me wrapped in her dressing gown with full make-up and hair complete. She already looked sensational. Sarah sat crossed legged on the living room floor with a glass of wine in one hand and her straighteners in the other. It had always amazed me how she expertly managed to do those two things at once without A) spilling a drop of her wine or B) giving herself third degree burns. She had a gift, no doubt. I could hear Ben walking around upstairs, but by the time I had put my bag down and placed my Karen Millen jacket over the banister, he was halfway down the stairs.

It sounds cliché, but Ben, like Claire, was family. We had grown up next door to each other, so technically, I guess we had been friends our whole lives (although for obvious reasons I could not remember the first year or so). Ben's parents owned the local Italian restaurant, and given the long hours they worked, he had spent much of his childhood at our house. Many a night he would have dinner at ours and then end up sleeping over at the foot of my bed. At one point, mum even splashed out on a camp bed so that he could get a good night's sleep. I always felt a bit protective over him, even though he was a year older than me. He missed that traditional family upbringing that Claire and I were fortunate to have. He never once moaned though, he always said that we were like his adopted family, and that he was lucky to have two sets, that some people did not even get to have one. He had always been such a soft, kind-hearted person. As a boy, he was always rescuing some poor, stray animal, and bringing it home to our house to look after. He wanted to save the world and everything in it. When Claire and I decided to go off to university to study marketing, he took a gap year and went to Botswana to help build a village school. When we went on holiday to Ibiza, he went backpacking around eastern Europe volunteering in the orphanages with Save the Children. He was pure of heart and soul, and one of the few truly good guys to walk the earth. Nowadays, he worked for a children's charity in central London, helping disadvantaged young adults get back on their feet, helping them to find work, accommodation or finish their education. Just thinking about what he did made my heart swell with pride. He was quite literally an angel.

"Ah, there she is, what took you so long? Do you want a glass of wine?" Dressed only in a grey towel and still dripping wet from the shower, Ben bounded down the stairs towards me like a playful St. Bernard who had not seen its owner all day. He threw open his arms in a playful gesture.

"Don't even think about it, you're soaking wet!" I squealed. This only made him more determined, and he practically swept me off my feet in a huge, wet embrace. "Ben!" I shrieked, slightly miffed, although it was impossible to be truly mad with him. Physically, he had changed so much since the early days. Dad used to joke that his legs were hollow because he could eat for England but never managed to put on any weight. He had always been athletic and was on every sports team, but he was always slighter than the other boys. When he got back from Botswana, he was like a different person. I did not recognise the man we picked up from the airport, he had shot up by about two foot and filled out. He looked nothing like the young boy we had stood and emotionally waved goodbye to the previous year. "Yes please, I will have a glass" I finally replied as he put me down. He scuttled off to the kitchen dripping a trail of water behind him.

I plonked myself down on the floor next to Sarah, kissing her on the cheek "Hi darling!" She was the newest member of our tribe. We met her at university where she was studying economics. Back in the day she was fierce, and a real live wire. Thinking about it, not much had changed, she just knew how to contain the beast a little better these days.

We initially saw her at a fresher's event and bonded over apple sours and shots of tequila. In awe of her ability to drink and dance until the sun came up, and then head straight to a 9am lecture and take full and comprehensive notes, Claire and I knew she was a keeper. She was also the sole reason for me achieving my degree and for my student loan not being a complete and utter waste of money. Her love of partying had never left her, and a night out with Sarah was a guaranteed good night. Now though, instead of heading straight to a lecture, she would go and chair a meeting of her fellow brokers in the city. Of all of us, she had by far been the most successful career wise and had the best paid job. She had been in banking since leaving university and in recent years had outperformed may of her superiors and been promoted numerous times. She made the three of us look like a bunch of useless under-achievers.

"Can you do those loose, bouncy curls you did for me last time?" she begged, craning her neck to look at Claire.

"You'll get what you're given and be grateful" she replied jokingly. "Now, drink up, we have to leave in half an hour."

"Half an hour! Shit, I haven't even had a shower or a glass of wine yet" I moaned as I ran out the living room snatching one of the glasses that Ben was carrying. I hated not having enough time to get ready properly.

I managed to shower, blow dry my hair and apply (or should I say trowel on) an ample layer of foundation, blusher, and highlighter, whilst covering my eyes in a smoky hue, a flourish of black eyeliner, and a coating of mascara which promised me 'killer lashes'. Now, I could not say whether my eyelashes were indeed 'killer', but for a fifteen-minute makeover, I did not look too shabby. All that was left was to decide what to wear. There were only two real choices. A black YSL dress which I had picked up in an uber posh charity shop, or a pair of faux leather trousers and matching bandeau which I had recently purchased online. To be honest, I did not really care which one I went for, it was all about the shoes!

"Wear the dress, it looks great on you" Ben offered as he rushed past the door clumsily buttoning up his shirt.

"Hmm… maybe you're right" I mused, staring at both options again. He was right; the dress was the one to go with. It was quite plain and understated, suitably short enough not to look like a dress you would wear to a funeral, but long enough that I would not flash my undercarriage should I need to hop up onto a bar stool. It was the perfect blend of classy and high-end escort, and more importantly, would give everyone a clear view of my Sophia Websters. I reached down into the bottom of my wardrobe and carefully retrieved the pale pink shoe box, daintily lifting the lid and caressing the tissue paper lining with the tips of my fingers before pulling back the protective sheath and exposing the treasure beneath. Using my thumb and index finger, I hooked one sandal out at a time, turning them in the air to get a glimpse of them from all angles. They were as light as a feather. Without a doubt, they were going to be the most comfortable pair of 'going out' shoes I had ever owned. For a second, I felt like a little girl in a shoe shop trying on her first pair of princess shoes, you know, the ones that had the hidden key in the soles? As a woman I could not only feel the same sense of magic I had felt all those years ago, but I could truly appreciate and marvel at the exquisite craftmanship that had gone into making these works of art. Anyone who dared say that these babies were not worth the nearly four hundred pound price tag were either jealous, stupid, or both.

I rummaged frantically through my underwear drawer, trying to lay my hands on the most appropriate pair of Bridget Jones pants I could find. As I yanked them up to within an inch of my armpits, I gasped as six pounds of unwanted fat disappeared within a second. I sincerely hoped that the person who invented these was sitting back in their country retreat, sandwiched between a Nobel prize and a Chinese takeaway for four, because they truly deserved it. However rich they had become off the back of this horrifying looking contraption, I would bet my life, that there was not a woman or drag queen on this planet that would begrudge them a penny of it. The heterosexual male population might not be so generous with their praise. No man really wanted to take on the challenge of extracting his date from her shapewear, even if he did come prepared with a crowbar and a healthy dollop of Vaseline. I know I keep harping on about it, but this just highlights my point about inventions needing to have a valid place in the market– LJT would be wise to take a page from Kimmy K's business model. Love them or hate them, the Kardashians know their shit when it comes to product placement and captivating an audience. A product can be ugly as hell, but if it works, if it fulfils a need, it's going to make you a fortune. Couple that with a killer hot bod and some expert photoshopping, and you are well on your way to global domination. RIP Spanx, hello SKIMS. I made a mental note to get myself an upgrade.

My dress fell effortlessly over the top, all lumps and bumps masterfully restrained, my outer appearance giving away no clues as to the trussed-up chicken that lay hidden beneath. Did I look like a Kardashian? No, but maybe I would with some new shapewear (see, the power of marketing!). I decided to keep my hair loose, and although I did not have time to give it a hip 'bouncy' blow dry, I had to admit that it did not look too bad by the time I had whizzed the dryer over it. I grabbed my clutch, put a few essentials in it (lip gloss, powder for when my face got all sweaty as it invariably always did, some chewing gum, my bank card, and my phone) and aimed for the door.

"Wow! You look great" said Ben as we almost collided on the landing.

"Thanks Mr. You don't look half bad yourself" I admitted, running my eyes over his dark blue jeans, slim fitting white shirt and pale grey jacket. I could see why he was a hit with the ladies. He was a good-looking guy. Six foot plus, good body, dressed well, smart and had a heart of gold. "You might even pull tonight!" I joked, patting him playfully on the shoulder.

"Not bloody likely" he replied. "It's far more probable that I'll be stuck babysitting the three of you! I'm fairly sure that's the only reason you invite me to these things. That, and to pretend to be one of your boyfriends when you get hit on by someone too poor, too boring, or too ugly to entertain."

"Ouch! You hurt my heart, Ben Angelino. I'll have you know that I've been out with plenty of dull people!" I flashed him a cheeky grin. "Remember Simon the chartered accountant? He had a face like Zac Effron, but the personality of Lurch. He used to talk to me about profit and loss statements and the benefits of fixed long-term investments after sex!"

"Jesus Jem, I'd rather not have that image in my head if it's all the same to you!" he scoffed.

I could not help but chuckle at his obvious discomfort. "Come on you," I linked my arm in his and together we bounded down the stairs like two pinballs in a machine, dodging the obstacles which coincidentally, were still in the same positions as this morning. The girls were waiting impatiently by the door.

"Come on, the taxi's been waiting for ten minutes already" Claire scorned.

"Okay, okay, we're coming! I just had to give Ben the sex talk in case he pulls tonight. It took a bit of explaining which is why we're running late!" I could not help mocking him sometimes, that is what siblings did. He rolled his eyes at me, refusing to engage in the joke.

❖ ❖ ❖

Never had I had to queue to get into a restaurant before (unless you counted the kebab shop on the High Road at the end of a night out). When we pulled up, there was a line of scantily clad people snaking around the corner of the building, chatting excitedly. It looked like they were queueing to get into a fancy club rather than a restaurant.

"Jeez, I wasn't expecting to have to queue" Sarah exclaimed in dismay from the front seat of the cab.

"Me either" I chimed in. "How can you have a table booked for a certain time if you then have to join a mile long queue?"

We asked the taxi driver to pull up round the corner to avoid the gaze of everyone waiting in line. Once out of sight, we bundled out the car and grudgingly joined the end of the queue. It was hard to get any real impression of the place from so far back, but as we moved closer, the unmistakeable thud, thud, thud of music moved into earshot. A bit closer still, and you could peer over the window decals which were clearly designed to keep prying eyes and photographers out. A half-hearted attempt at providing some privacy for those nearly famous diners who constantly peered over their shoulder to see if anyone had recognised them. A warm glow emanated from the huge gold contemporary hanging lights within. I had to admit, I was quite intrigued. By the time we made it to the front of the queue, my ever so comfy, practical going out shoes were starting to let me know that going out shoes were not meant to be comfortable. And although I never would have admitted it, I was secretly looking forward to sitting down. Claire had positioned herself at the front of our group (she was self-designated group leader tonight), and she gave our reservation details to the immaculately dressed guy behind the desk. With a dramatic flourish of his wrist, he beaconed over an equally pristine (and exceptionally beautiful) South American looking girl who genially waved us in and led us to our table.

"Wow! This place is incredible" I breathed, following her through the room. Groups of people chatted animatedly over their food, the noise level not deafening but certainly louder than a normal restaurant, giving that club vibe that was so popular these days. Looking around, I could see that I had been mistaken about the lights. They were not gold, but in fact a rich, burnt copper, which I now saw matched the rest of the colour scheme for the interior. It appeared that practically every surface, whether it be a table, bar, door, or wall was made of the same opulent material, all of it helping to reflect the light from above. The floor was a deep, rich mahogany, a stark contrast, and a welcome relief from the ostentatious copper. Camilla (our hostess' name as I later discovered) wound us through the main dining room and through a hidden copper door which led to a smaller, more dimly lit, private area. If it were at all possible, this room was even more sensational than the last. In the corner, a DJ played a song which sounded like it came straight from the dance floor of a salsa club in Havana. The music was not as loud as in the previous room, which implied it was there more for atmosphere than it was for listening to.

"Here is your booth ladies and gentleman." Her lips lingered on the word 'gentleman.' Not even Stevie Wonder could fail to see the serious fuck me eyes she was giving Ben. He gave her one of his affable smiles in return, acknowledging the move, but planting his feet firmly in our camp. A polite rebuttal, one which said, had it been another time, I might have taken you up on your offer. "Your reservation was amended this afternoon from our standard dining to our VIP experience. Manni will be looking after you this evening, so if there is anything you require, please do not hesitate to let him know."

"Oh, um… I think there has been a mistake" Claire stuttered. "I haven't made any changes to our reservation today, there must be mix up. We'll stick with the standard dining if that's okay?" Although the light in the room was muted, I could see that the colour had completely drained from her face. The realisation that this little 'upgrade' was going to cost us a small fortune ever so quickly sinking in.

"No mistake" Camilla replied kindly. "A gentleman called us earlier and made the changes on your behalf. Your bill for this evening has been taken care of." She extended her arm towards the booth, ushering us in and then swiftly turned around and sashayed away. The four of us sat dumbstruck in the plush leather seat.

"Fuck, this is going to be one almighty expensive mistake guys" chuckled Sarah. With that we all burst into fits of nervous laughter. There were worse mistakes that could happen, I am sure.

"Jesus. We're all going to be eating beans for the rest of the month if that girl's got it wrong" chirped Ben.

"Look on the bright side" chipped in Sarah. "I could do with losing a few pounds, a month of starvation might not necessarily be a bad thing. Besides, a night here might be cheaper than doing the Dukan diet."

"That's true" I agreed. "Let's just make the most of it, and if she's wrong, we'll just have to do a runner. It's not like we will be coming back here any time soon is it!"

With that, a small, dark-haired man walked confidently over to our table. He had a pleasant, smiley face and was holding a copper bucket which had an expensive looking bottle of champagne poking out the top.

"Good evening, everyone! My name is Manni, and I am here to make sure you have a fantastic evening with us. I will shortly bring you your menus, but in the meantime, I have been asked to give you this." He gestured to the champagne and placed it in the centre of the table. "Which one of you is Jemma?" Everyone turned to stare at me, eyebrows arched in curiosity. I raised my hand reticently, slightly afraid of what was coming next.

"Ah, hello Jemma!" he smiled affectionately. "The gentleman

who called earlier, also asked me to give you this." He handed me what looked like an awfully expensive white compliment card. "I'll just get your glasses."

I turned the card over in my hands. It was beautiful. Thick white card stock with a guilt edge border and delicate gold font which read 'Sanchos'. Simple yet elegant (it probably cost as much as a glass of that fancy champagne). I turned it once more to look at the back. There was a handwritten note. Incomprehension spread across my face as I re-read the words, my eyes not believing what was written in front of me.

"What does it say?" Claire asked excitedly.

"Err…" I read it again once more just to make sure I hadn't made a mistake.

"Jem!" she shouted more aggressively this time.

"Umm…it says … Have a wonderful evening with your friends, you deserve it. Jake… and a kiss."

"Jake?" Sarah looked confused.

"Jake, as in your boss Jake?" Ben added with a tinge of distaste.

"I don't know" I replied dazed. "I guess so. I don't know any other Jakes, but I can't think why he would do this."

"Who cares!" sang Sarah happily. "Now we know it's not a mistake, we can actually get on with enjoying ourselves!"

"Sounds a bit suss to me" quipped Ben.

Manni returned a second later with four elegant champagne flutes in his hands. He expertly popped the cork and deftly poured the exquisite pink fizz into them. "I'll be back in a minute with your menus."

"Let's raise a glass to Jem, and to whatever it is she's done to get us a free VIP experience," Sarah said winking, holding her glass aloft for the rest of us to meet it.

"I bet I can hazard a guess" muttered Ben under his breath.

"Excuse me? What do you mean by that?" I asked, a little perturbed, and more than just a bit snappy.

"Well, what guy pays for dinner for a group of people he doesn't know without there being something in it for him?" He sounded genuinely irritated.

"Ben, I don't know what you're insinuating or why you're being such a dick, but I can assure you that I haven't done anything to warrant this." I sat back in the seat and took a long slug of my champagne. It was divine. Cold and crisp, the bubbles danced on my tongue as I swallowed it. This was going to go down way too easily.

"I'm sure it was just a thank you for all the hard work you've put into this pitch" Claire offered, trying to diffuse the tension.

"Probably" I smiled sarcastically, quaffing back more champagne whilst staring angrily at Ben. What was his flipping problem?

"I'm sorry" he said, as if reading my mind. "You're right, that was a dickish thing to say. It's just been a long day. Let's enjoy ourselves" and with that he raised his glass again. "To Jem!"

"To Jem" everyone repeated.

Manni returned with our menus, offering suggestions and explanations for the dishes. He was a master of his craft and made each menu choice sound delicious. So much so, that I wanted to try everything. It transpired that the chef patron came over from Cuba in the 1970's as a child and longed for the comfort of the food from his homeland. Obviously, in the seventies the ingredients were not readily available, and his mother often struggled to re-create their dishes. Alejandro had vowed to his parents that one day, he would open a restaurant in their honour and serve the food of their ancestors, expressing his love for them and his country through his cooking. Heartbreakingly, his father passed away unexpectedly during the pandemic, so the restaurant had been named posthumously after him in commemoration. Now, whether this story was complete bullshit, I do not know. But I have always been a sucker for sentimentality and a happily ever after, so I hoped it was true. If not, it had still successfully sucked me in, and I would happily have spent a few hundred pounds to aid Alejandro's dream (although luckily for me, thanks to Jake, it was not my money that was now going to have to do it).

We all chose the same starter. It was similar to a fish taco, although our comparison had left Manni slightly affronted. He assured us that it was completely different. When they arrived, they looked nothing like the ones I had consumed before at Taco Bell. An almost perfect circular pillowy flat bread sat in the centre of the delicate white plate. Atop of that sat a carefully arrange mound of seared swordfish, adorned with vivid flashes of red and green and finished with the most vibrant green oil. It was a piece of edible art. What was more surprising was the fact that it tasted even better than it looked. Clean and fresh with punches of chilli heat that gave a real kick but did not overpower the delicate, flaky swordfish. It was heavenly. The four of us were unable to speak, looks of pure ecstasy covered our faces, and only primal, guttural noises echoed round the table. Anyone looking from the outside in might have mistaken our table for the famous scene from When Harry Met Sally.

The first bottle of champagne disappeared all too quickly and was swiftly and discreetly replaced with another. I wondered if Jake had instructed the team to keep the drinks flowing in his usual commanding way? I dreaded to think how much this was going to set him back. Ben had also taken the liberty of ordering a round of Mojitos shortly followed by another of Cuba Libras. My head was starting to spin a little but not in a bad way. It was more like that warm fuzzy feeling you get when everything feels fantastic, the world seems so much more beautiful than it was when you were sober, and you are so much funnier than you were at the start of the evening. This was only going to end one way – in disaster, but right now I was loving every minute of it. From out of nowhere, Manni placed four little glass dishes in front of us.

"This is our Mojito sorbet, a palette cleanser. The coldness of the ice and the freshness of the lime should help clean your palette in preparation for your main course. Enjoy!"

"Wow!" I exclaimed, digging the tiny silver spoon into the freezing ball. I had had many sorbets before, some of which had been quite disappointing. But this did exactly what is said on the tin. It was fresh, vibrant, clean, and tasted exactly like a Mojito (not that I needed any more). Unlike other sorbets I had had, it was as smooth as silk and slipped effortlessly down my throat, leaving it revived and ready for more delicious food.

"Shit, this is good" replied Claire, still clinging to the spoon in her mouth.

"Mmm...." agreed Sarah

As with any top restaurant, Sancho's struck the perfect balance between not rushing the food out too quickly and not keeping customers waiting too long for it. There was just the right amount of time between courses to indulge in conversation and merriment (slightly more merriment and less coherent conversation in our case). By the time we had finished our sorbets, Manni had returned to replenish the cutlery and bought over a bottle of red wine which he had recommended to accompany our main meals. After clearing away our sorbet dishes, he disappeared only to return a second later with a young girl in tow, each of them carrying two plates. He deftly placed the two he was holding in front of Ben and Sarah, then relieved the young girl of the two she was holding and placed them in front of Claire and me. The smell coming off the plates was divine. He briefly reminded us of what we had ordered and then left us in peace to enjoy.

Claire and I had both chosen the Ropa Vieja, a shredded braised beef skirt steak, slow cooked in tomatoes, onions, and peppers, while Ben and Sarah had gone for the Lechon Asado – spit roast pork served in a spicy Cuban mojo marinade. I did not think it was possible to top the starter, but the main courses were out of this world delicious. I would go so far as to say that I had never eaten such succulent beef in my whole life, and the flavour was so intense it made my mouth water. Yet again, none of us really spoke until we had devoured the last morsel and had practically licked our plates clean (none of us had completely lost our student ways).

"I don't think I have ever eaten food as good as that before in my life" asserted Ben as he dramatically threw his napkin down on the table in mock defeat and slumped back in his seat. "How have I never thought about travelling to Cuba before?" he asked sounding completely ashamed of himself.

"Ooh let's all go next year" giggled Claire excitedly "I've always wanted to get down and dirty with a sexy Cuban in Havana."

Manni re-appeared looking quite smug at the scene laid out before him "You all enjoy your meals?" he asked, already knowing the response.

"Oh Manni, it was just perfect, thank you!" replied Sarah in a dreamy, half cut kind of voice.

"It was out of this world" I added appreciatively "Thank you so much!"

"The night is not over yet my lovely people. First there is dessert and then there is dancing!" he sang.

"I don't think I could eat another thing, I'm completely stuffed" joked Ben, puffing his cheeks out, trying to simulate looking full.

"Nonsense!" protested Manni. "You can't possibly leave before trying our famous arroz con leche!"

"What's that exactly?" I asked.

"You mean you've never heard of arroz con leche?" he sounded shocked.

"Afraid not" I replied feeling more than a little embarrassed at my lack of knowledge.

"My dear, do not worry. Do you like rice pudding?"

I cast my mind back to my primary school days and the beige, non-descript pool of nothingness that was served up at lunchtimes for dessert. I cannot quite recall whether it was rice pudding, semolina, or macaroni, I'm fairly sure we had all three at some point, but I could not have told you the difference based on what they gave us. I did not want to crush Manni who had nearly run out of superlatives to describe his national dessert.

I settled on "I haven't had it for a long time" hoping it would not give my true opinion of it away. It was like he read my mind.

"Forget everything you know about your beige, bland, stodgy English pudding. Arroz con leche is the most famous, most delicious dessert in Cuba. Yes, it is made with rice and milk like your version, but we infuse the milk with spices to give it a more complex flavour profile. Think Christmas with cinnamon and star anise, but with a fresh hint of summery lemon to cut through the sweetness. It's rich and creamy and warming to the palette. And above all, it is comforting, like a huge hug in a bowl." The way he spoke about this rice pudding was like he was recounting a favourite childhood memory. If a pudding could invoke those kinds of feelings, I was all up for giving it a go. Besides, I only had my own vivid memories of rice pudding, and it would be nice to replace them with a new one.

"Go on then, you've convinced me!"

"Me too!" replied Claire and Sarah in unison.

"I guess I can squeeze it in!" added Ben.

"Four arroz con leches coming right up!" Beamed Manni, as he practically skipped away from the table.

"That guy really loves his job, and he's amazing at it too" gushed Sarah appraisingly. I felt slightly guilty for my previous, unwarranted assumptions of the staff here.

Manni did not let us down. The Cuban rice pudding was a revelation. It was everything he said it would be and more. Creamy but not stodgy, sweet but spicy. Who knew rice pudding could be so grown up! The fact that it was served in a small mason jar with a cinnamon stick poking out the top only helped to highlight the difference between this version and my previous point of reference. Undoubtedly, this had cured my aversion to milk puddings.

We ordered a coffee and the obligatory shot of tequila to finish with and agreed that dancing on a school night was not in our best interests (not that Sarah agreed in the slightest). Manni seemed a little heartbroken that we would not be staying on but was brightened a little by the generous tip we gave him. After all, we had not had to pay for the meal, and he had been an absolute superstar. We thanked him, hugged him as if he were a close friend that we were not going to see for a while and then meandered our way through the restaurant and out on to the street. The air was warm outside, giving it a holiday vibe. Although it was nearly 11pm, the street was full of people, some of whom were only just entering the building (clearly these were the people who were not afraid to go dancing on a school night). Part of me wanted to go back in and join them, but the part of that could feel her pulsating feet and knew what she had to get up for in the morning, drowned out the little party animal inside.

I could honestly say that I had not given it too much thought whilst we had been inside, but as we stood waiting for our taxi, I really could not fathom why Jake had paid for the evening. I was sure Claire was right, and it was just a thank you for the work we had been putting in over the past few weeks, but it just seemed very generous, too generous perhaps. Maybe Ben was right. Maybe he did want something. Perhaps he was going to land us with another shit product that needed to be pitched, or he was about to make us redundant, and was trying to soften us up before delivering the killer blow? I hoped it was Claire who was right because I really could not face going to countless interviews or standing in line to sign on (if that was even a thing anymore).

That night, as I lay in bed, I could not help but think about Jake Bales. This man who had come bursting unannounced into our lives, who I knew nothing about (other than his name and the fact that he had stirred up feelings in me that I did not think were possible - or work appropriate). Obviously, I knew all the office gossip, which led me to believe that he was nothing but your archetypal man-whore who was trouble with a capital 'T'. But I could not help but wonder if there was more to him than that. I mentally kicked myself for even giving him a second thought. As if he would do me the same courtesy. He was probably out with a group of twenty-year-old Scandinavian socialites spreading his genital warts with gay abandon, or worse, scouring LinkedIn for my replacement. No. I would simply go into the office in the morning, thank him kindly for his generosity and carry on as normal. Simple. Sorted. With that fool proof plan in my head, and copious amounts of alcohol, I drifted off to sleep, vivid images of a naked Jake Bales running salaciously through my depraved mind.

• • • • • • • • • • • • • • • • • • • • • • • • • • • • • • • • • • • • • • • • •

# TUESDAY

I rolled over and peered at the alarm clock on my bedside table. "Urgh…" 3.35am. I was unsure whether the pounding in my head and blurred vision were due to alcohol or a blunt trauma which I had received last night and could not remember (courtesy of said alcohol). Either way, I made the executive decision to cancel my 5.30am alarm. No run for me today. I rolled back over and cocooned myself in my duvet, no doubt looking like a veritable human sausage roll. Last night was one of the worst night's sleeps I had had in ages. If I was not having inappropriate dreams about Jake, who incidentally, was Cuban, a fantastic salsa dancer and lived solely on fish tacos, I was having unconscious panic attacks about my upcoming presentation. Personally, I blamed the rice pudding. It was a well-documented fact that dairy before bed was a killer (it had absolutely nothing to do with the irresponsible level of alcohol I had consumed). The evening had been out of this world fantastic, but my god I was going to pay for it. My mouth was as dry as the bar at an Alcoholics Anonymous meeting (which is probably where I should have been heading), and my head and body felt completely detached from each other. Even though my mind was telling my arm to move, it was currently unresponsive, laying outstretched and motionless by my side, and no amount of effort was able to bring it round. I was caught midway between life and death, like the tormented husband in that 90's film Ghost, who refused to cross over to the other side. I started to head towards the light, a beautiful, serene light. A place which smelt divine, like strong coffee and croissants. *Is this what heaven smells like?*

"Wake up sleepy head." *Is that God talking to me?* He sounded much younger than I imagined (although I guess nobody really knows how old he is). "Come on, it's 7.30am." There was something about that last part which dragged me back from the light and forced me to sit bolt upright. Ben was sitting on the edge of the bed, coffee in one hand and a pastry in the other.

"You look like shit" he smirked, handing me the coffee.

"I feel like shit" I conceded, rubbing my eyes with my fists, trying to make the pounding in my head go away. "My head feels like it's about to implode."

"Hold on." He rummaged in his dressing gown pocket and pulled out two paracetamols. "Here, take these, if you don't throw them straight back up, they might just help!"

"Thanks Mr." I put them both in my mouth and took a swig of the coffee. "Fuck, that's hot!" I spat, almost losing the paracetamol.

"You'd moan if it wasn't" he explained, getting up from the edge of the bed. He knew me too well.

"True" I admitted reluctantly. "I'm going to be so late; I have to be at work in forty-five minutes and I currently look like a close relative of The Elephant Man and Quasimodo."

"Don't be too harsh on yourself, looks aren't everything, and you've got a great personality" he said smiling and heading for the door.

"I'm never drinking again" I pledged half-heartedly as he went to pull it up.

'I've heard that a million times before" he laughed. "Oh, and I've ironed you an outfit, made you some lunch and ordered you an Uber, so I reckon you have about twenty minutes to get your shit together."

"What would I do without you?"

"Smell like a donkey's arse and be late for work" he smiled, finally leaving.

Surprisingly, I was washed, dressed and in my recently ironed skirt and blouse within fifteen minutes, giving me a whole five minutes to apply some make up. As the saying goes, you can't paint a turd, but I am a firm believer that you can always add a bit of sparkle and mascara to it. I threw on my shoes and headed out to the waiting taxi, planting a kiss on Ben's forehead.

"Jesus, you cleaned the kitchen too!" I said in complete shock, my mouth agape, as I caught a glimpse of the now pristine room out the corner of my eye.

"All in a day's work" he beamed. I am not sure how he was not looking or feeling as rotten as me, I was convinced that we had all had the same amount to drink. Either way, I was super glad that he was not. "Have a good day and I'll see you later. I'll pick up a Chinese on my way home. Oh, and I popped a couple more paracetamols in your bag just in case you need them later."

I went back and kissed him a second time. "Love you."

"Love you too Jem."

As I lowered myself gingerly into the cab, I deliberately threw the smiling driver a look that said, "Not today, Derek, not today." I loved the way that Uber kindly notified you of your driver's name, it made not speaking to them so much easier. Poor old Derek obliged, despite looking in the mood for conversation, and we drove in absolute silence to the office. Each turn of the steering wheel sent a wave of nausea coursing through my body. Today was going to be a long arse day and those paracetamols were going to be much needed. As we pulled up outside the office, I thanked Derek for his service (and his silence) and delicately exited the vehicle. Claire had a dental appointment first thing, so I was riding solo for a few hours.

Like every morning, I made my way through the throng of people milling about in the foyer. Today's short journey to the lift was a tad more sedate since I did not want to vomit on any unsuspecting co-workers. Luckily, some people had just exited so there was an empty one waiting patiently for me. I stepped in and hit the number twenty-two (I also hit twenty-three and twenty-four thanks to my shaky hands and continuing blurred vision). The doors were just starting to close when a tanned arm appeared out of nowhere, reaching in between them, halting them in their tracks. Had a forearm ever looked so divine? Thick wrist, check. Long elegant fingers, check. Expensive watch, check. Fanny flutters, check, check, check.

"Room for one more?"

Oh, sweet baby Jesus! In all the scenarios which had played out in my dreams last night (and there had been quite a few let me tell you), meeting Jake in the lift whilst looking like shit on a stick was not one of them. This was surprising when you consider that in most romantic comedies (not that I am suggesting I am a character in a romantic comedy), the fantasiser always bumps into their crush in the lift. Caught midway between sheer blind panic and wanting to sound completely nonchalant and unaffected by his presence, I produced the only response I could think of. "Umm… yeah, sure." Nailed it.

"Great, I don't think I could face taking the stairs this morning!" His broad, penetrating smile and the closeness of his body was disarming and proved to be the catalyst for my downfall. Out of nowhere, the lift suddenly felt hot, and when I say hot, I mean ridiculously hot, like the belly of a volcano hot. I could feel the blazing heat rising from my blistered feet (alas, I can confirm that my Sophia Websters were not dissimilar to all my other excruciating going out shoes), up through my legs and spread to my face like wildfire. Where there was once one astonishingly beautiful man stood before me, there were now several, and it was impossible to decipher which one was real.

"Is it warm in here?" My voice sounded strange - breathless and disorientated. The lift started spinning and my mouth began to fill with liquid, the awful precursor to vomiting. *Oh God, please not now, not here, not in front of him of all people!* My prayers were in vain. With legs that now resembled a pot of Rowntree's fruit jelly, I grabbed onto the handrail and tried to steady myself.

"Are you ok Jemma, you don't look too good." *Not everyone can look like you, arsehole* I thought to myself as I tried to focus on taking in deep breaths and remaining vertical.

"I'll be ok" I lied, hoping the nausea would pass. "I just need some …. fresh ……air" I stated, frantically pressing at the buttons on the panel to get the doors to open. It transpires, that for safety reasons, lift doors tend not to open midway between floors, so my valiant attempt to break free was futile. Given the choice, I would have happily signed any necessary disclaimer and scaled the lift shaft like a Navy Seal, just to escape being in such close proximity to him. But as was so often the case, life gave me the middle finger, pulled up a pew and decided to let the scene play out in full. What happened next was hazy. I vaguely remember stumbling and the feeling of being scooped up in a pair of strong, muscular arms (every girl's dream, right? – except for the stumbling part obviously). And then there was the smell, his smell, fresh and woody, and oh so masculine. Heaven. And then nothing. Naff all, just darkness, like the black hole of Calcutta. From heaven to hell in the blink of an eye.

Amid the darkness, a hand moved tenderly across my forehead, and a calm voice said something indistinguishable in the distance. It was muffled, as if I were listening to it from deep under water. For a moment, I imagined I was Ariel from the Little Mermaid, floating through azure seas, the voice of Prince Eric calling me up to the surface. *I'm coming Eric, I'm coming!*

The hand continued to stroke my face, and with time, the voice became louder, clearer. I managed to prize open an eyelid and instantly regretted it, quickly clamping it shut again. Goddamn Disney and their happily ever after's. The fear that had gripped me earlier returned a hundred-fold. Feeling like a panicked octopus, arms and legs flailing everywhere, I attempted to get up.

"Hey, how are you feeling? You gave me quite a scare there." Eric's, I mean Jake's hand brushed lightly over my forehead. *God that felt good.*

"What…happened? Where am I?" I replied weakly, giving the whole eye-opening thing another shot.

"Don't worry, you're in my office. You passed out" he paused. "But not before throwing up over both of us" he smiled kindly, motioning to a discarded shirt on the floor which looked like it had been in a fight with a rabid toddler. The look of terror on my face prompted him to add "Don't worry, I keep spare clothes in the office for just such occasions." How could he joke at such a time?

"Oh God, I'm so sorry, I have absolutely no idea what happened. Does this mean I'm fired?" It was the truth; I had no clue how all of this had come about. I also knew that it did not matter what the reason was, if you threw up on your boss, your job was already being advertised internally.

As I tentatively pulled myself up on to my elbows, I could see that I was laid out on the sofa in his office. It dawned on me that in the few months that he had been here, I had only been in his office a handful of times, and on each occasion, I had been so eager to get out as quickly as possible, that I had never really paid much attention to what it was like. I was quite taken back. It was beautiful. The shell of the room was much like a glass fishbowl, with huge expansive windows overlooking the London skyline, with only some aluminium blinds to provide privacy from the prying eyes within the building. The one solitary solid wall was adorned with two gigantic pieces of modern art, there were two jade green informal comfortable chairs, plus the plush navy sofa I was currently sprawled across, and an array of soft furnishings and fresh flowers at every turn. Either he was an undercover interior designer (or the woman he was seeing was), or worst-case scenario, he was gay and was about to break a thousand hearts in the office (except maybe Frank's). He must have caught me looking around and fathomed what I was thinking (hopefully not about the being gay part).

"I spend so much time here" he gestured to the room "I wanted to make it as homely as possible" he offered, almost embarrassed.

"No, it's beautiful" I replied, a bit too quickly. I was sitting level with him now, and the realisation that I had just vomited and smelt like a toxic waste bin, hit me. I tried to pull myself up further so that I was not breathing noxious fumes directly in his face. "I really am so sorry" I said again, trying to inconspicuously cover my mouth with my hand. "Please let me pay for your dry cleaning."

"Honestly" he chuckled "Please don't worry about it, these things happen." He paused for a second time, as if trying to remember the last time he had been thrown up over by an employee. "Well, I mean I guess they don't happen that often, in fact, I don't think it's ever happened to me before. But at least I can say you were my first!" His eyes sparkled like two black gemstones. Although he was quite clearly taking the piss, he did it in such a charming way, that I forgave him instantly. In fact, come to think of it, now was the first time since he had arrived that I did not feel uncomfortable around him – so ironic given the shit show of a morning I had given him front row seats to. I smiled, appreciative of his kindness. He returned the favour with an award-winning smile of his own, warm, genuine, and full of pearly white, equally sized veneers. *Oh, to be so perfect.*

"Unfortunately, my spare clothes don't extend to anything that would fit you. So, unless you want to don an oversized M&S suit, you may as well call it quits and head home."

"Sorry, what?"

"I said you might want to head home and rest up, I don't think you'll get much done here today now," he said in a slower more pronounced voice, misinterpreting my confusion.

"No, about the suit? Did you just admit to shopping at M&S?" I managed a wry smile.

"After all the horrifying things I've just told you, that's what you took away from that conversation?" he laughed playfully.

"I beg to differ, shopping at M&S is far more humiliating!" I scoffed. "I'm confused though," I added, trying to paint a picture of genuine puzzlement across my face. "I thought M&S was reserved solely for middle aged women who value function and quality of fabric over and above style?"

"You forget comfort" he added easily, looking deadly serious. "M&S clothes are extremely comfortable, and never underestimate functionality and the feel of a good cotton trouser suit." His face was deadpan. So much so, that I could not work out if he was being honest or still taking the piss. That was, until he cracked another one of his killer watt smiles. I wondered how many women he had managed to disarm and get into his bed with one of those. My guess was a thousand plus, but the thought made me feel a bit icky, so I tried to block that thought from my mind.

"Grab your coat and I'll drop you home. I don't think I could subject a poor, unsuspecting cab driver to a repeat of the horrors I have just witnessed, plus my mother would never forgive me for abandoning a lady in need."

"Oh, so you're a mummy's boy as well as a secret M&S superfan?!"

I could not tell you where this bravado was coming from, I can only assume it was connected to my recent dalliance with death, and apparent newfound approach to throwing caution to the wind. That and the fact that if my job was lost already, I may as well go out with a bang!

"Didn't your mother ever tell you not to judge a book by its cover?" he said raising an eyebrow in jest.

"Unfortunately, not, I never knew my mother" I replied faintly, casting my eyes to the floor.

"Oh shit, I'm so sorry Jemma, I had no idea. I'm such an arse." He looked genuinely distraught.

I lifted my head, unable to contain the widening grin on my face. "Not really, my mother is very much alive and kicking, and I saw her a mere seventy-two hours ago!" I laughed "But you should see your face, it's quite a picture!"

"Jemma, I honestly thought she was dead, or that you'd been adopted! You are a horrible, horrible person" he chortled, shaking his head as though he could not believe he had fallen for my joke.

"I've been called worse" I admitted

"Me too!" he concurred, laughing.

"I can imagine!" I said raising my eyebrows, imagining all the hurt and angry men who had had their wives and girlfriends whisked away from under their noses by this beautiful man. I was starting to feel slightly less troll like, but as I took to my feet, my legs buckled beneath me. Instinctively, I reached out and grabbed him, the way an unsteady toddler grabs a parent or sofa when learning to walk. Our faces were just mere inches apart. There was no way he could avoid inhaling my death-dealing breath from this angle.

"Here, let me help you" he said softly, ignoring the poisonous green haze emanating from my mouth. In one swift and ever so gentle movement, he pulled me back to my feet, wrapped his arm supportively around my waist, picked up my bag and gestured to the door. And there it was again. The smell. It was intoxicating. I closed my eyes and breathed it in (clearly not in a sexy way like they do in the movies because it made him panic).

"Are you ok Jemma, are you going to be sick again?" He sounded concerned. Not least because he was fresh out of clean spare clothes, but also, in case I was about to re-decorate his immaculately designed office.

"No, I'm good" I replied, hating myself for being a simpering wench yet again.

"Did you eat something this morning?"

"Er, no, I was running late so didn't have time. I'll grab something when I get in." That is when it hit me, why I had been late for work. Last night. I had completely forgotten to thank him for last night! How could I have been so rude?; he must have thought I was such an ungrateful cow! I felt genuinely ashamed of myself and utterly mortified – again.

"Jake" I turned slowly to face him. He was so close that I could feel the rapid beat of his heart through his shirt. Unconsciously, I let my hand hover over the area, drawn to it, feeling the rhythm quicken the longer it stayed there. "I wanted to say thank you for last night. I was going to come and see you first thing, but I didn't get a chance, given that I was too busy breaking all sorts of professional and personal boundaries with you instead! I don't want you to think that I didn't appreciate it, because I did, I mean I do." I could feel the heat rising ominously up my body again and knew that if I did not take a breath soon, lightening would indeed strike twice.

"You are very welcome" he smiled, his hand resting on my

shoulder, "But you worry too much. Did you have a good time? It looks like you might have done if this morning is anything to go by!" he laughed.

"It was perfect" I replied weakly, humiliated that he suspected the reason behind my current state.

"Perfect, wow, I wish I'd been there too!" I was momentarily stunned by his response. Was he not cross with me? What did he mean about wishing he had been there? Did he mean that he wished he had been there with me, or just wished that he had been at the restaurant? Was I reading way too much into things again? More than likely, yes, but I needed to know something.

"Jake…why did you pay for last night?" I hoped I was not overstepping the mark.

"I wanted to say thank you for all your hard work on this project. I know it's been a tough couple of months, but I appreciate everything you've done." His eyes lingered on mine, hesitation passing over his face. "I was wondering …" he trailed off, staring at the ground, as if considering his next move. "When you are feeling better, would you let me take you to dinner… just the two of us?" There was a tinge of nervousness in the way he asked his question. Shit. My bravado from five minutes ago disappeared. I was transported back to my formative teenage years when I was first asked out by Iain Blackman (who it transpires is now gay), and the way my body froze when he had asked the very same question (not that a McDonalds takeaway paid for by his mother, could be considered going out for dinner). Anyway, I'm not sure how long I stood there in silence not answering, but it was obviously uncomfortably too long. "Sorry, I shouldn't have asked you now. That was wrong of me, I don't want you to think I'm taking advantage."

"No!" I blurted out.

"Okay, no problem at all." He looked wounded.

"No, I mean, no, you shouldn't not have asked me, or yes, you should have asked me, whatever the correct way of saying it is. Oh shit, I mean, yes, I would love… I mean I would like to go for dinner with you Jake." Well, that was all kinds of horrifying.

"Really?" he sounded surprised.

"Yes" I smiled. "I mean, God, I thought I was about to get fired, so this is a complete bonus!"

"So, you're only saying yes because it's a better option than being fired?"

"No! Not at all, that's not what I meant!" I stuttered. *Someone put me out of my misery!*

"I'm just kidding Jemma. I'll get something booked."

This was all too much. "Cool beans!" What. The. Actual. Fuck. Had the man just offered to take a twelve-year-old out for dinner? Who even said "cool beans" anymore? Even back in the day, it was only ever pre-pubescent kids, or skateboarding man-children who thought that baggy denim cut-offs, socks pulled up past their knees and a battered pair of Vans were the epitome of cool that would have dreamt of uttering those words. As I was neither, that phrase should never have left my mouth.

"I'm glad the prospect of dinner with me has the ability to cause such a reaction!" he joked. My face and neck were beyond flaming, and the stench of cooking vomit was rising from beneath my blouse. "Right, we'd better make a move otherwise people are going to start wondering what we are up to in here!" he said, carefully turning me in the direction of the door.

He re-took his position next to me and guided me over to the exit. I had not appreciated how peaceful it was in his office until the door flung back and the noise from outside filled the room. I was reminded of that nineties TV programme my mum used to watch religiously - Stars In Their Eyes, and that iconic moment when the contestant would say "Tonight Matthew, I'm going to be…" and then they would step through the smoke and out on stage, dressed in the most outrageously awful costumes, looking more like the old woman from next door than the star they were trying to impersonate. I was supremely aware that I was now that person, only I was still me, and I was not dressed in a crap costume, I was in my own vomit encrusted attire. The eyes of the whole office were on us, and I immediately tensed up. Jake tightened his grip slightly around me, as if sensing my trepidation, wanting to reassure me of his support. Together, we walked slowly past the rows of tightly packed desks which ran alongside his office, past the famous photocopier, where women congregated to discuss their latest X-rated dreams about our boss, past Frank's desk who was midway through a bacon roll and currently mopping up tomato ketchup from his lap, and towards where my teams' desks were situated. Helene looked up as I shuffled pathetically past.

Her eyes were like saucers behind her black framed glasses. "Shit the bed Jemma, what happened to you?" her concern was matched by her disgust at my appearance.

"I'll fill you in tomorrow" I said, offering a limp wave of my hand.

Claire, who had just arrived from her dental appointment, was hurriedly making her way over to us.

"Jesus Jem, what happened? Are you okay?" I must have looked like crap because she seemed genuinely worried.

"She's okay" Jake said trying to comfort her "She just took a bit of a turn first thing. I'm going to take her home to make sure she gets back safely." I do not know who was more shocked by his statement, her, or me, but judging by her open-mouthed expression, I am guessing it was her.

"Oh, okay, I'll give you a call a bit later" she called after us.

"Yep, speak to you later" I replied weakly.

Every ounce of my being was screaming to get out of the office, I could feel the pairs of eyes boring into the back of my head, and it was suffocating. I could already hear the rumour mill going into overdrive. Jake hit the button for the lift and helped me inside when it arrived. He did not take his hand from around my waist until the doors opened at the underground car park and he had to search his jacket pocket for his key.

"You don't have to do this you know; I can get an Uber."

"I know, I want to though" he replied sweetly. "It's funny, I think I have spoken to you more today than in the whole time I've been here. It's nice to get the opportunity to get to know you a bit better."

"You might be right about the talking bit" I smiled, embarrassed. "But please don't judge me on this morning's little performance, I am so much more than puke and adolescent conversational skills," I joked, hoping to inject a little lightness into the situation, wondering whether that statement was true or not.

"I think I knew that already Jemma, although I can't deny that it hasn't been a welcome trip down memory lane this morning. Who knew that people still used the phrase 'cool beans' anymore!" I wanted to die. Sniggering, he pointed the key off into the distance. I heard the unmistakeable click of the central locking system open on an impressive looking pale, matt grey R8 Spyder.

"Are you absolutely sure that you shop at M&S, because in my experience, people who drive a car like that tend not to frequent such establishments!"

"Like I said, never judge a book by its cover" he smiled, opening the passenger door, and carefully helping me into the seat "You, okay?"

"If you mean, am I going to throw up in your fancy car, then yes,

I'm okay."

"Thank God" he joked "I only had it cleaned last week, and it's impossible to get the stench of vomit out of leather." I could see him chuckling to himself as he closed the door and made his way round to the driver's side.

● ● ● ● ● ● ● ● ● ● ● ● ● ● ● ● ● ● ● ● ● ● ● ● ● ● ● ● ● ● ● ● ● ● ● ● ● ● ● ● ● ● ● ●

◆ ◆ ◆

There was no explaining it. The overly confident, quite frankly arrogant man who had joined our company had been temporarily replaced by this kind, gentle, funny human. How could one person change so much? Moreover, could a person change that much? Which version of Jake Bales was the real version? In the words of Eminem, "Would the real Jake Bales please stand up."

"You're very quiet" he said as the engine roared into life "What are you thinking about?"

"Honestly, I'm a bit confused" I admitted, turning my head to face him. *God he is even more beautiful from this angle.*

"What are you confused about?"

"You. You seem different to how I imagined you would be."

He looked quizzical. "Is that a good or a bad thing?"

"I don't know" I admitted. "I can only go by what I've heard about you, but that doesn't seem to match up to what I've seen today."

"That sounds ominous" he chuckled. "What have you heard?" I did not dare tell him about the rumours currently circulating around the office.

"Oh, nothing really" I choked unconvincingly.

"So, you haven't heard the story about my genital warts or me sleeping with a seventeen-year-old in HR?" he replied with a wry smile on his face. He turned to look at me, but I was too mortified to meet his gaze and I shuffled uncomfortably in my seat to face the front again. How did he know about that? "Jemma, it's my job to hear everything" he said wistfully. "It's one of the plus and minus points about being the boss, I don't let it get to me. Most of the time, I just let people get on with it. I don't care what they think, and I don't really want them to know the real me anyway, so I let them spread their stories. They'll get tired soon enough and move on to someone else. But I want you to know that none of what they say is true. I have never slept with anyone. Well, not anyone, but certainly not at work, and I am happy to say that I am completely wart free!" My face burned at the thought of his penis, wart free or not, and I crossed my legs to stop the tingling sensation from taking hold. Things just got extremely uncomfortable. An awkward silence crept over the car. What should I do? Think of something witty to say? Keep staring out the window so that I did not look at his crotch? After what seemed like an eternity, he spoke.

"Anyway, enough about me. Tell me about you. Who is the real Jemma Lucas, and for the sake of today's car ride, where does she live?" His tone was light. Phew, that was better, I could cope with serious, non-genital related questions.

"She lives at 114a Eastwick Gardens, Chiswick. But who is she?... that's a bit more complicated to answer, I may need to come back to you on that one" I giggled, feeling some of the tension dissipate.

"Sounds intriguing" he laughed as he put his foot to the pedal, and the car darted forward out of the car park on to the main road. He masterfully weaved in and out of the traffic, dodging pedestrians, and other road users with ease. If it were possible for a car to be the embodiment of a person, then this car was just that. It was sleek, bold, confident, capable, and commanding, but it was also calm, quiet, and thoughtful. A contradiction in terms you might say, much like the man sitting next to me.

We talked non-stop all the way home, and by the time we pulled up outside my front door, I realised he was right. I had learnt more about him in the last couple of hours than I had in the whole time since he arrived. Before, I had just thought he was hot (which I hasten to add, I still did), but now I realised there was so much more to him. I might even like him as a person. I found out that he had grown up in Hampshire with his parents and his twin Charlie (yes, there were two of him! I must remember to tell Claire). By the sounds of it, he had had quite a charmed upbringing, splitting his time between the family home and the South of France as his mother was French (hence the killer tan). He had studied business at Warwick University and had graduated with a first. When he finished, he was not sure what he wanted to do, so he took a couple of years out and went over to Provence to help on his grandparents' vineyard (as you do). The time he spent there sounded idyllic. He must have been happy there, because as he spoke about it, his face lit up. He recalled everything with such fondness and said that one day, he would like to live there again. Anyway, his rural idyll had come crashing down when he received news of his father's unexpected death. He flew home, took up the mantle of head of the family, got a sensible job in the city, worked his way up the career ladder, and here he was, my new boss at Taylor Marketing! (a slightly condensed version of events for your benefit). I was now wishing that I had not been so elusive with my own life story when he had asked, I feared it may have given him the impression that it was full of drama and excitement, when it had been perfectly dull and 'normal'. The engine switched off and we sat for a second or two in silence.

"Thank you so much for today, Jake, and I really am so sorry that you've had to babysit me" I unclicked my seatbelt and went to open the door.

"Wait!" he tentatively put his hand on mine. "Are you free Thursday after the presentation?" I considered all the things I would not be doing on Thursday evening.

"All evening" I admitted, slightly embarrassed.

"Would you be free for dinner afterwards?" He seemed more confident this time, more self-assured.

"You're sure that after this morning, you want to risk taking me out in public. I'd be happy enough just to keep my job" I giggled childishly.

"Your job is safe, trust me, and I think I want to take you out more because of today" he chuckled adorably.

"In which case I would like that very much." I extracted my hand from his which was now buzzing from the contact, undid my seatbelt and exited the vehicle.

"Good. Now, make sure you rest up and remember to get something to eat!" He called, craning his neck to see me.

"I will, I promise. Thank you again Jake." I closed the door and floated up the path to the house, a spring in my step which could not have been mustered earlier. I turned the key in the lock and pushed open the stiff door. Ben was waiting expectantly on the other side.

"God Jem, are you okay? Claire called me and told me what had happened." He took my bag and coat off me as he spoke. "Go and jump in the shower and I'll pop the kettle on."

"Why aren't you at work? I thought you had a meeting?" I called out as I began ascending the stairs.

"It got cancelled, so I thought I'd work from home today" he shouted from the kitchen.

"Cool!" I turned on the shower and peeled the clothes from my putrid smelling body. Quite how chunks of the stuff had made their way into my bra was beyond me and to be honest, I really did not want to imagine how they got there. It was best I could not remember otherwise I would never have wanted to set foot back in work again. The water felt divine, and I stood there unmoving for what felt like hours (it was no more than ten minutes in reality). I wrapped one of Ben's oversized towels around me and made my way back to my room. As I trundled across the landing, the smell of bacon cooking wafted up the stairs. It smelt delicious. Years back, I had contemplated going vegetarian, but the thought of not being able to have a bacon sarnie killed the idea off pretty quickly. I threw on my sweatpants and a hoodie and headed down towards the smell of fried pig. Ben was coming out of the kitchen holding a tray laden with mugs and sandwiches.

"Movie day?" he asked hopefully.

"Don't you have work to do?"

"I'm sure they can cope without me for a few hours. Besides, you're more important." He placed the tray on the coffee table and we both sank back onto the sofa. "Right, what do you fancy? Thriller? Rom Com? Marvel?" He listed every genre he could think of but we both knew there was only one choice.

"Marvel!" I squealed excitedly.

"From where we left off?"

"Abso-blimmin-lutely!" I insisted. Ben and I had been Marvel fans for as long as I could remember. I had lost count of how many times we had watched and re-watched their films. He had recently discovered the correct chronological order in which to watch them, so we had started from scratch and were now about half through the list. Do not get me wrong, I loved a rom com as much as the next person, but superhero films were my absolute favourite. I pondered whether there might be a real-life shield wielding Captain America out there somewhere for me. Then quickly realised that with my track record with men, I was more likely to bump into a universe destroying Thanos than some kind, earth saving, hottie. Ben pressed play on the Sky remote and handed me my sandwich as the opening Marvel comic strip intro started for Avengers Civil War.

"You need to take better care of yourself Jem. You're always running round at a hundred miles an hour; you're going to get ill if you don't slow down a bit." He looked genuinely concerned.

"I will, I promise." My mouth was full of sandwich. "This is so good!" I said appreciatively, patting his leg. He flashed me a wide smile, proud of the reaction his sandwich was getting.

When I finished, I pulled my legs up onto the sofa and snuggled down under the blanket he had got out for me. I held it up slightly, offering for him to get under too, which he did, and that is how we spent the rest of the afternoon.

"Thank you" I whispered as I cuddled up to his side.

He kissed my forehead. "Anything for my favourite girl."

Claire and Sarah arrived home just after six, so a full and in-depth description of what had happened earlier was demanded. All Sarah wanted to know was where Jake was taking me for dinner on Thursday, and all Claire cared about was being introduced to his twin brother. Ben left us to have some 'girl time' while he went to get the Chinese. My appetite had returned with vigour, and when he returned laden with three carrier bags, I ate enough food to feed a small family (something which I felt slightly guilty about, but not enough to stop me from eating my fourth piece of prawn toast). The thing was, as soon as I had finished, I was ready for bed. Whether it was the crap night's sleep I had last night, or my brush with death this morning, I did not know, but I was exhausted.

"I'm going to split I'm afraid guys" I said pulling a pretend sad face.

"Typical" replied Ben. "Disappearing just as the dishes need doing."

"Leave them for me, I'll do them in the morning" I added kissing them all goodnight.

"Sleep tight" they replied in unison.

# WEDNESDAY

That night, I slept like a baby after a warm bubble bath and a Calpol and Nurofen cocktail. It was amazing what a solid ten hours of glorious, uninterrupted, comatose-like sleep could do for a person. So, when my alarm went off bright an early, I bounded out of bed, feeling fully revived and ready to face the world. Filled with the energy of twenty eager Energiser bunnies and the enthusiasm and conviction of someone on the first day of their Slimming World journey, I threw on my gym gear, and headed straight for the door, making sure to grab my black cap on the way out as my hair was akin to that of Medusa's. Glancing in the mirror in the hallway, I also made a mental note not to stop and talk to anyone given that my teeth were covered in a generous layer of yellow fur and my breath smelt like that of a feral animal.

Although summer was on its way, the morning felt cooler than the previous few. A breeze gently rustled the trees in peoples gardens and along the roadside, the wet dew on the ground implying that it had been colder during the night too. The unmistakeable soothing voice of Otis Redding singing 'Dock of The Bay' played through my earbuds and carried me gently round my route. Although not my usual go to running music, he was helping my relaxed approach to this morning's outing. I was not trying to break any records today; I was just glad to be back outside and feeling myself again. Whether it was down to the cooler weather I do not know, but there were less people about. I smiled at a few fellow joggers and dog walkers (remembering not to expose my furry pegs), but in general I had the free run of the place.

As I rounded the corner of the lake, the pop-up coffee van came into view. No matter what time of day, you could always guarantee that there would be someone queueing patiently for their freshly ground caramel macchiato or chai soya latte, and today was no exception. A small queue had formed by the open serving hatch, and at the front stood a tall, dark-haired man wearing tight running leggings under some skimpy shorts. He was impossible to ignore. As he turned around, my heart stopped dead. Fuck. Really? Of course it was him. What kind of sick divine intervention was this? Someone up there hated me for sure. There, in all his beauteous Lycra clad glory, was Jake. All freshly washed, with clean teeth and immaculate hair. Not even a hint of imperfection in his appearance. Was me hurling over him not enough? Did he really need to witness me looking like this too? I may have had a shower since then, but in no way, shape, or form was I was I looking my best. Hell, I barely looked human. I was so not ready for a second encounter just yet. There was no way he could see me looking or smelling like this (although in fairness, he must be getting pretty used to both by now). My mind went into overdrive. I was too close for him not to notice me. I had two, possibly three options at best. 1) I pretended that I had not seen him, turned around, and ran back the way I had just come (although as I just pointed out I was too close not to have noticed him and would seem extremely rude if I did not say hi). 2) I sped up and ran past him as quickly as possible (as per point 1 though, I was too close to say I hadn't noticed him, plus it was highly likely that in doing so, I would look like a silly little school girl trying to run as fast as she could to impress a boy, which I was not, and in addition, was likely to fall in the process or do something even more humiliating). 3) I dropped down dead on the spot and then did not need to worry about the pitfalls of options one and two, but this was highly reliant on further divine intervention, or a hidden heart defect that had gone unnoticed, rearing its ugly head within the next ten seconds. *I'm screwed.*

"Jemma is that you?" Too late. Options one and two had gone out the window, and unfortunately, my heart was still functioning perfectly.

"Morning!" I mumbled behind pursed lips, feigning surprise.

"God, are you okay? What's wrong with your mouth?" he asked, looking concerned. How did you tell someone that apart from practicing poor dental hygiene and currently smelling like a badger's arse, you were fine and dandy?

"Oh, what this?" I laughed, gesturing to my mouth which was currently looking like a feline's anus. "I'm just practicing a new breathing technique I read up on. It's all about limiting the amount of air intake whilst running" I explained, moving my hand over my mouth. Even I was acutely aware that this sounded ridiculous, and I could tell he was not buying it either.

"Sounds dangerous" he replied with a knowing smile.

"What are you doing here? Do you run here a lot? I haven't seen you here before!" I had intended this to be a very brief, light-hearted conversation, but it came out far more aggressively than I had expected, and it sounded more like an interrogation than a friendly chat. He was clearly finding my neuroticism amusing.

"Umm…. I usually go the gym before work, but one of the guys there mentioned that he comes down here because it's a good place for a run. I thought I'd switch things up a bit. Is that… okay with you?" he joked. *Oh great, now he's mocking me.*

"Absolutely! Great idea! Fine by me!" I said waving my arms animatedly in the air. Dear god, I had gone from SAS interrogator to Broadway actor, all smiles, wide eyes, and jazz hands within an overly dramatic blink of an eye. I hated the effect this man had on me. I was a wreck (emotionally and physically).

"Yeah, it is" he chuckled. "Even better now I've bumped into you" he continued calmly, watching for my reaction.

I pulled my cap down lower over my face to try and hide the beetroot colour it had quickly turned. "Hmm... well, I'd better keep going, I've got a new boss and don't want to be late in to work." I grimaced but quickly followed it up with a smile to prove that I was only joking (just in case he decided to change his mind about the whole firing thing).

"What's he like? Is he a jackass?" Crap, he was playing along. I had not expected that.

"I'm not too sure" I replied honestly "I'm still trying to figure him out."

"Sounds like the sensible thing to do. He's probably just a normal guy though, maybe you should give him a chance to prove that he's not a complete idiot? You never know, you might even get to like him!" His eyes were kind, almost pleading. How was I supposed to respond to that? Should I admit to having watched his every move since he arrived? Tell him how I had repeatedly imagined myself underneath him on numerous occasions and could not stop wondering how he looked naked?

"Maybe I will" I smiled, trying to get the image of his naked body out of my head for the fifth time today already. "See you later," and with that I started to move away, suddenly conscious of how I was running and how I might look from behind.

"You will indeed!" he called out after me, his voice laced with a smile.

◆ ◆ ◆

When I got back, I realised that I had sprinted the entire way home. Whether I was just desperately trying to escape the awkward situation in the park, or whether I had been so consumed with re-playing the scene over and over in mind that I had paid no attention to how quickly I was running, I have no idea. Claire and Sarah were both sat at the breakfast bar in their dressing gowns holding steaming mugs of coffee when I walked in. Out of all of us, it was only me who got up before 7am. The others all agreed that an extra hour in bed was far more favourable than burning off an extra few hundred calories.

"Ooh, is there any more coffee left?" I asked hopefully.

"Yep, there should be some in the pot, I've only just made it" Sarah replied, taking a gulp of hers.

"Fab!" I poured myself a cup and then swivelled myself on to a bar stool.

"How was the run this morning?" asked Claire.

"Don't ask" I said shaking my head. I should have known by now that telling Claire not to ask was like showing a red rag to a bull and was never going to end with the desired result. By the time I had told them about the whole debacle, they were laughing uncontrollably, and said that my invite to dinner was more than likely now rescinded based on my earlier performance. I was just explaining how Jake had asked me to give him a chance when Ben stumbled in through the door.

"Give who a chance?" he mumbled searching for a clean mug.

"Jake!" the girls shrieked excitedly.

"Why are you giving him a chance?" he turned round to face us. "I thought you said he was an arrogant womaniser? Why would you want to get caught up in that?" He sounded like an overprotective parent.

"I don't know" I said wistfully. "I think he might be different. Maybe I got him wrong? I don't know." I really did not know. I was starting to question everything.

"In my experience, your initial gut instinct is usually right" he asserted, pouring himself a coffee.

"Well, my gut instinct says that even if he is an arse, I bet he's fucking awesome in bed, so what's she got to lose?" joked Sarah.

"You would say that" replied Ben coldly. "You've never had a relationship that lasted beyond breakfast. Maybe Jem isn't looking for that."

"Oh, give me a flippin break!" she chortled, not taking his words to heart. "What woman doesn't want mind blowing sex with a beautiful man?"

The girl had a point, and if that were the worst-case scenario, (if the beautiful man did indeed want to have amazing sex with me), would it be so bad? The only thing was, I could not get the nagging feeling out of my head that maybe Jake was more than that. Of course, any sensible person would point out that I did not know him, and indeed, Ben was more than likely correct. I did, however, have an opportunity to get to know him (that is if my dinner date was still on), surely there was no harm in that?

"Of course, there isn't Hun" Claire reassured me when I voiced my thoughts. "If you think you like him, you've got to give it a chance. It's only dinner. You might think he's a complete knob after that and then you can forget all about him. Well…, I mean you can't really forget about him, because he's your bloody boss and you're going to have to see him every day at work which will be super awkward, but at least you won't always be picturing him with an erection!" Claire was nothing if not brutally honest, which is why I loved her. It was settled, I would give him a chance to show me just how 'normal' he was.

Since I had looked like a displaced hobbit when we bumped into each other this morning, I decided to make more of an effort with my appearance than was usual for a day at work. Do not get me wrong, I was not going to be like the other women in the office who dressed solely for his approval, although I was hoping he would think I looked pretty. I was doing it for …. nope, that was the sole reason I was doing it. Claire and I were going into the office together, and as was always the case when we did, she was stood waiting for me by the door, chiding me about my tardiness. I shuffled uncomfortably downstairs in my patent black Dune heels and high wasted black pencil skirt, teetering on the edge of falling face first down the last few steps. Not only was my skirt super tight (the term figure hugging does not even come close), but it was also impractical and almost painful. I mentally kicked myself for being such a slave to fashion and for bowing down to the stereotypical image I had accused so many of the girls in the office of being. On the plus side, it made my waist look super tiny and my bum perfectly peachy! The real downside was that there was no room for cinnamon buns today. I paired my skirt with a sleeveless olive silk blouse with a pretty bow necktie which I'd somehow managed to tuck into my shrink-wrapped skirt. I had taken the time to blow dry my hair properly and was much more careful with my make-up application than normal. This was as good as it was going to get. As I neared the bottom of the stairs, Claire looked up, and in that typical way that girls give each other a head-to-toe examination before forming an opinion of them, ran her gaze over my upscaled worked attire.

"Shit, you really are trying to get his attention aren't you!" she smiled deviously.

"I don't know what you mean" I replied innocently.

"Like hell you don't! Well, one thing's for sure he won't be paying any attention to what you say when you run through your presentation with him."

"That's the plan" I said honestly, and it was not for the reason she thought either. I genuinely doubted whether he would think it was good enough. Suddenly, Ben's face popped into my mind. What was it he had said about gut instincts this morning? He was always so clever. He always followed his heart and refused to compromise. I wish I could be that brave, and not have to rely on Jake not listening to my presentation to get by.

Effie was already sat at her desk looking as pretty as ever when we walked in. She was staring intently at something on her computer but tried desperately to click out of it as she clocked us approaching. I caught a brief glimpse of Jake's LinkedIn profile before it was replaced by the company's homepage. What was wrong with everyone? *He is just a normal guy, just a normal guy* I repeated over in my head.

"Wow, look at you!" she exclaimed sounding shocked. "Someone's had a bit of a glow up since yesterday!"

"Thank you for the back handed compliment Effie. Tell me, have you booked refreshments for the meeting tomorrow or are you not yet finished looking at Jake's LinkedIn details?" *Touché Jemma.* I would not normally bite; but her overly intrusive interest in Jake had irked me (the words pot and kettle sprang to mind, but I did my best to ignore them).

"Yep, all ordered!" she replied not appreciating my sarcasm.

I lowered myself slowly and deliberately into my chair. Movement today was going to be a challenge. No flinging my arms and legs around with gay abandon, it was small, considered movements all day.

As the clock ticked nearer to 11am, I thought I would make the most of my nervous energy (and my bouncy curls which would no doubt drop out any minute) and see if Jake was free to go through my notes. I gathered up my laptop and made my way tentatively over to his office.

"Good luck!" whispered Claire, making a crossed fingers sign with both hands. I knocked on the door and waited for a response. The blinds were shut.

"Come in!" he called, sounding calm and confident – like a real grown-up boss.

I peered round the edge of the door "Hi, are you free now?" He looked up from his laptop.

"Hi! Yes of course, come on in" he said with a wide grin, beaconing me over with his hand.

I pushed the door fully open and stepped inside, closing it quietly behind me. I was suddenly very self-conscious. I had forgotten how big his office was, and it took me at least ten seconds to make my way over to him (in normal circumstances it might have only taken two, but the skirt really was bloody tight). As I walked towards him, he sat silently watching. He did not smile or make any gesture with his face, he just watched intently. It was unnerving.

"You weren't late this morning then?" he said as I sat down, smiling at the private joke between us.

"Nope. Couldn't be really, I bumped into my boss first thing, so wouldn't have had an excuse" I replied, returning the smile.

"Hahaha" he chuckled, looking completely relaxed, except that I noticed his hands were clamped around the arms of his chair like a vice.

"How was the rest of your run?"

"Good thank you." *Not that I can remember anything after the point of seeing you.* "How about you? Did you enjoy your coffee?" The polite chit chat was killing me.

"Great, thanks. I was a little distracted though after our meeting" he confessed sheepishly.

"Oh" I stuttered, surprised by his comment, hoping it was a good thing and not because he had been horrified by my appearance. We both went to open our mouths to speak again. "Sorry, you first" I apologised.

"Umm…" He suddenly sounded a little uneasy. This did not bode well. "I know I mentioned about taking you to dinner tomorrow night …" he trailed off. Oh great, the girls were right, this morning's face to face encounter with me looking like a rabid dog had killed off my dinner invite. He was cancelling on me, the superficial, misogynistic pig! He gazed at me more seriously and continued "I have a work thing this evening, it's probably going to be boring, but I can't get out of it. An old client of mine is holding an open evening for a new art exhibition of his in the city and he's asked me to go along." He stopped again and took a deep breath. "I was wondering if you would like to accompany me?" Okay, I was not expecting that. Ignore my previous comments. I straightened out my skirt, taking a second to steady my nerves.

"How can I say no when you make it sound so exciting!" I smiled, looking up at those beautiful dark eyes which watched me intently.

"Does that mean you'll come with me?" he replied, leaning back in his chair, and giving me that beautiful smile of his.

"Consider it a date! No… not a date, you know what I mean!" *Really? Again?*

"I'll consider it a non-date then!" he laughed, seeming relaxed once again. Had he been nervous to ask me? "It starts at 8.00pm so I'll pick you up at 7.30pm? Oh, and its black tie I'm afraid, is that going to be okay at such short notice?"

"No problem at all. I'm sure I can rustle up something, even if it is a binbag!" I was wishing now that I had gotten the full details before committing. What the hell was I going to wear?

"Why don't you finish a bit early today, give yourself a bit more time to get ready?"

"Are you sure? What do I tell people if they ask where I'm going?"

He pretended to think about it for a few seconds then said "Just tell them you're accompanying me to a client meeting. They don't need to know the details. Unless you particularly want to tell them?"

"Okay, thank you." I did not know what I was thanking him for. The invite, being allowed to leave work early, or the plausible explanation for doing so. Either way I was thankful.

"No" he smiled, "Thank you." He held my gaze, and it felt like the world had stopped turning. The image of him laying naked in bed was all I could see, and in that moment, I wanted it, I wanted it more than I had ever wanted anything else. The thought of touching him and being touched by him made my cheeks blush.

Oh, how I wanted to feel his body move over mine, to feel the weight of him pressed against me. How I wanted to feel the warmth of his skin under my hands. Would he be rough or gentle? Take his time and be considerate or go at it like a crazed animal. *Feel free to do either*. The door to his office sprung open and in walked his assistant, her arms full of files. I practically jumped out of my skin. Did she not think to knock?

"Sorry Mr Bales, I did try knocking but there was no answer. I just wanted to pop these on your desk" she said apologetically motioning to the files, looking back and forth between the two of us, a look of confusion on her plain face. She placed them on the edge of the table, and then headed back to the door in a hurry.

"Er… thanks Erin" Jake called, sounding slightly flustered. "Right," he said as if trying to re-group. "Let's take a look at this presentation, shall we?" He cleared some space for my laptop. Was I imagining it, or did he just re-adjust his trousers?

"Yes, of course" I replied, feeling like I'd just been caught red handed watching porn. I instantly shut down the image of Jake tied to my bed in nothing but a blindfold and opened my laptop. *What is wrong with me?* I found the file containing the presentation and handed it over to him. He flicked through the slides, suggesting small tweaks and offering up advice, but overall, he thought it was a solid pitch, and was pleased with the level of detail and amount of evidence I had included to support our ideas. When he had finished, he pushed the laptop to.

"So, how have you felt about this project" he asked earnestly.

"Umm… what do you mean?" My response was cautious.

"I mean have you enjoyed it, have you had any difficulties, is there anything you would do differently if you had to do it again?"

I was not sure where he was going with this. "Honestly?"

"Yes" he smiled, "honestly." He sat forward in his chair, placing his elbows on the desk.

"Okay, if we're being honest. I've not found it easy." I fidgeted in my seat, the waistband on my skirt digging painfully into my hips.

"How so?"

"If I'm being totally honest, I don't believe in it" I replied apprehensively, my eyes cast down towards my lap at the admission.

"Why not?" I felt like I was being interviewed. Was this payback for this morning? I thought for a second before responding.

Looking back up to face him I answered as calmly and as honestly as I could. "Because I've always thought that marketing was a bit like magic. You get given an idea or a product and you have an opportunity to make it into something amazing. You have the power to make people want and need something, even before they themselves know they need it. And I know you can't always love what you're selling, heaven knows it was hard to pitch an eco-friendly dog chew last year, but you must at least believe that it has a place in this world or a purpose, surely. Otherwise, how do you convey that passion, that message to millions of people? I just don't know whether I believe in this" I said solemnly. "It's not unique, it's not really offering anything new, and I genuinely believe that in this instance, removing the human interface from the process is not a positive thing." I realised I was rambling. "Sorry, ignore me. That was a bit too much for a Wednesday morning. I've overstepped the mark. My opinion won't affect tomorrow's presentation I promise" I said, trying to reassure him.

"No" he said softly, a genuine warmth in his eyes. "Listening to you just then, made me realise why I love my job. Marketing for me is a form of escapism, a way to leave the real world behind, where eco-friendly dog chews can make non-pet owners want to go out and buy a dog! It is powerful and exciting, and it has the capability to change things – people's opinions and perceptions."

There was a pause. "Their desires" he added, a sparkle in his eyes. *Oh god, please do not speak about desires right now.* I crossed my legs, a feat in itself, given my attire. "The thing is" he continued, abruptly halting my vision of us undressing each other and having passionate sex over his desk. "As much as we want to love our work and have it make a difference, we are also bound by the needs of the business, which ultimately, is to make money. Sometimes, we must put that before our own hopes and ambitions."

"I know" I agreed reticently. "I'll go back and make the amendments you've suggested. Unless there's anything else you want to add in?"

"I think, you've got it covered Jemma. It's great, honestly."

"Thanks" I smiled. "I'll leave you in peace. See you later though." I stood up gingerly, not realising until that moment that where my skirt had cut off the circulation to the bottom half of my body, both my legs had gone to sleep. I had to physically pick them up and move them to carry myself out of the office. Not the ideal situation.

"Looking forward to it" he called, stifling a laugh.

"So… how did it go?" whispered Claire eagerly before I had even made it back to my seat.

"Really good" I replied dreamily.

"I'm talking about the pitch, not the flirting" she chortled sarcastically.

"Oh, shit. I told him I thought the idea sucked."

"You didn't!" she looked both gobsmacked and impressed. "What did he say? I take it you've still got a job and you haven't been given five minutes to pack up your things before he has someone escort you from the premises? I hate to ask, but if he does sack you, can I have your desk?"

"Of course, you can" I smiled "But he agreed me with me in a roundabout way. Anyway, he's invited me to a gallery opening this evening with him. Totally work related before you get any ideas," I added hastily more for my benefit than hers. Claire sat there, her mouth agape.

"Shut up!" she screeched. "Work related my arse! I've seen the way he looks at you. He could have asked any woman and about seventy-five per cent of the men in this office to go with him, and all of them would have jumped at the chance and probably offered him a blow job by way of thanks. But he asked you! This is one hundred per cent NOT work related! Please tell me you said yes?"

"Yes, I said yes!" I giggled. "But now I'm shitting my pants. What if I screw it up? What if I wear the wrong thing, it's bloody black tie! What if I embarrass myself, or worse, him! I'll have to give up my job and go and work in a supermarket where nobody knows me."

"Why a supermarket?" she replied, homing in on that one thing, ignoring the rest of what I had just said.

"I don't know, it was the first place that sprang to mind" I laughed nervously.

"Calm down Jem, you're not going to have to go and work in a supermarket" she said reassuringly. "You are a beautiful, intelligent woman, and he's bloody lucky to be taking you. This is what you do, you're great with people. You will have a brilliant time." She lowered her voice. "I guarantee you'll be horizontal with him pounding your lady bits before the stroke of midnight! It will be like a modern day Cinderella story. Except hopefully without the mice or the housework, because let's face it, you're not good with either!" We both burst into fits of childish giggles.

"You are so vulgar" I spluttered, wiping the tears away from my cheeks.

"What's the joke?" Helene span round from her computer, eyeing us both with a suspicious glare.

"Oh nothing" I said trying to compose myself.

I achieved bugger all the rest of the day. I managed to order some last-minute refreshments for the meeting (it transpired that Effie had ordered a delivery for the following week instead). By 3.30pm I was beginning to clock watch, and the excitement of earlier had descended into a nervousness unlike anything I had known before.

"I'm going to make a move Hun" I whispered to Claire. "I'll see you at home."

"No probs, I'll see you later" she mouthed whilst on hold to someone on the phone.

I grabbed my bag and jacket and headed off.

❖ ❖ ❖

By the time I got back, I was feeling positively sick. What had I been thinking? This whole thing was utter madness! People like me did not go on dates (if this even was a date) with their gorgeous bosses (although I am guessing some did which would account for this country's higher than average divorce rate and the vast number of in-office relationships). Only one thing could save me now. Wine. I grabbed a bottle of white from the fridge, and poured myself a huge glass, necking half of it where I stood without even flinching. I topped the glass back up, went to put the bottle back in the fridge before thinking better of it, and taking it upstairs with me to get ready.

I wallowed in the bath's hot, soapy water for an hour, reliving every moment and every conversation with Jake from the past few days. I revisited every look I thought he had given me, and every clue to prove that I was not imagining this. My head told me it was all strictly business, but my heart dared to hope it might be something more. A bottle of wine later, I forced my wrinkly body to get out and dry off. The nerves had dissipated a little but were dangerously close to resurfacing every time I thought about what I was doing. My black-tie wardrobe was a little limited to say the least, it not being a pre-requisite for a Friday night Dominoes or a cheeky midweek Nando's. But I did have one dress that I hoped would suffice. I had bought it in a Donna Karen sale in New York a few years ago but had never had the opportunity to wear it (or indeed take it out of its bag). It was a gorgeous mid-length, black bandeau style dress, tight fitting with a silk-like sheen. I was praying it still fitted otherwise I would be fashioning that bin bag (and from memory, we only had the khaki green ones left). The dress was a bit too revealing to wear alone, so my plan was to team it with a new white tailored, silky jacket with big shoulder pads, which I'd recently purchased from an up-and-coming designer, and a pair of black satin peep-toe stilettoes, that were my go-to for more formal occasions. I'd already decided to wear my dark hair up, hoping it might make me look a bit more 'businessy' and sophisticated, and make-up wise was going for a natural glow with a smoky eye (easy to achieve in theory, but I somehow always managed to look more like an upset panda than the dark and mysterious image I had in my head). I wanted the overall look to seem effortless, even though more effort was going into it than on nights when I did want to look like I had tried (the irony was not lost on me).

It took me two hours and another glass and a half of wine to finish getting ready. When I stepped back and looked in my full-length mirror, I had to concede that I did not look like a total disaster (no upset pandas tonight!). The dress thank God did still fit, and the jacket sat perfectly over my shoulders, highlighting my neckline which I had accentuated with a delicate diamond pendant my parents had bought be for my birthday last year. My hair was tied loosely in a messy bun. I was sure that Jake had been accompanied to many events by far prettier girls than myself, but from a personal perspective, I was pleased with the finished article (and even if I was not, it was too late to do anything about it now).

I heard the unmistakeable purr of his car pull up outside our house, and my nerves threatened to overspill.

"He's here, he's here!" Sarah called up in a shrill, excited voice.

"Sweet mother of Satan, would you look at him" followed Claire, "It's like watching a scene from a James Bond film! Is it me or is he walking in slow motion?"

Sarah chuckled "I think it's just you, you fool! You realise how sad and desperate the pair of us look perving on him through the blinds like this, don't you?"

"Not at all" replied Claire sounding offended. "It is our duty as friends to do our due diligence and make sure that Jem isn't going on a date with an ugly psychopath."

"Well, I can't tell from this angle whether he is a psychopath or not" Sarah offered seriously, "But I can confirm that he's certainly not ugly!" she snorted, bursting into fits of giggles.

A few seconds later and the door knocked, my desire to run to the bathroom and throw up overpowering. *Deep breaths, deep breaths*. I could hear the girls fighting over who was going to open the door. Sarah was obviously victorious.

"Hi!" she said in her posh finance voice "You must be Jake. I'm Sarah, and you already know Claire." I could imagine the scene unfolding downstairs.

"Hi Sarah, pleasure to meet you" replied Jake politely. "Hi Claire, how are you?" he said slightly louder, implying she was still standing in the kitchen.

"Oh, er... I'm good thank you" she replied, sounding flustered. "Jem, are you ready? Jake's here!" just in case I had missed their little performance.

"Coming!" I called, taking one last lingering look in the mirror. There was nowhere to hide now. I was too old and too trussed up to escape out of the window, plus there was a part of me that was desperate to see him. I took another deep breath, gathered my nerves, and headed for the stairs. Holding on tightly to the handrail, I gingerly descended the first step. It creaked loudly signalling my descent. All three of them looked up to where I was. Claire and Sarah were closest to me and were obscuring my view of Jake. I saw their reactions first. Sarah's mouth was agog, and I saw her mouth the words "Shit" and "Wow" whilst Claire had her proud mum face on and was slightly more poetic with her appraisal.

"You look absolutely beautiful Jemma" she whispered in my ear as she leant in to give me a kiss on the cheek. "Have a wonderful time tonight." She stepped aside and for the first time I saw him clearly.

It was like the wind had been knocked out of me, the breath stolen from my lungs. He stood perfectly still, watching me closely the way he had done this morning. Dressed in a black tuxedo and bow tie, he looked every inch the dapper gentleman, one who coincidentally, had just stepped straight off the cover of Vogue magazine. My eyes scoured quickly over him, wanting to take every inch of him in. I could not ignore the way his trousers fit perfectly around his thighs, and how his shirt fit snuggly into his waistband (lord only knows what was going on beneath that). His jacket skimmed over his broad shoulders highlighting his toned chest and muscly arms. But it was his face that I was drawn back to, his eyes in particular. They were so dark and mysterious, and although they were kind, there was something much more there, something I could not read. They were penetrating my very soul. Had we not needed to be somewhere, and had Claire and Sarah not been stood there, I could have stared into them forever.

"Hi" I finally managed, trying to ease the palpable tension in the room.

"Hi" he responded, a smile growing on his face. He took an assured step forward and offered me his hand.

"Shall we Miss Lucas?" I took it without question. The touch of his smooth skin on mine sending shockwaves through my body, as a waft of his intoxicating smell drifted past my nose. I thought my legs might give way as he led me towards the door.

"Goodnight, ladies" he called behind to the girls, who were now whispering animatedly between themselves.

"Night you two" bellowed Sarah "Don't do anything I wouldn't do!" The notion of that made me chuckle inwardly, knowing there was little she would not do, first date or otherwise.

As the door closed and we headed down to the waiting car, he turned to look at me with those delicious dark eyes. "You look absolutely beautiful" he whispered, leaning in.

I blushed at his words, my heart thrumming loudly in my chest. "Thank you, you scrub up well yourself. M&S?" I giggled.

"No, not this time" he smiled, bending down to open the passenger door. As he came back up his body brushed gently against mine. "I'm so glad you agreed to come with me tonight" he said quietly.

"I'm glad you asked me" I replied breathlessly, holding his gaze, feeling giddy. He helped lower me gently into the car, closed the door and then made his way round to the driver's side. I watched him transfixed as he made the short journey. Everything about him was mesmerising, the way he looked, how effortlessly he moved, he had an aura that was distinctly his, and it did something to me that I could not explain. I'd forgotten how cosy the Spyder was inside, and as we went to fasten our seatbelts, our fingers grazed each other's unexpectedly. Whether it sent the same feeling through his body as it did mine, I do not know, but he turned to face me again, his hand lingering on mine.

"Jemma, I know I said this was a work-related thing tonight" he looked suddenly unsure of himself, "but I must confess that I asked you to come with me because I wanted to spend time with you, as well as getting your professional opinion of course. Do you mind?"

"I don't mind at all" I said, smiling like a goon.

The engine sprang to life, and we hurtled off down the street. There was something so very sexy about watching him drive this car. The way he handled its power and expertly manoeuvred it despite the amount of traffic on the road. I watched as his hands caressed the steering wheel, wishing that they were holding me in the same way. As we drove through the streets, he filled me in on what to expect that evening. Jacques Lucerne was an art dealer and an old client of Jakes at his previous company. Tonight, was the official opening of his London based gallery, and he had asked Jake to attend so that they could discuss ideas for the Paris gallery which he was hoping to open next year. According to Jake, tonight's event would be full to the brim with supermodels, investment bankers and other arseholes who knew nothing about art, but whose sole motivation to attend was so that they could be photographed arriving and leaving to boost their social media presence. There was a real tone of distain in his voice as he spoke.

"The thing is" he griped, "These people aren't going for the art. They couldn't distinguish between a Picasso and a Turner even if they were offered a million pounds. They care nothing for the way art can make you feel, the talent of the artists, nothing. They are going purely for the champagne and the paparazzi." I considered for a moment that I probably could not distinguish between a Picasso and a Turner but thought I would leave that bombshell for another occasion. No point ruining a first date (and I was fairly sure this might be a first date now).

"You seem extremely passionate about this" I mused.

"I am" he said smiling warmly. "Jacques is a great guy, and he works with amazing artists. Each one of them is supremely talented. I hope you'll get a chance to meet a few of them this evening." He sounded genuinely excited. I had not had him pegged as an art connoisseur, but then so far, he had been nothing like I had imagined. I wondered what else he would surprise me with.

The car journey flew by in an instant, and before long, we were pulling up outside the gallery. I can only describe the scene in front of us as being like something straight out of Hollywood. I do not know what I had been expecting, but it certainly was not this. Two uniform rows of six-foot golden torches lined a scarlet red carpet which led up to the most ornate set of wooden doors I had ever seen in my life. Huge, grand, and imposing. The building itself was ostentatious but classic, cream render and Grecian style pillars stood stoically either side of the doors, transporting it back to a time long ago. An orderly queue of cars waited patiently for the valets to park them discreetly out of sight, whilst the beautiful people who had arrived in them paraded down the luxurious carpet desperate to be noticed.

"Oh... dear...God" I said petrified, as I stared hopelessly out of the car window.

Jake placed a reassuring hand on mine. "You're going to be fine" he said softly. "You look sensational, and just remember, once we're inside, it's just a gallery."

"Mmhmm..." I replied turning to face him.

"I'll be right here next to you" he whispered squeezing my hand a little tighter, and there was something in the way he did that that made me believe everything would be okay.

Two six-foot blonde Russian looking supermodels in couture gowns and towering heels exited the Rolls Royce Phantom in front of us, and sashayed down the carpet like they were working the runway at New York fashion week.

"See," said Jake mockingly "Twenty pounds says they aren't here to buy a painting."

"Well, by looking at them, I'd say they aren't here for the food either" I joked, my mood lifting slightly.

A young boy came over and took the keys to the car whilst

Jake opened my door and held out his hand "Mademoiselle." The whole thing was surreal, like being in a dream.

"Why, thank you kind Sir."

He was true to his word. Once out of the car, he did not leave my side. In fact, he stayed so close, that I could feel the beating of his heart, which strangely comforted me and slowed the racing rhythm of my own. He carefully placed his hand at the base of my spine and walked me confidently up the carpet towards the entrance. To everyone looking on, we were just like every other couple that had walked before us. Only I could feel the gentle circular motion his thumb was tracing over my skin, and the blistering heat it was causing between my legs. Could he feel it too? He continued walking, his eyes fixed ahead as if nothing was happening. *Nope, just me then.*

As we entered the great hall, teams of servers stood expectantly with silver trays lined with glasses of champagne. Others glided effortlessly through the throngs of people offering refills and canapes with an elegance that you just did not witness at your local Wetherspoons. We both took a glass of the pearlescent fizzing liquid.

"To art." I raised my glass. "May we never confuse a Picasso with a Turner, and may we always appreciate it even if we do not understand it." I smiled, chinking my glass with his.

"Spoken like a true master." An older gentleman with silver hair and a thick French accent strode confidently over to us with his arms outstretched. "You must be Jemma" he said wrapping them around me and kissing me three times on the cheeks. "Jake, I'm so pleased you made it! Come here my boy" he said releasing me and transferring his affections to him. The way they held each other was more like long lost friends than old work acquaintances. It was touching to see two grown men so openly affectionate towards each other.

"Sorry, Jemma this is Jacques" Jake offered apologetically.

I could not help but instantly warm to this genial man. "A pleasure to meet you Jacques" I beamed.

"Mais non, the pleasure is entirely mine" he professed. "Jake has told me so much about you, that I told him to bring you along so that I could finally meet the person he speaks so highly of!" It was now Jake's turn to blush. Why had he been speaking about me?

"Okay, I think you've embarrassed me enough. Don't you have other people to speak to" he said jokingly.

"You're right, I do, but none as important as you. I'll be back later!" He turned on his heels, but before leaving added "Jemma, I'd value an opportunity to speak with you later to discuss your thoughts on the evening and run through some ideas with you."

"Of course, the honour would be mine Monsieur Lucerne."

"Enchante Cherie, please, call me Jacques."

"Avec plaisir" I smiled broadly. My inner Parisian had been awakened and there really was no stopping her now. That was, until I remembered that Jake was half French and probably fluent. I prayed the conversation did not go beyond my GCSE qualification and expose me for the charlatan I was.

"I know I'm going to like you very much indeed my dear. Now, if you would excuse me, I must go and ingratiate myself with some social climbers and inconsequential aristocrats who are only here to quaff my champagne." With that he turned and disappeared into the crowd.

"He's fantastic!" I beamed.

"Yeah, he really is something" Jake replied fondly. "He's been like a father to me since mine passed away."

"Oh, I'm so sorry, I didn't realise, I thought he was just an old client of yours."

"He is, but he's also been a family friend for years. He's more like family. Right," he said breaking the train of conversation "Let's get another drink and have a wander round the exhibits."

"Perfect" I smiled "You can educate me on the differences between Turner and Picasso!"

"I might need to take you to a different gallery for that" he smiled. "Jacques does however have a piece from one artist in particular I'd like you to see. In fact, I think he's going to be here tonight, we might have an opportunity to meet him."

"Really? Who's that? "I asked keenly.

"His name is Quentin Soloss. He is a modernist painter. He specialises in bold prints using various mediums and is renowned for his use of texture in his work. He's quite revered within the industry and is a huge talent." His face came alive, his eyes were bright and his smile wide as he spoke about this man.

"You really are passionate about all of this aren't you?" I said gesturing to the walls of artwork surrounding us. "Can I ask you a question?"

"Of course, anything" he replied earnestly.

"If you love art so much, why are you not doing something with it? Why are you working in marketing when this is clearly your passion?" Of all the questions I could have asked, I don't think he was expecting that, and for a moment, he looked slightly taken off guard. He pondered his response for a second before replying.

"You're right, art is my passion. Ever since I was a young boy, I loved the escapism that art could bring. I loved knowing the story behind a piece as much as I loved the work itself. I was obsessed with knowing why an artist created something, so that I could understand it and appreciate it even more. It is so much more than just visual; it has the power to create feeling and emotion. Art can sate all the human senses."

"What about taste and sound?" I asked genuinely curious "Surely art can't sate those senses?"

"Art takes so many forms. Music is art. Food can be art. We

assume that it is only paintings, drawings, or sculptures, but there is art all around us." He waved his arms around the room and then paused for a moment, his mood altering a little. "When my father died, I made a promise to myself that I would forge a successful career so that I could take care of my mother and Charlie if I ever needed to. I couldn't take the risk of following my heart and it not working out, so I went into marketing." My heart broke at the sound of his confession. The more I knew about him the more I liked him.

"I'm sorry" I said, resting my hand on his arm.

"Don't be. I have a brilliant life. I wouldn't change any of it, and over the years, I have come to love my job. There are parallels between art and marketing too you know. Besides, I wouldn't be stood here with you now if my life had taken a different path." He leaned in slowly towards me. "I really am so glad you came tonight." He was tantalisingly close, and the woody smell of his aftershave was intoxicating. Instinctively, I tilted my head to look at him, my heart thrumming out of control beneath the black fabric of my dress.

"I'm glad I came too." Even in heels he was much taller than me.

"Jemma... there is something I've been thinking about since I first met you..." We were so close; I could feel his delicious breath on my face.

"Oh God, what's that?"

He looked suddenly flushed. "How it would feel to kiss you," he whispered, raising his hand to my cheek.

"Oh..." *I might have given it some thought once or twice ...*

"What would you say if I did?" he asked, staring intently at my mouth with those huge, deep brown eyes of his.

A fire raged in the pit of my stomach. Who was I to deny this god-like human a kiss, if that was what he so desperately wanted? "I think I would say that I'd like that very much" I replied unable to prise my eyes away from them. Both his hands reached up to cup my face, and as his full lips met mine, I was struck by how incredibly tender he was. How gently his mouth moved. I was even more surprised when his tongue slowly stroked mine. I could feel my body melting into his. The warmth of his hands on my face, the closeness of his body, the sound of his breathing. It did something to me. It stoked a feeling deep in my core which I had not felt before. I had never experienced a kiss like it. It was divine, he was divine. *Oh shit, oh Shit, oh shit, I'm kissing Jake Bales!* He retreated slightly, a smile on his face. "I've wanted to do that since the moment I first saw you" he admitted like an embarrassed teenager.

"Really?" I managed, shocked at his confession. "And now that you have?" *please don't say it was crap, please say it was the best kiss you have ever had.*

"I think I'd like to do it again" he smiled, his face drawing closer again, his lips re-connecting with mine even more gently than before. In that moment, I forgot that we were in the middle of a crowded room, surrounded by prying eyes. All I could feel was the pounding of our hearts beating in unison, all I could see was him. It was like he had lifted me up and transported me to a place far away, where it was just him and I. He held the side of my face in his palm, his mouth now mere millimetres from mine. "You are so beautiful Jemma. I have thought that since the very beginning."

My mind was working overtime, not quite able to catch up to where we were. "My face was covered in cream cheese frosting the first time you saw me." I remembered the encounter well and blushed. We had all been gathered to witness the arrival of our new CEO, I however, had been midway through a cinnamon bun (no shock there), and unbeknown to me, was wearing more of it than I had consumed. When Jake made it round to Claire and me, he discreetly pointed out that I had something on my face and offered me his hanky to help remove it. I remembered thanking him for the gesture but using my finger instead to remove the offending article (and then praying that a huge sinkhole would open up and remove me from this earth).

"I know" he smirked. "Most women would have been mortified at the fact, you just seemed happy that there was still some left!"

"I was mortified!" I admitted, recalling how angry I had been that the earth beneath our building had proven itself so solid. "But there was no point crying over spilt icing" I concluded.

"Exactly" he said, still holding on to my face. "I thought you were the most beautiful woman in the room. I couldn't take my eyes off you." His honesty took me by surprise.

"Why?"

"Because you seemed different."

"Every girl's dream" I scoffed, still gazing into those molten pools of lava.

"I mean, you were more than just beautiful. You seemed smart and funny. I saw how you rooted for your team, how you wanted the best for them, you cared. Not many people do."

"I had no idea you were watching."

"That makes me sound like a creep!" he laughed.

"I don't think you're a creep.  A bit creepy perhaps, but not a creep" I joked.

"That means a lot, thank you."

"I genuinely had no idea though" I smiled.

"Really? I was so worried that I'd made it too obvious, and that you'd run a mile."

I was confused. "How were you obvious and why would I run a mile?"

"Did you not notice how I always found an excuse to come over to your desk, how I could never seem to get my words out when I was around you? I didn't think you would be interested because of all the rumours about me." He looked crestfallen.

"Not once. I never thought you would be interested in someone like me. And the rumours? Well, they were just that, rumours. Why would I have listened to them? Maybe I would have liked to get to know the real you?" Now was not really the time to admit I had passed a couple of those rumours off as gospel myself.

"Would you?" he said hopefully.

"Yes, I would. It would be nice not to be a quivering wreck around you for a change!"

"Do I make you nervous?" His thumb stroked the side of my face.

"Mmhmm...." My eyes closed of their own accord whilst I luxuriated in the feel of his touch.

"I don't want you to be nervous around me" he whispered in my ear.

At that moment, one of the elegant servers interrupted us. "Champagne?"

"Oh, yes please!" I stuttered, clearing my throat, and taking a glass from the tray. Jake helped himself to a water.

"Come" he said stifling a laugh and taking my hand. "We've been here an hour nearly, and we haven't seen any of the exhibits yet."

"I'd almost forgotten where we were" I confessed, ashamed.

"Me too" he smiled. He led me through the throngs of people, zigzagging between various pieces, explaining about the artists and their work. He was incredible, and he was correct, the more you knew about the back story, the more you understood and appreciated the art.

"Ahh, now this piece...." He halted in front of a beautiful watercolour. It depicted a mother and her young child sitting by a lake. It must have been set early in the morning, as the reflection on the water showed a breath-taking sunrise in the background. It was so peaceful and serene.

"It's beautiful" I admired.

"Yes, it is" he replied a little sadly. "This is the only piece the artist ever painted. Her son died unexpectedly in 2018, and afterwards she retreated from the world, not able to cope with his loss. She locked herself away in a cabin by that lake and painted this. She said it was only her overpowering need to finish the painting which kept her going through her darkest hours. And although she credited the work for saving her life, she couldn't bring herself to paint again, because she said no subject matter could ever be as important." A little plaque next to the canvas read 'Until we meet again' by Angela Seaton 2019.

"That's heart-breaking." A wave of emotion washed over me, and I could feel my eyes welling up. I looked back to the painting. It was like seeing it for the first time. Yes, it was still the same beautiful watercolour, but now I saw how the mother was holding the child, almost clinging to him, how her forlorn, empty face was staring bleary eyed out over the water, and the sunrise was not a sunrise, but a sunset. How had I not noticed that the first time around?

"See, that is the power of art" mused Jake, noticing my eyes and squeezing my hand slightly.

"It's so sad."

"It is, but it proves that grief can be creative as well as destructive. One might argue that without that profound heartache, she would never have been able to create something so incredibly heartfelt."

"True" I agreed, "but I bet she would give it all up for one more day with her baby."

"Without a shadow of a doubt. I doubt there isn't a person on this earth who wouldn't trade their soul to have one more day with a loved one," he smiled ruefully, like he understood what that was like. We stood and stared for a moment longer before slowly walking on to the next exhibit. In stark contrast, it was a vibrant display of colour and texture, unashamedly celebratory. It was entitled 'The Real Me.' This was the first piece created by the artist since coming out as gay. It was an expression of his freedom and symbolised his escape from the shackles of spending a lifetime pretending to be someone he was not. It was joyous.

"Amen to that!" I exclaimed raising my arms. "We could all do with something like this in our homes. Wait, don't you have something similar in your office?" I tried to recall the two paintings I had seen hanging on the wall yesterday.

"How very observant of you" he smiled. "Jacques gave me one for my birthday a few years ago, and then I bought another one last year. I thought that since I spend most of my time at work, I'd get more enjoyment out of them if I hung them in the office."

"You know it's not healthy to spend all your time at work, right? Have you not heard about this new thing called work/life balance?" I teased.

"Haha. I guess I just haven't had a reason not to put work first for a while. Who knows, maybe that will change?" He gave me a smile that was playful and full of promise. I could feel the colour rising in my cheeks. What was he implying? Was he saying that I could be the 'something' which dragged him away from his work? I mentally gave myself a slap for being so pathetic, but secretly hoped that that was exactly what he meant.

"You okay? you looked flushed."

"I'm good!" I replied, feeling flustered again. How could this man have such an effect on me?

There must have been at least a few hundred people milling around the gallery, what was surprising, was that as Jake had predicted, most of them were gathered in the centre of the room, chatting in groups close to the champagne rather than the round the outskirts, taking in the exhibits. He noticed me taking in the scene. "See, I told you why they were here."

"Why did Jacques invite them if he knows they aren't interested in the gallery itself?" I asked genuinely confused.

"Because, like any business, you must play the game. These people might not be interested, but they attract the media, and that is priceless. Jacques knows that." He smiled. "If this event gets reported about in tomorrow's papers or on someone's social media, chances are real art lovers will see it and they will then visit."

"It all makes sense. At least he's not expecting me to purchase something tonight. As much as I'd love to, it might be a little out of my price range." I snorted and then instantly felt embarrassed, covering my mouth with the palm of my hand.

Jake laughed. "Don't be embarrassed, it's endearing." He pulled my hand away and turned it over in his affectionately. "Are you ready to leave now?"

"Er… yes. If you are?"

"Yeah, I am, it's been a long day" he replied sounding tired for the first time.

"Ah, there you both are. I was wondering where you had got to!" bellowed Jacques who was standing near the main door with a tall, dark-haired gentleman who was gesturing animatedly to the extravagant chandeliers overhead. Jake placed his hand round my waist as we crossed the room towards him. "So, what do you think?" he asked, sounding like a little boy asking for his parents' approval.

"I never doubted you" replied Jake before placing his free arm round his shoulder.

"And you Jemma, what about you? Jake here is biased, but you will give me an honest answer."

"I think the whole evening has been magical. It's been a rollercoaster of emotions, a real treat for the senses. Who knew that art could be so powerful?" I gushed. "You have created something wonderful Jacques" I said with a genuine smile.

"You are very kind Cherie; I am so glad you came."

"So am I" I replied, sheepishly looking up at Jake, who squeezed my waist gently in his hand. Not paying attention, Jacques took my hand in his and planted a kiss on it.

"I hope I will see you again very shortly. Will you be accompanying Jake to Paris this weekend?"

"Paris?" I replied confused.

"Sorry, I haven't got round to discussing it yet." Jake rushed. I was not sure if he was speaking to me or Jacques. "I'll speak to you tomorrow to confirm details" he continued. Again, I was not sure who that was aimed at. "Brilliant evening Jacques, congratulations again" Jake said pulling him into a manly embrace and kissing him twice on the cheeks. You could tell they shared a strong bond just by looking at them. It was quite touching. "Right, shall we?" He gestured to the exit. I pulled my jacket closer around me as we stepped back out through the ornate doors. It was much quieter outside now, although there was still the odd photographer lurking around, no doubt trying to get a picture of a drunken heiress or a randy old Duke. Needless to say, they paid us no attention whatsoever as we headed to the waiting car. The valet opened the door, and I lowered myself into the seat. By the time I had manoeuvred myself into position, Jake was already behind the wheel and the engine had thrummed into life. There was something so exhilarating and overtly sexy about that sound and the sheer power it alluded to.

"I think Jacques liked you" Jake said as the car accelerated.

"I liked him too" I replied honestly watching the oncoming cars disappear into the distance. "He seems like an amazing man. You're lucky to have him in your life."

"I am. I owe him a lot," he paused. "Enough about me though, you promised you'd tell me more about you."

"Me? There really isn't much to tell. My life has not been as exciting as yours."

"You're not getting out of it that easily! Please, I want to get to know you better." It was impossible to say no to this man!

"Hmmm…okay, but don't say I didn't warn you. Just make sure you don't fall asleep behind the wheel" I snorted again before rushing to put my hand over my mouth in horror.

"So that's like a thing, is it?" he chuckled, turning to look at me.

"Yep. So, first thing you should know is that I have a tendency to snort when I laugh."

"Does it happen often?" He pretended to sound concerned.

"It can do" I giggled, pulling an apologetic face.

"Okay, I can live with that. What else?" *He can live with it!*

"Umm…… I LOVE Marmite, but I have to mix it with butter because otherwise it's too strong."

"Now that I can't accept." He scrunched up his face in mock disgust. "Everyone knows that Marmite is the food of the devil."

"Don't say that!" I pretended to be offended. "You just need to persevere with it. It really is a revelation, especially with cheese!"

"Okay, I'll try it. On one condition."

"Name your price."

"You come to Paris with me this weekend."

"Pardon?"

"I was going to ask you yesterday, but I didn't pluck up the courage. Jacques wants me to go over to look at a venue for another gallery. It's only from Friday evening until Monday. We'd have separate rooms. I'm not suggesting that we should share." *Damn it, that was the main incentive to say yes.* "I appreciate its short notice and you've probably already got plans." These moments of self-doubt surprised me. I could not imagine that someone like him would be so unsure of himself. From the way he was at work, I had assumed he was arrogant and self-assured. I pretended to think long and hard about the things I would not be doing this weekend.

"I'm so sorry Jake, I would love to, but I'm busy this weekend." I hoped I sounded convincing.

"Honestly, don't worry, like I said, I know it's short notice." He looked a little disappointed and I felt awful.

I could not prevent another little snort from escaping my mouth. "Sorry, I couldn't help it, you left yourself wide open! Of course, I would love to come to Paris with you. The only thing you've interrupted is a night in with a Domino's pizza, a face mask, and a bottle of wine." I laughed.

"Are you being serious? I can never tell with you!"

"Yes, I'm being serious. I'd love to come." *But please don't make me sleep in a separate room.*

"Brilliant!" he beamed. "I promise there will be wine too. I can even provide pizza and face masks, so you don't feel like you're missing out" he smiled.

"You've got yourself a deal then" I grinned.

"I'll get everything booked in the morning. Jacques will be so pleased; he's been hounding me to come and take a look at this project for months!"

The car weaved effortlessly through the traffic. Considering it was late, there were so many cars still on the road. It was one of my favourite things about London. It never slept. I paid little to no attention to where we were, something my mother had always warned me about as a teenager. "Always make a note of your location" she said in a dire voice one day. "That way, if you get kidnapped, you'll stand more chance of being found." She had watched one too many crime thrillers where kidnap victims had been able to pass on subtle clues as to their location in their captors' ransom videos. I did not have the heart to tell her about the statistics on kidnap victim recovery rates. The only other piece of solid advice she gave me was never to leave home without a lipstick. Thankfully, the latter had proved far more useful.

"Whereabouts, are we?" I asked, not recognising any of the roads and wondering whether I should have paid more attention. Jake turned to look at me, his eyes glinting in the moonlight. My breath caught somewhere in my chest and goosebumps spread over the surface of my skin. I shivered.

"Are you cold?" he asked.

*Nope, just seriously turned on.* "I'm good."

He indicated left. "I hope you don't mind, but a night out isn't a proper night out without a kebab at the end of it. There's this amazing little place just down here if you fancy it?"

"Wow, I didn't have you pegged as the kebab eating type!" I laughed. "You are full of surprises!"

"You have no idea" he joked.

"A gallery opening and then a kebab. You really are giving me the full spectrum of experiences!"

"Variety is the key to life. Caviar is great, but sometimes only a kebab will do."

"You are preaching to the choir Mr, although I should probably warn you that I eat way more kebabs than I do caviar." The car slowed and veered across the road to a space between two cars on the other side. Jake expertly parallel parked and as had been the case the past couple of days, ran round to open my door. "Thank you" I said, taking his outstretched hand.

"You're very welcome."

We walked over to the typical looking kebab shop and joined the back of the queue. I had forgotten that we were not really dressed for the occasion, something which did not go unnoticed by the crowd outside. "Right, what do you fancy?" Jake said, ignoring the mutterings going on around us. How did I tell him that what I really fancied was him, but in the absence of that a lamb donner would suffice?

"Umm… what are you having?" I replied trying to shake off the desire to tell him that what I really fancied was him.

"Well, I usually get a lamb donner with chilli sauce but it's all pretty good here" he replied honestly.

My soul sang. "Really? That's what I usually have too!"

"Ah, see, we have more in common than you think!" *We are a match made in heaven.* Once we had ordered, we took the food back to the car. Jake started to feverishly unwrap his.

"You know this is going to make your car stink!" I said sounding shocked.

"It's fine, it's going in for a valet tomorrow morning. Besides, you can't eat these things cold" he said picking up a piece of meat between his fingers. I could not help but watch him. *I wonder if he would eat me with such enthusiasm?*

"Okay Mr but don't come complaining to me tomorrow that you've found lettuce and chilli sauce on your car mats."

"I won't I promise" he smiled with his mouth full. With that I tucked into my kebab.

"God, this really is good" I said appreciatively.

"Told you!" We sat in perfect silence as we devoured everything within the cream paper wrappers.

It turned out we were only about fifteen minutes from home. We chatted all the way, about anything and everything. It felt so comfortable, like I had known him forever. I had to keep reminding myself that I had not, and to not read too much into everything he said. As we pulled up outside my front door, the engine silenced. We both undid our seatbelts, and Jake, swivelled round in his seat to face me. "I had an amazing time tonight."

"Me too" I said, feeling a little awkward. There was a quietness descending over the car, but the air fizzed with something undeniable. Need. Desire. It was unmistakeable. It touched every corner of the space, every hair on my arm. My heart thudded so loudly in my chest I thought he might hear it. The anticipation was overwhelming, almost too much to bear. His eyes danced over my face, his soft, full lips calling to me like a siren. What should I do? Did I open the door and leave? Did I kiss him good night? Was I supposed to invite him in to have mind blowing sex with me? That would undoubtedly be the best idea, but I did not want to come across as easy. Or did I just sit there, mute and unmoving?

His hand moved slowly towards mine; his warm touch trailing a scorching line across my skin. "You look deep in thought."

"Sorry" I replied. "I just wasn't expecting any of this, I'm not really sure what to do." In his presence I felt inexperienced, unsure. I was no virgin, but this man made me feel things I did not understand.

"Please don't apologise," he said gently "I wasn't expecting this either." He edged his body forward, closing the gap between us. God, he was beautiful. His thumb caressed the side of my face. "All I know, is that I've never wanted to kiss anyone as much as I want to kiss you right now." His words came out gravelly, as if it almost pained him to say them.

"Even though I have kebab breath?"

"Especially because you have kebab breath" he laughed, releasing some of the tension.

"In which case, I'd like to kiss you too." Once he had permission, he made his move, holding my chin between his thumb and forefinger, studying my lips as if he was formulating a plan. "You are so beautiful" he whispered against them, his thumb, pulling at the lower one, opening me up to him. That was it, I was done, my mind and body nothing but a puddle on the floor. His lips clung tenderly to mine, whilst his tongue parted my mouth further. In and out he delved, slowly, confidently and masterfully, his hands moving to the nape of my neck, nestling in my hair, his breathing rapid. My body reacted instinctively, meeting him move for move, seeking him out, encouraging him to go further, to give me more. An urgency crept over us, our gentle touches growing more fervent with every second, a blinding heat that could not be sated. His touch too much and yet not quite enough. I needed more of him, and his body was seemingly happy to oblige. And then as quickly as it had begun, it was over. The searing heat replaced with a painful coldness as he withdrew. I opened my eyes to see what was wrong. He was still frustratingly close to me, his hand still entwined in my hair, his breathing still ragged, but something had changed. It was as if a light had gone out in his eyes. A look of regret was etched across his face. My heart ached at the sight of the changed man before me. What had I done wrong? Why had he stopped? I sat motionless for a moment, trying to make sense of everything, my eyes full of questions and incomprehension.

He retreated, desperate to force some space between us. "I'll walk you to your door" he said softly, tracing his thumb from my chin over my cheek. It felt like he had slapped me across the face, his touch burning as it trailed downwards. What had I done wrong? Perhaps the kebab breath had been too much after all.

"No need, I'm good. Thank you for tonight. I'll see you tomorrow." The words were clipped and emotionless, but my insides were reeling. I wanted nothing more than to scream and shout and demand he tell me why he had stopped, but my pride would not allow me to humiliate myself further. I stepped out of the car, closed the door, and walked purposefully up to my front door, refusing to look back. Only when I was inside and hidden behind the door did I crumple to the floor and burst into tears. How could I have been so stupid? How could I have been naive enough to believe that he wanted me in the same way that I wanted him? I had practically put myself on a plate for him, no, I had thrown myself at him, and he had rejected me. I was mortified, heartbroken even, but not really surprised.

"Jem? What's the matter?" Ben came bounding into the hallway to find me slumped on the floor against the door. "What's wrong? What did he do to you." He was seething. "I'm going to fucking kill him!" he spat with venom, reaching for the handle as if he were going to run out into the street after him.

"No, no, it's not what you think. He didn't do anything honestly. It's me, I'm just an idiot" I cried, clinging to his jumper so he could not escape.

"Jem, tell me what happened." He got down on the floor next to me and wrapped me in his arms. There was something so comforting in the gesture that it made me cry even harder. In hindsight, it did look like something awful had happened. How did I explain to him that the reason I was bawling like a toddler was because I'd wasted an hour of my life shaving my legs - past the knee I might add, only for Jake to decide he did not want to take full advantage of my silky smooth skin, and he most definitely did not want to do the things to me that Ben was clearly accusing him of.

"I just need to go to bed Ben, it's been such a long day and I'm knackered" I sobbed, getting to my feet.

"Okay" he said reluctantly. "But let me carry you upstairs." With that he scooped me up and took me to my room. "Have you got clean PJ's?" he asked as he plonked me down on the end of my bed.

"Not out. There should be some in that drawer though" I said motioning to my dresser. He opened the top drawer and pulled out a clean t-shirt and shorts combo.

"Here you go" he said handing them to me. "Put them on and get straight in to bed."

"Thanks" I smiled gratefully up at him. "Night Ben."

"Night you. Are you sure you're ok?" he asked, concern still etched on his face.

"Yeah, I'm fine, honestly."

"Ok, well get some rest" he said pulling the door shut.

# THURSDAY

"Well, well, well, if it isn't the office floozy! You look like you've been banged more times than a car door" squealed Sarah excitedly as I walked into the kitchen. "Tell us every sordid little detail. I want to know how big his cock was, what he did with it, and when he's going to do it to you again."

"I'm sorry to disappoint you ladies, but nothing happened" I replied solemnly, washing out a mug in the sink and pouring myself a coffee.

"Don't give me that bullshit! Stop being coy and tell us what really happened! He's up there right now waiting for round two isn't he!" chided Claire who was sitting at the breakfast bar patiently waiting for an autopsy of last night.

"I'm being serious" I said, turning round to join them. "He dropped me back, kissed me, then acted all weird and left." The thought of him pulling away from me, still stung, and as much as I tried to pretend it did not hurt, I could not get rid of the ache in my chest.

"Are you fucking serious?" slammed Sarah. "What a dick!"

"Yep" I mouthed staring into my coffee mug searching for an explanation.

Claire draped her arm around me. "His loss. On the bright side, at least you won't catch genital warts" she smiled, trying to lighten my mood.

"Oh, he doesn't have them" I replied absentmindedly. "He said that was just a rumour."

"Well, if he hasn't got them already, I hope he gets them soon as punishment for being such an arse to you" added in Sarah who slammed her mug down on the counter in a show of solidarity.

"Thank you," I smiled half-heartedly at my two loyal defenders. I appreciated their efforts to cheer me up, even if it was not really working. "Right, I'd better get my act together. You okay if I jump in the shower first? I can't go in looking like a steaming pile of crap this morning."

"Course. Go and make yourself beautiful and show him what he missed out on last night."

Regardless of last night, I had been dreading this day for weeks. Now, I was unsure if the feeling of dread emanating from the pit of my stomach was solely to do with the presentation, or partly to do with making an arse out of myself with Jake. The thought of seeing him again made me want to retreat to my bed and hide. Maybe I could wrap myself tightly in my duvet and wait for my body to become mummified. I'd only leave the confines of my room when I was being transported to a research facility for carbon dating.

As appealing as that was, I knew it was not an option. Nobody else knew my presentation well enough. Instead, I jumped in the shower and tried to wash the memory of last night's embarrassment off me with a generous squeeze of shower gel and a loofah. Alas, not even the heartiest of scrubs could wash away the stench of rejection. The sound of the water splashing off my skin did, however, help to drown out the negative and persistent voice inside me, telling me to not go into the office.

Today was not the day for tight skirts and bouncy curls. Let's face it, they hadn't really worked yesterday anyway. I had already decided on my black trouser suit and fitted white blouse. I wanted to be taken seriously, so natural make-up and hair up. Although I did add a bit of sparkle in the form of my favourite Vivien Westwood diamond earrings and pendant – I needed something to stop me from looking like an extra in Men in Black. As I glanced at the finished article in the mirror, I wondered whether it would be enough to convince LJT to sign a contract with us. My train of thought was derailed when there was a knock on the door and Ben walked in apprehensively.

"Hey, you. How are you feeling this morning? You scared me last night you know." He looked genuinely worried.

"I'm sorry, I didn't think anyone would be up" I replied guiltily.

"Don't apologise. I just wanted to make sure you got in okay. Look, you know you can tell me anything right? I'm here for you. If you want to chat …or if you need me to cut the brakes on his poncy car or send him a letter filled with anthrax, you just have to say."

"Thank you" I giggled, "But I don't think that will be necessary."

"Okay, well if you change your mind, just let me know."

"You will be my first port of call for anything criminally minded, I promise." I could not help but smile at him. He was always there for me. Ready to jump in and do time in prison for me when necessary. If only all men could be like him.

"Good luck for today, you're going to smash it" he said as he pulled the door to. I wished I could have been as positive as him.

◆ ◆ ◆

Claire and I travelled into the office together, using the time in the taxi to go over the presentation one last time.

"You're going to be great Jemma. You've covered everything that you need to. Just remember to keep calm and deliver it in the way that I know you can, and they will go for it." She said resting her hand on my lap reassuringly.

"Right, let's do this!" I said trying to muster up some courage and false bravado as we pulled up alongside the main entrance. There was a real frisson of excitement around the building this morning. As the doors to the lift retreated, the group of us who had been crammed in since the ground floor, spilled out on to the office floor in all directions, like marbles escaping from a bag. I went one way and Claire made a beeline for the new IT guy. Apparently, she was in dire need of help (of that there was no argument). Whether it was because we were a few minutes late, or because everyone else had arrived early, I was not sure, but the office was already buzzing with noise and anticipation. Effie sauntered over wearing a stunning jumpsuit, her hair piled high on top of her head in one of those impossibly hard to achieve, just got out of bed looks (clearly, she did not wake up in the same state as me), and her make-up looking as if it had been applied by a professional make-up artist.

"Morning!" she chirped. "Pastries are laid out in the conference room, as are cups, saucers, glasses, tea and coffee, and Lucy on the front desk is going to call up when they arrive, so that we have a heads up!" She seemed so proud of what she had achieved. "We are still waiting for Mr Bales to arrive though; do you know where he is?"

"No, why on earth would I know where he is?" I replied a little too sharply and a tad too defensively. It was an innocent question; she had no idea what had happened last night. "Sorry Effie, I'm just a bit stressed. I don't know where Jake is I'm afraid. Well done for getting everything set up though. I really appreciate it."

"No probs!" she smiled, completely unaffected by my churlishness.

Helene looked up from her desk. "What's rattled your cage this morning?" she enquired in her usual sarcastic tone.

"Nothing, I'm fine" I replied unconvincingly.

"Are those fuckers here yet?" Claire asked breathlessly as she came bounding over to her desk.

"No, not yet. Did you get the help you needed from Mr IT?" I smiled wickedly.

"Nope, not yet, but we're going out tomorrow night, so hopefully it won't be long! Right, I'm gonna pop downstairs quickly and grab a coffee. Anyone want one?"

"Ooh, yes please, I'll have a cappuccino" replied Helene without looking up from her screen.

"Can I have my usual please and a pain au chocolate?"

"Make that two" chimed in Helene still engrossed in what she was reading – Yoga for the over 50's.

"Cool, I'll be back in five. Give me a shout if they turn up and I'll make sure I stay down there a bit longer!" With that she headed back towards the lift, phone, and purse in hand. Jake was filtering out as she stood waiting to get in. I could feel the chill in the air from across the room.

"Morning Claire" smiled Jake a little tentatively.

"Morning." Claire, averted her gaze, giving him the proverbial cold shoulder. She was so loyal; it melted my heart.

I watched him stride casually across the floor and noticed the dozens of other pairs of eyes also tracking his journey. This is what I had become, just another pair of eyes. How humiliating. As he came closer, I tried to busy myself.

"Morning." He hovered uncomfortably by my desk.

"Morning" I replied looking up, trying to keep my tone neutral.

"How are you?" he asked, a pained expression in his eyes.

"Good, everything's ready to go" I avoided answering the real question and tried desperately not to burst into tears or beg him to tell me why he rejected me. I may have been a pathetic loser, but I was not about to give him the satisfaction of knowing how hurt I was, or risk being the subject of office gossip.

"Good" he replied, a faint smile on his face, but a look of something else in his eyes. Was it regret again? Hurt? Fear? Was he worried I might go to HR and report him? *Jerk.*

"Was there anything else?" I asked politely. Hell hath no fury like a woman scorned.

"Er... no, just wanted to check you were ok."

"Like I said, everything is good here" I smiled brightly. He walked away, his head low, looking like a pitiful child who had had his new toy taken away from him. Good, I thought, he deserved it, he deserved to feel shitty about last night. I was not going to let him off just because he had had a change of heart. Erin, noticing he had arrived, came rushing over and ushered him over to his office to sign some documents which were needed for the meeting. I stared at him as he walked away, the ache in my chest returning with every step he made.

"I'm going to check the meeting room," I said more for my benefit than anyone else's. I needed to snap out of it and focus otherwise today was going to be a bloody shambles. All credit to Effie, the room looked great. Everything was set up just as I would have done it myself. Who knew, maybe she did take in some of the things I told her! Pastries, fruit and drinks sat resplendently on top of the huge sideboard by the window, and the meeting table had been furnished neatly with water glasses, coasters, pads, and pens. As I stood looking at the room, a wave of nausea hit me. There was no turning back now.

"Jemma..." The familiar voice rooted me to the spot. The door closed softly, and I could feel him tentatively edging closer, unsure how to proceed. "Please, talk to me." A new wave of sadness washed over me.

"I'm fine" I managed, not able to turn and face him. Knowing that if I did, I would crumble.

"Please, Jemma." His hand reached out and he pulled me round so that I was facing him. The smell of him hit me first, the woody aroma of a pine forest in winter, and then I saw the look on his face, a pained expression that I had not seen before. Taking both my hands and drawing me closer still, he pulled me into him, the warmth of his body washing over me like sunshine on a summer's day. I hated how good it felt. "I owe you an apology." His voice sounded strangled, as if he were struggling to get his words out.

"You don't owe me anything" I replied stoically, staring into his mahogany brown eyes, hoping my resolve would not falter.

"But I do ... and I owe you an explanation." The last thing I wanted was his pity. I had gotten the wrong end of the stick. End of. I would just chalk it up to experience and never talk to another man as long as I lived. Simple.

"I can't do this Jake, not now" I said, taking a step back.

"When then?" he pleaded. God, did he have to be so bloody beautiful? Why did being so close to him hurt so much? It was not like we had even been dating. This was nothing. Nothing. Nothing. So why did it not feel like nothing?

"I don't know."

As I pulled my hands free, Effie came bounding in through the door. "They're here!" she called excitedly. Oblivious to what she had just walked in on, she turned around and left as quickly as she came, notifying the rest of the office of the imminent arrival too. Jake stood there silently, dejected, watching me for a moment before Helene, Claire and the rest of the team slowly filtered in, taking their place at the back of the room. He quietly positioned himself by the door so that he could personally welcome the group from LJT, and I sat down on one of the chairs Effie had laid out next to the projector, staring at the ground in front of me, my mind a complete blank. I heard voices approaching in the distance.

"It's showtime everyone!" warned Jake from the doorway. And just like that, he flicked a switch and went into full charm offensive mode, the previous five minutes erased from his memory. It was frightening, how quickly he changed. How was he able to compartmentalise his emotions like that? He had left me a quivering wreck and he was completely unaffected. That was telling.

"Geoff, good to see you again!" he boomed, shaking an older gentleman's hand vigorously.

"Jake, it's been a while" he replied jovially, matching Jake's vigour. Both were clearly fans of the old school belief that a handshake was somehow an indicator of how a person performed in the boardroom (and possibly the bedroom). It was a bit like watching two alpha males get their cocks out and compare sizes. For a split second, I contemplated again what Jake's might look like and then mentally slapped myself for even caring. Geoff, being the CEO, was the person we really needed to focus on today, not Jake's beautifully proportioned penis. *Oh, for God's sake, stop fantasising over something you're never going to see.* Other than the firm handshake, there were many similarities between him and Jake. Both were impeccably dressed, had an air of self-importance about them, and could no doubt command a room full of people. And although Geoff was probably nearing sixty, he was a good-looking chap. Tall, with salt and pepper hair now, but who I am guessing had similar colouring to Jake's in his younger years. I am sure he had been a real hit with the ladies. In fact, judging by the way Helene was ogling him, I would say he still was (so much for the menopause turning her off men). He was accompanied by a group of six other guys, all of whom were that generic, city slicker type, and one, young beautiful blonde who I assumed was his assistant.

"Gentlemen… Andrea." Jake greeted them all with an award-winning smile. Andrea responded by taking his hand and giving it a warm squeeze rather than a formal shake. Why did that gesture irk me so much?

"Great to see you again Jake" she smiled effortlessly. Clearly affected by him. How did she know him? A pang of jealousy coursed through my veins.

As the group took their seats, Jake moved purposely to the front of the room. His confident gait hiding any insecurities he may have had. Despite hating him, I could not help but take in his appearance. It was the first time I had really noticed what he was wearing. He had veered away from his usual navy and dark grey suits and had on instead a very pale grey one with slim fitting white shirt. He looked breath-taking. Of course, now that I hated him, it did not affect in me in the same way as it would have done twenty-four hours ago. Ignore that. Who was I kidding, it affected me in just the same way, more in fact, because now I had had a taste of him and wanted more. *Arsehole.*

"Good morning, ladies and gentlemen" he began. "I'd like to formally welcome you all to Taylor Marketing. We all know why we are gathered here this morning," he extended a dramatic arm towards the projector which showed the title page of the presentation. "It is our intention to take you through our vision for the marketing strategy for your company's new app. We have spent countless hours and given great consideration to developing a proposal which we believe will best place your product within the market, helping it to not only gain traction, but market dominance within twelve months of its launch." Cue dramatic pause, as the faces around the table drank in his every word. The guy could sell condoms to nuns he was that good. "Without further ado, I would like to introduce you all to Jemma Lucas, she has been the lead on this project, and it is her innovative ideas which form the cornerstone of our strategy. Once she has run through the presentation, I will then take questions from the floor. Jemma, over to you." And there was that dazzling smile once more, only this time, I could see it did not reach his eyes. It was all pretend.

"Thank you, Jake." *Douchebag.* I stood up, my pre-rehearsed, confident smile matching his. If there was one thing I was good at, it was concealing how I felt inside. "We all know that the property market is extremely competitive" I stated confidently, pointing to my first slide which showed a pie chart depicting the main players and their current market share. "Over the past ten years, we have seen a huge shift towards web-based companies, and a move away from the more traditional focus of people and premises. Technology has never been so important. For a new company, product, or app to be successful, you need to harness this technology and make the offering dynamic, innovative, and worthy of a place in the world. This is not an easy task given that most of the current players are making variations of the same thing. The question is, how do we make your app stand out from the crowd? The answer I believe, is by doing this." I clicked to the next slide, pausing for a second to allow the room to see what was on the wall. "These are all household names" I gestured to the Rightmove, Zoopla and Purple Bricks logos. "We all know what they do, and whether what we know about them is good, bad, or indifferent, there is no question that we have all heard about them. They are synonymous with the property industry. This is the first thing we need to achieve for you. Brand awareness. From the research we have done here, there is one blinding thing that makes your app different from these, and going forward, it will be your USP. Where all these other companies fall short, is that they do not provide an all-encompassing end to end experience. At some point, an external entity, be it a separate solicitor, financial advisor, agent or so on, needs to step in to complete the transaction. If we look at Rightmove for example, the UK's leading property search engine. They do not deal with the sale of the product, they must hand that over to an estate agent, similarly with Zoopla. Conversely, purple Bricks although an online company, still uses such portals to help advertise their properties. What you have is a tool which will give you complete control over the entire process, thus increasing efficiency and increasing profitability." I flicked quickly to the next slide. "It is our vision to market your app as a one-stop property shop. The world knows that moving home is one of the four most stressful aspects of life, behind birth, death, and marriage." There was a murmur of agreement from around the room. "We aim to show people that by using this app, not only will it save them money, but it will be more efficient, less stressful and ultimately, free up more of their time to deal with the other three stressful aspects of life." I smiled at this notion and the room responded to the intended humour. "Mr Thomson, your technology has the capability to revolutionise how we buy property." If I had learnt anything over the years, it was that massaging old men's egos was always a sure-fire way to get their attention. Bingo. Forward to the next slide. "Of the two thousand people we interviewed, eighty-nine per cent of them said that they would prefer to buy through a company that could facilitate the whole customer experience. To my knowledge, there is no company on the market that can currently does this. Once the legal teams have devised a framework in which the auctioning and bidding system can operate, the conveyancing can be done, the transfer of large sums of money can be safely transferred and the GDPR guidelines can be adhered to, we would be looking at setting up your app in a similar way to the way in which eBay operates. Obviously, your product offering is a little more specific, but the same bidding process would be used on both platforms. eBay is a trusted brand that people feel safe in using. They trust that due diligence is being done behind the scenes, that there are robust processes in place to protect the consumer, and that the safety and satisfaction of their customers is paramount to their core beliefs. This is something we believe you too should harness. Now, if I can ask for a few more minutes of your time, I would like to show you how we intend to do all of this in a little more detail." I stepped back towards the laptop and hit play on the next sequence of slides.

Looking around the table, it was impossible to gauge their reaction. Eight impassive faces looked up at the screen, not an ounce of emotion etched on any of them. I glanced over to Jake for support.

"You were great" he mouthed silently. A sense of relief swept over me. I had not realised how nervous I had been whilst I had been standing, but as I sat down, my legs shook uncontrollably. I took a mouthful of water from my glass to try and steady myself. We watched patiently as the slideshow ended, and then Jake took to the floor once more. He took several questions from the delegation, answering all of them with a self-assured confidence, not only in his own ability, but in the knowledge that this really was the best course of action for them. He really should have been a salesperson because the way he spoke about the app, he even had me believing it was going to be a roaring success. As the questions finished, and the meeting came to a natural end, Geoff Thompson peeled off from the group and made his way over to Jake and me.

"Thank you both for all your efforts on this. We'll head back to the office now to discuss things and will be in touch. I do believe that your proposal has immense potential and merit and is something we will give careful consideration to. I'll come back to you in a few days once the team and I have had time to discuss things. Jake, great to see you again, and Jemma, it was a pleasure to meet you." He held out his hand as a parting gesture.

"You too Mr Thompson. We look forward to speaking with you shortly" I said accepting his hand. The rest of his team trailed out the door after him, followed by our team who had waited patiently at the back.

"Bravo you fabulous bloody woman!" squealed Claire as she made her way to the front. "You fucking nailed that! I bet the big GT was creaming in his pants at the very sight of your pie charts!" She grabbed a Danish pastry from the sideboard and shoved it in her mouth, completely blanking Jake as she sauntered out the room. Everyone else had filtered out too and were making their way back to their desks, chatting excitedly as they went. Only Jake and I remained in the room, him clearing the glasses from the table, and me turning off the projector.

"I can do that" I said, hoping he would leave the room too.

"It's okay, it will only take a minute. You were amazing you know." He looked up from the table over to me. Part of me wanted to run to him and throw my arms around him, the other part wanted to smash one of the glasses he was holding over his head and run screaming from the room.

"Thanks" I said, disconnecting my laptop and making for the door.

"Jemma, wait…" he called urgently after me, but I was already several steps safely onto the office floor where I knew he could not follow me. I quickly made my way to my desk and sat down, Claire watching the whole thing from her vantage point behind me.

"What was that about?" she whispered.

"Nothing" I replied, trying to quell her desire to start a conversation about it. Jake exited the room moments later, his steely gaze fixed on his own office. A few people tried to catch his eye, but he stopped for no one, slamming his door behind him as he reached his destination.

"He looks pissed, what's up with him" commented Helene perceptively.

"He's just annoyed that Geoff Thompson's got more money and a bigger dick than him" joked Claire, diverting attention away from me. I kept my eyes firmly on my computer screen, silently thanking her for having my back once again.

◆ ◆ ◆

My heart rate was finally showing signs of returning to normal when my computer pinged, signalling receipt of an email.

**From: Jake Bales**
**To: Jemma Lucas**
**Subject: meeting**
**Sent: Today at 12.04pm**

**I need to talk to you. Come to my office in 5 minutes.**

Shit. No hello, no please, no 'From Jake'. He sounded furious. God, this was getting out of hand. I had a sinking feeling in the pit of my stomach, that feeling you get when you know the inevitable is going to happen. I stared at the screen hoping to find some softness in his words, some kind of hope that this was not going to end in me being escorted from the premises. Nope. Nothing. It was as bad on the hundredth time of reading it as it was the first. Fuck. I closed my Outlook and like a prisoner on death row, decided to meet my fate head on, the famous phrase 'Just do it!' (which I had only just discovered was not invented by Nike), whirling round my head. I got up slowly from my desk and walked vacantly towards his office, stopping momentarily before knocking on the door.

"Come in." His voice was cold and measured. There was no warmth or familiarity in it. My stomach churned. How had it escalated to this so quickly? I tentatively pushed open the door and stepped inside. "Close the door behind you." He was standing over by the window, hands in his pockets, looking out over the skyline. He had lost his jacket, so I could see how his shirt fitted his body like a glove, skimming over his muscular shoulders and back like it had been made specifically for him. As much as I tried to convince myself that I hated him, I could not pretend that I was not affected by him. Every time I saw him, something inside me came alive, and the distance between us was physically painful. I wanted to run my hands over him, wanted him to hold me, to tell me he had made a mistake. But there was nothing. He stood there staring for what seemed like an age, not acknowledging my presence.

"You wanted to see me?" I managed. It was barely audible. All my strength and resolve had been used up bringing myself before him. I felt like a naughty child who had been sent to the headteachers office. He turned to face me, running his hands through his hair as he did so.

"I did" he replied as coldly as before, looking me square in the eye. This man was dangerous. Dangerous because he made me want things I should not want. Dangerous because he made me feel things I should not feel. My skin itched to be close to him, but at the same time, the way his eyes were boring into me, I knew I needed the distance between us to remain safe. He was a hunter, and I was his prey. I was helpless. Why was he so angry? He left me, not the other way round.

"Wh… what did you want?"

"I wanted to talk but you've been avoiding me all day." His eyes were blacker than the night, his pupils completely submerged in the darkness which surrounded them. "I didn't know how else to get you by yourself."  With his admission came a change in his tone. He stalked slowly towards me. "I just need a chance to explain what happened last night."

God this was mortifying. Did he really feel the need to have to spell it out to me? "I told you; you don't need to explain anything. I got the wrong end of the stick. Can't we just leave it there and pretend none of this ever happened?" I begged him.

A frustrated laugh escaped his mouth. "Jemma, for God's sake, you didn't get the wrong end of the stick, and no, I can't just leave it there, I'm fucking crazy about you! Can't you see that you're driving me insane!"  He turned towards the window and started pacing backwards and forwards, his hands clenched. He reminded me of a lion in a zoo. "I think about you every second of the day, I can't switch off from you. Do you have any idea what that's like?" He looked directly at me, clearly agitated.

*Erm, yep, got a bit of an idea how that feels.* He turned away again, unable to look me in the eyes and stalked back towards the window, where he stood, his hands stretched out over his head, resting on the pane of glass, staring out. Every muscle in his back was taught, every inch of him raging. I was captivated.

"If that's true, then why did you leave me last night?" I muttered, utterly bewildered, unable to connect the dots.

"Because I panicked."

"Panicked?" What a load of bullshit. A man like him did not panic, he caused panic in others. "Just be honest Jake, please" I begged.

He prowled over to me, his fists clenched, his jaw firm. "I am being honest" he growled. "I panicked because I knew if I carried on kissing you, I wouldn't be able to stop." He looked tormented, like he was physically hurting.

"What if I didn't want you to stop" I whispered sadly, recalling the feeling of rejection I had felt in his car.

"You don't understand. I didn't want to be the guy that they all think I am." He gestured wildly to the office outside. "You've heard the rumours! I wanted to show you I was nothing like that, I wanted you to be able to trust me. If I hadn't left when I did, I would have proven them all right. I wanted to be better than that. I wanted to be better for you." His confession shocked me. It sounded so genuine, so heartfelt. He seemed deflated. "I wanted to give you time to think about things before going further."

"Jake," I said taking a shaky step towards him. "I didn't want time to think, I just wanted you. I still want you. I don't care what anyone thinks. When I thought you didn't want me, I ..."

"Jemma." Abruptly, he took my face in his big hands. "I want you more than I have wanted anyone in a long, long time. I want you so much that I don't know what to do with myself" he admitted. Our faces were so close they were practically touching, his words were nothing more than a whisper. His forehead rested against mine, and for a second, he just stood there, watching me, imploring me to believe him.

"Me too" I breathed, my hands resting on his chest, feeling the thrumming of his heart which was beating rapidly. "Jake I ....," but before I could finish, his mouth was on mine, his tongue parting my lips, delving expertly in. My tongue met his, dancing to a rhythm that only we could hear. My hands roamed over his body as they had done last night, but this time he did not pull away, instead, he pulled me closer, pulled me in so close that I could feel everything. The strength of his arms, so big that they encased me, the wall of thick muscle beneath his shirt which twitched and tensed, and the unmistakeable bulge in his trousers which he pressed unashamedly against me. I gasped for air as he bit gently down on my lip, sending a wave of unimaginable pleasure coursing through my body. It felt like flying. Like I was soaring through the air, with only the wind beneath me and the heavens above. It was even better than I had imagined it would be. It was everything.

"I need you" he whispered, holding my gaze, gently stroking my cheek. "I never should have left last night." He paused, those dark orbs pleading. "Say you'll give me another chance, say you'll still come to Paris with me."

I wanted to shout at him, to tell him how much he had hurt me, to make him feel just a little of the pain that I had when he drove away last night. But the words would not come out. None of it seemed to matter now. All I could feel was hope and possibility, and I would not give that up for anything. 'Yes,' I replied weakly, incapable of a better response.

His eyes appeared to mist over. "Thank you." With one hand still on my cheek and the other at the nape of my neck, he pulled me gently back in towards him. The kiss was soft and gentle, slower than the previous one, like a feather brushing over my lips. "There's so much I want to show you" he breathed, interrupting his heavenly assault. Heat rose in my body at his touch and at the promise in his words. Whatever it was he wanted to show me, I wanted to see it.

"I can't wait" I managed, my breathless tone exposing my desire for more.

"Neither can I" he replied with a smile, his fingers moving to the base of my spine, tilting my hips towards his with just enough force that I could sense his own excitement again. The feel of it stoked the flames within me, and an almost inaudible moan escaped my hungry mouth just as his tongue came crashing back down on it. I was losing control. Sensing my unravelling, he slowed the pace with which he was playing me, his grip on my back slackening to allow me to breathe more freely. "Not here" he groaned, self-doubt etched in his words, the bulge in his trousers clearly disagreeing. "I don't want it to be like this. I don't want a quick fuck in my office. I want to give you so much more." Steely determination mixed with wanton desire was scribed on his face.

"How much more?" I teased, trying unsuccessfully to regain my breath.

"If you knew how much, you'd run a mile" he smiled.

"If I promised not to run, would you tell me?"

"In time, maybe… but just know that I want you, all of you." He sounded so certain, so confident. A girl could be in danger of risking everything for words like those. I am sure many would risk everything for far less.

"You, Mr Bales, are a confusing contradiction" I smiled, searching for my composure.

"You have no idea."

"Right, well I should leave before people start talking!" I mused, prying myself from his arms, straightening my trousers and patting down my ruffled hair.

"Are you embarrassed to be seen with me then?" he joked with mock offence.

"Absolutely."

"Ouch! Go gentle on me Miss Lucas. You'll give me a complex!" I smiled over my shoulder as I closed the door. *I'll give you more than that if you'll let me!*

Claire watched on avidly from her desk as I made my way back across the floor. "You'd better tell me everything when we get home" she hissed in hushed tones. "I've been going out of my mind worrying about you since last night, and I'm pretty sure it's now affecting my productivity!" I shot her a look which made it quite clear I did not believe that that was the reason for her reduced output. Truth be told, she was overqualified for the job and was bored. The trouble was, I loved working with her and did not want her to leave, so I was more than happy to put up with her below par productivity to keep her with me.

◆ ◆ ◆

By 5pm most people in the office had started to head home. Effie had dashed off to go to some sweaty Bikram yoga class, and Helene had popped to Waitrose to pick up some carrots for tea as her elderly mother was coming over. Neither of their evenings sounded particularly appealing to me. Sarah had called Claire earlier for a gossip update and to check that I had not been locked in the toilet crying my eyes out all day. She suggested we all meet at the pub for something to eat and a bottle (or two) of wine for a debrief. Thankfully, things were not looking as dire as they had done this morning, and there was fresh hope for my new satiny thighs and fuzz free lady bits. A debrief did not sound as horrendous as it would have done had it been suggested at 8am.

"Right, you ready to get the hell out of here?" asked Claire, already switching off her computer and putting her jacket on.

"Two secs" I promised as I too closed my computer. "I just need to say goodbye to …"

"Loverboy!" she finished for me, with a wicked grin. I gave her a disapproving look, snatched my bag out from under my desk and ran pathetically over to his office, knocking before entering.

"Hello, you!" he smiled, looking up from his computer. "You off now?"

"Hey" I answered shyly. "Yep, Claire's waiting outside for me. You leaving soon?" I hated the thought of him staying late by himself. Although I guess he always did, and I had just never really thought about it before. Why did I suddenly feel so protective of him?

"In a bit. I've got a couple of bits to tie up first. Is it okay if I call you later?"

"Of course, it is. Do you have my number?" I asked, surprised that he felt the need to ask permission.

"I'm sure I can find it" he smiled, knowing full well he had access to all my personal information. "We can talk more later" he continued, "I was thinking maybe I could pick you up in the morning so that we can head straight to the airport after lunchtime?"

"That would be great, thank you" I said looking back nervously over my shoulder towards the door. "I'd better go, I think Claire is about to come in here and physically carry me away" I replied, conscious that she was waiting impatiently outside.

"We don't want that do we!" he replied, looking half serious. I got the impression he was terrified of her.

"Speak to you later" I laughed pulling the door to.

"Look forward to it."

"Hurry up you, I'm bloody starving" yelled Claire across the office.

"Okay, okay, I'm coming, I'm coming!" I squealed, running over to her. "Let's go, I need some chips and a large glass of wine!"

It turns out that Thursdays are officially the country's most popular date night. It also happens to be the preferred evening out for most of the city folk. As a result, the Kings Arms was packed to the rafters with couples and groups of people when we arrived. Luckily, Sarah and Ben (who already looked like they were a few glasses of wine in) had secured us a table. As per usual, they had bagged us one of the high bar tables with stools at the edge of the room. Sarah always preferred to sit there so that she could spy on people. The rest of us went along with it because it was easier to acquiesce to her demands than it was to go against them.

"Hey!" we greeted them before engaging in a round of friendly hugs and kisses.

"We got wine!" sang Sarah happily as she raised the bottle in the air as proof "but we've drunk most of it I'm afraid" she said feigning a sad face.

"No probs, I'll go grab another one" I said cheerily. "Same again?"

"Yes please!" they all chorused.

The queue was three deep at the bar, and it took fifteen minutes for me to return with the drinks, by which time they were deep in conversation.

"What did I miss?" I said wiggling onto my stool and placing the bottle of wine down on the table. They all looked up guiltily. "Hmm…. are my ears burning?" I joked.

"It's nothing bad" replied Claire trying to sound nonchalant. "I was just filling them in on your stellar performance this morning." The others nodded in agreement.

"I wouldn't call it that exactly. Anyone for a top up?" I started pouring the bottle evenly between the four glasses before receiving an answer.

"A toast to Claire and Jemma" signalled Sarah holding her glass aloft. "To taking the marketing world by storm and for being a genuine pair of badasses!" We all raised our glasses and chinked to that.

"I'm famished" said Ben putting his glass down and perusing the menu. "Is everyone eating?"

"Too right we are!" said Claire picking up a second menu from the middle of the table and taking a look.

"I already know what I'm going to have, I've been hankering after them all day."

"The dirty fries?" guessed Sarah correctly.

"Am I really that predictable?"

They all nodded in agreement. "Yep."

Like the drinks, there was a wait for the food, which gave the girls plenty of time for their interrogation.

"Right…" Claire started, settling down on her stool like we were going to be a while and she needed to get comfy. "What we really wanted to know was what he was like in bed but given that you've not yet done the deed I guess I'm going to have to ask you to start from the beginning and give us all the boring details. I wouldn't want my halo to slip or my saintly image to be tarnished, so for the sake of posterity, let's keep it clean" she winked. Ben sniggered at the part about her saintly image, but quickly covered it up when she glared at him with dangerous intent.

"First of all, tell us about the gallery. What was it like? Did you see anyone famous?" Sarah sounded genuinely intrigued, Claire however had already zoned out and was waiting for certain buzz words (probably relating to a man's anatomy) to pique her interest again. Ben sat quietly flicking through his phone. It was more of a girlie conversation. I often forgot that he probably didn't want to hear the three of us talking about other men. I told them everything, from Jake telling me I was beautiful and to asking permission to kiss me, to the sad painting of the mother and her child (which left Sarah teary eyed and Claire completely unaffected), finally, to his rejection outside our house at the end of the night and then how he apologised to me today. Claire's ears pricked up when I mentioned the kiss in his office and chided me for not giving him a blow job there and then.

"It sounds like something from a movie" interjected Sarah dreamily, resting her elbows on the table.

"Don't you think this is all moving too fast?" questioned Ben, looking up from his phone. Clearly, he had been listening to the conversation all along.

"Possibly." I looked down at my lap and played with the bracelet on my wrist. "But something feels different with him. I can't explain it. He is so much more than I originally thought. He's kind and funny and so clever…"

"And he looks like a god and has a massive bank balance and probably a huge dick to boot!" butted in Claire.

"I wouldn't know" I smiled sheepishly, my cheeks flaming, "I just know that he makes me feel different. I feel like I've known him for forever" I added feeling embarrassed.

"But you haven't!" argued Ben. "Jem, you don't know him at all. I don't trust him. You're going to get hurt."

"Ben," I said reaching out to grab his hand. "I appreciate you looking out for me, I do, but I'm not going to get hurt. He feels the same way I do."

"This is ridiculous, I'm going to the loo. Same wine again?" he asked sounding agitated as he got up from his stool.

Sarah looked at me perplexed. "Yes please! What's up with him tonight?" she mouthed as he walked away.

"I don't know" I replied wistfully. "I just wish he'd be happy for me."

"I'm sure he is. You know what he's like, he's always looked out for you. He's like this with every guy you bring home" she said holding my hand reassuringly.

"Maybe," but deep down I did not think that was the reason for his outburst. Several alternative reasons were mooted, none of which seemed plausible, until Claire stumbled upon the most ridiculous one yet.

"Maybe he's jealous" she muttered whilst taking a sip of her wine.

'Jealous? Don't be daft! I'm like his little sister." I paused to consider what the real reason could be. "No, there's got to be an explanation. Ben always sees the best in people."

"Well, here's your chance to find out."

"Find out what?" he asked as he sat back down with a new bottle of wine.

"Why you don't like her hot new love interest" Claire replied brazenly. If it were possible to shoot someone actual daggers, there would have been a million flying across the table towards her at that very moment. Her lack of filter still managed to astound me even after all these years.

"Just leave it Claire" he said matter-of-factly.

"Come on, you can't get out of it that easily" she continued, ignoring the stark warning in his tone.

"Claire, I said leave it. It doesn't matter!" His voice was stern, the level raised so it was almost a shout. Ben did not get angry very often, but he was angry now.

"It matters to me" I said solemnly, reaching out, imploring him to look at me. His hands gripped the edge of the table like a vice, and he struggled to meet my gaze.

"I just don't trust him, and I don't think you should either" he snapped, refusing to look up.

"Why?" I probed gently, feeling desperate to know more. The girls looked on anxiously, sensing my discomfort.

"For God's sake Jem, please just drop it." His tortured voice was pleading. Whatever the reason, he really did not want to share it. But something inside me could not let it go. I had to know.

"I can't drop it Ben, I need to know. We've always been honest with each other, whatever it is, you can tell me." He sat silently for a second, contemplating his response, before finally looking up and staring at me, a mixture of fury and anguish painted over his face.

"Because he's playing you for a fucking fool, that's why!" he barked. His words were cutting, laced with pity and contempt and stung like a fresh wound.

"What do you mean?" I whispered numbly, not sure if I wanted to know the answer or not.

"Come on guys, stop this" begged Sarah.

"Ben, I need to know," I begged, unrelenting. He looked at me, the anger gone, just pity remaining in his kind eyes.

"Because I saw him with another woman," he struggled, as if it were physically killing him to say the words aloud. Of all the things I was expecting, for some reason, that was not one of them. Ironic really, given the man's reputation.

"What? When?" I asked, a sinking, hollow feeling washing over me.

"Tuesday night. I went out with the boys for a bit after you went to bed" he replied solemnly, his pained expression intensifying.

"Where?" It was immaterial where, but I needed to try and picture the scene.

"At a bar in town." His answers were becoming more stilted with every round of questions.

"Was she pretty?" I am not sure why I even asked that. A dull ache in my chest was threatening to take over my whole body. Would it have made it better if she were ugly? Abso-fucking-lutely.

"Jem… please." I could tell from the way he looked at me, and his inability to give me an answer, that she did not fall into the 'she has a face for radio' category.

"Why didn't you tell me?" I asked hurt, and embarrassed, my tone accusatory which unwittingly sparked his anger again.

"Because I didn't know you were going to fall in fucking love with him in 48 hours did I!"

"Neither did I," I admitted lamely.

"Look," interrupted Claire, seeing that things were spiralling out of hand. "It was probably a work meeting, Jake meets people outside of the office all the time, you know that. Jem, he's mad about you, you'd have to be blind not to see the way he looks at you. I don't think he would do anything to hurt you. There has got to be a logical explanation." I could tell from the tone in her voice that she was not as certain about that statement as she would like to be.

"Listen to yourselves! Do you know how stupid that sounds? You're three intelligent women, trying to convince yourselves that there is a plausible explanation for Jake cosying up to another woman. Nobody has work meetings at 10pm in a bar, and they seemed to know each other very well. You need to wake up and see this for what it is. What do you actually know about this guy? It could have been his wife for all you know! He's playing you for a fool and you need to steer clear of him. He's exactly the kind of guy you all thought he was originally."

"I need to get some air" I said instinctively, staggering to my feet and grabbing my bag.

"We'll come with you" motioned Sarah, picking up her things and glaring at Ben.

"No, stay, eat. I'm just going to go for a walk and then head home. I want to be by myself for a bit."

"Are you sure?" asked Claire, looking worried.

"I'll be fine, honestly" I replied, ignoring Ben's attempts to catch my eye. "I'll see you back at home." I headed numbly towards the door, my legs feeling like they were wading through treacle. Every step required a Herculean effort, every move forward stripping me of my resolve and determination to hold it together. It did not make sense. Surely Ben had been mistaken?

But how? He knew what he had seen. As I pushed open the heavy door and exited out on to the street, the stark realisation of what had just happened hit me. I had been a fool. A fool to think that someone like Jake Bales could ever like someone like me. A fool to fall so head over heels for someone I did not know, and moreover, I was a fool to think that there was a plausible explanation for it all. The tears free flowed down my cheeks as I walked along the pavement, Gloria Gaynor's 'I will survive' aptly blasting out of an apartment window across the street. *Too soon, way too soon.* My phone buzzed in my bag pulling me briefly back to my senses, but I let it ring off, wanting to be alone in my thoughts.

In contrast to my mood, the evening was beautiful. A balmy, early summers evening, the type where people decided to go for strolls or congregate in the parks until the light faded. Although it was approaching 8pm, the streets were vibrant and alive with people. As I ambled past couples holding hands and groups of friends chatting animatedly, I realised how alone I felt. My phone vibrated frantically once more, but I ignored it again, losing myself in the comforting warmth of the air and the hum of distant conversations. How I wanted to be one of those people right now, basking in the last drops of the amber light, oblivious to everything I had just been told. My body acted instinctively and took me back home through the park. I could not tell you how I made it back, but I did, and I made a note to be more present when walking alone next time. I turned the key in the lock and headed straight for my room, closing the door behind me, and slumping down on to my bed. Fat, wet tears soaked into my pillow. I pulled my blanket up around me, seeking refuge from my pounding head in its softness. My phone buzzed again from inside my bag.

"Go away!" I screamed wildly at whoever it was trying to reach me, overwhelmed by gut wrenching pain and abject humiliation. I did not know what was worse, the fact that Jake was seeing someone else, or the embarrassment of having people know about it and feeling sorry for me. How had I let this happen a second time? I was just a sucker for a line and a pretty face, that was how. I buried my head into my damp floral pillow, recounting the week, searching for clues that I had missed. I analysed our conversations repeatedly, the looks he had given me, the snippets of information he had told me. How had I got things so wrong?

The house was dark and silent now, all but for a glimmer of light from the streetlamp outside which shone through the crack in the curtain, creating menacing shadows on my wall. It took me back briefly to my childhood when I had been terrified of the dark. I had always slept with a bedside light on. When Ben stayed over, I pretended it was for his benefit. He never questioned my reasoning, but looking back, he always knew who it was for. Ben, one of the few constants in my life. My rock. My go to in times of need. He had been so angry tonight. Without lifting my head, I stretched out an arm and turned on the chrome bedside lamp. The warm light may well have stopped the eery shadows in their tracks, but it did nothing to quell the haunting images of Jake with a mystery woman from whirling unchecked around my head. I imagined what she might look like. Blonde, leggy, prettier than me of course, and immaculately dressed. I envisaged her in a tight-fitting dress, all tits, coy smiles, and matching pearly white veneers, not a wonky tooth between them. I felt physically sick.

I could not say what time it was, but eventually, I drifted off into a restless, tormented sleep, riddled with strange dreams. Originally, the banging formed part of one of those dreams, but as it persisted, it grew louder, and as I started to come to, I realised that it was not a dream, but someone pounding on the front door. The girls in their drunken state could not locate their keys. It happened more frequently than you would think. The only saving grace was that this time, I was on the inside and could make it stop far quicker than if I had been out there with them in a similarly inebriated state.

"I'm coming!" I called out as I bundled down the stairs, stepping on one of Ben's upturned football boots as I went. "Motherfucker!" The studs stuck into the ball of my foot leaving behind an angry red mark. I stumbled towards the door, fumbling with the lock as I rubbed the throbbing spot on my right foot.

"Why didn't you answer your phone?" The terse voice halted me in my tracks. It was not the girls. Jake stood there filling the doorway waiting for an answer.

"Why are you here?" I managed, rubbing the sore patch on my foot, not sounding nearly as bristly or as cutting as I would have liked.

"I was worried about you" he replied more softly.

"Well, as you can see, apart from the bloody hole in my foot, I'm fine. Now if you don't mind, I'd like you to leave."

"Why? What's happened?" He sounded perplexed.

"What's happened? Oh, nothing!" I sang sarcastically. "I just found out what a philandering arsehole you are, that's all. Now if you'll excuse me, I have had one hell of a shitty day and I want to get back to bed!" I went to slam the door on him, all dramatically like they do in the movies, but his strong, muscular arm reached out, stopping me in my tracks. *Just give me this one thing, please!*

"Hold on a minute. You don't get to call me a philandering arsehole without explaining what you mean! I deserve that much surely?" he said sounding slightly amused. Was he laughing at me?

"You deserve an explanation? That's rich, I thought it was me who deserved one." I could hear my voice becoming shrill and more manic with every word spoken.

"Look Jemma, I don't know what the hell is going on, but can we talk about this inside?" He didn't wait for an invite, and stepped calmly past me into the hallway, closing the door behind him. The nerve of the guy. "You need to tell me what's happened because I can't keep up. Things were great just a few hours ago, and now you're acting like this." He held out his arm gesturing towards me. Anger coursed through my body; how dare he make me out to be the one in the wrong here!

"Okay Casanova, I'll give you a bloody explanation!" I screamed. "Why didn't you tell me you were with someone? Who was she, your wife? Your girlfriend?"

"What?" A blank expression painted his face. God he was good. I could almost have believed that he did not have a clue what I was going on about. I wanted to laugh in his face.

"I said... why the fuck did you kiss me if you were with someone?" I waited for an admission of guilt, but it did not come.

"You know I'm not with anyone."

"Don't lie to me! It's bad enough I fell for your bullshit before. I won't fall for it again!" There was no hiding my fury; my body was shaking, colour rose in my cheeks and my hands fisted in readiness for a fight. I was done with men making me feel stupid, he was going to get it from both barrels. *How dare you treat me this way. How dare you stand there and lie to my face!* Jake was next to me in a heartbeat, his hands holding the tops of my arms, steadying me.

"Jemma, I don't know what you think you know, but I promise you, I haven't been with anyone in a long, long time." He looked at me with a penetrating stare.

"I guess Tuesday is a long time ago given how quickly you move" I replied flippantly, trying to free my arms. It was no use, they remained pinned to my side.

"For God's sake, what are you talking about? What do I have to do to make you believe me?"

"You were seen Jake, cosying up to another woman, please don't deny it!" My voice cracked hearing it said aloud. "I don't want any part in this game you're playing. Please, just go back to whoever she is and leave me the fuck alone." I begged, my eyes welling up with tears.

His hand reached up and cupped my cheek. "You're wrong" he whispered, "You are so, so wrong. How could I be with someone else when I only see you?" His touch was warm and gentle, and his words stoked a feeling in the pit of my stomach which belied my protestations. "If you're referring to Tuesday evening, which I'm guessing you are," he smiled faintly still staring into my eyes, "Then you should probably know that the woman I was with was not my girlfriend, my lover or my wife... she was my sister Jemma." That last part hung in the air for a moment before I could take stock of what he had said.

"What?" That was not what I had expected to hear. Unsure whether to punch him or believe him, I erred on the side of caution. "You don't have a sister" I said, recalling the conversation we had had about himself and his twin brother. There was one hundred per cent, no mention of a sister.

"What do you mean, I told you about Charlie the other day." Both his hands were resting on my face now, urging me to remember.

"Charlie?" *oh dear God.* "But I thought... Charlie's... a girl?" I stammered, the cogs in my brain turning, slowly putting two and two together, the realisation of what he was saying hitting me like a freight train.

"Yep" he smiled.

"And so, Charlie is ..."

"Short for Charlotte" he added, the edge of his mouth turning up.

"So, you don't have a girlfriend?"

"Nope."

"Or a lover?"

"Nope."

"Or a wife?"

He hesitated for a fraction of a second, "Nope."

I could feel the colour drain from my face. "Oh, sweet baby Jesus!"

He laughed sadly, tenderly stroking my face with his thumbs. "Do you still think I'm a philandering arsehole?"

"No, but I think I'm a fucking idiot. Jake, I …."

"Don't. Please. Life is too short. Listen, I'm not sure what this is" he said pointing his finger between the two of us. "It's taken me completely by surprise. I don't really know you, and you don't really know me, but I want to get to know you." His forehead rested against mine and he breathed out slowly. "My god, I want to get to know you. I want to know everything there is to know about you; your favourite colour, your favourite food, what makes you happy and what makes you sad. But until I know all that, and until you know everything about me, believe me when I say I would rather die than hurt you." Tears pricked at my eyes once more. "I know I'm asking a lot, but I need you to trust me. Do you think you can do that?"

I wanted to. I really wanted to, but could I? My traitorous heart answered on my behalf. "Mmmhmm." Before I could think too much more, he picked me up in his arms, wrapping my legs round him and carried me towards the stairs.

"Good" he smiled. "Now, if it's okay with you, I'd like to do what I should have done the other day."

"Oh, and what's that?" I asked, hoping it was the exact same thing I was thinking of.

"Spend the night with you" he smiled, kissing me deeply and enveloping me in his strong arms. I breathed him in, pine needles and wintery forests, my new favourite smell.

"I would like that very much" I admitted, returning his kiss, and clinging on to him tightly as we ascended the stairs.

I hadn't noticed until then, but he was dressed in a grey tracksuit and trainers. It suited him. He looked like he might have come straight from the gym. His hair was damp, his dark waves scraped back off his face and there was a hint of minty shower gel mixed with his usual scent. The casual look made him seem so much younger. He was mesmerising. A different man altogether from the professional powerhouse of earlier in the day.

"You are so beautiful" he whispered, pulling me into him and tilting my chin up so that he could see me better. His confidence was alluring. "I know this is happening quickly, but you've turned my world upside down Jemma. You've made me feel things I didn't think were possible" he confessed as his hands gently tugged at my scrunchie, allowing my hair to fall around my face and his fingers to interlace with the curls. His voice was hushed and gentle, but his eyes conveyed the same dark, urgent look as they had done earlier in his office. My heart ached at the sound of his confession. Was it too soon to admit that I wanted him more than I had ever wanted anyone in my life? His eyes closed as his lips met mine. The kiss that followed was all consuming, passionate, and expert. His tongue masterfully prizing open my lips, delving in to conquer the deepest parts of me. It was like he was seeking something in me, but what I did not know. My body succumbed without question, my hands clinging to the back of his head, a confidence growing in me with every touch of his hand. Holding his gaze, I reached for the zip on his tracksuit top and gently pulled it down, exposing his bare chest underneath, tracing the line of the zip with my fingers over his warm, silky-smooth skin. I had never seen a body like it. I had imagined how he might look, but nothing could have prepared me for the reality. It was unnerving how perfect he was. Thick muscle coated his stomach, the defined lines and dips separating them moving with the rise and fall of his chest. Once he was free of his top, my hands wandered over his tanned torso. I stepped back, permitting myself an uninterrupted view of him. He stood watching me.

"Are you sure you want to do this?" he asked. I nodded, unable to drag my eyes away from his body. I thought that V below the hips only existed on Ken dolls and body builders.

He brushed his thumb tenderly over my cheek "Okay, but we can stop at any time, you just have to say."

"Jake… kiss me" I demanded breathlessly.

"My pleasure," he replied as he lifted me effortlessly in one arm, quickly pulling my vest top over my head with the other and laid me tenderly back on the bed so that he was towering over me.

"Don't move" he ordered in an authoritative tone. I closed my eyes and did my best to do as I was told, but he made it so incredibly difficult. His tongue began to explore every inch of my skin, tantalising and teasing as it made its painfully slow descent from my neck down to my breast where he gently bit and sucked my nipple. My body squirmed under his touch. Raging heat coursed through me.

"I thought I told you not to move!" he scorned playfully.

"I can't help it… I…." words failed me as the intense feeling continued to eat me alive. Every nerve tingled; every inch of my skin was on fire. Had anything ever felt this good before? Did it feel the same for him, or was he like this with every woman he slept with? My chest ached at the mere thought.

"I don't know how long I will last this time Jemma, but I promise to make it up to you all night long if you'll let me" he said in a ragged, almost deranged tone. *Umm… okay, if you insist! Perhaps he is not like this with everyone.* His breathing was shallower, his eyes darker than I had seen them before. He cupped my breasts in his huge hands, kneading and stroking, savouring them and revelling in the effect his touch was having on me. He began his descent lower; his tongue tracing circles over my flushed skin. His name fell from my mouth over and over again as he worshipped my body. I was in heaven.

"Hearing my name on your lips is something I've dreamt a lot about. You have no idea what that does to me" he groaned. Having discarded my shorts, his fingers delicately traced the line of my lace knickers against the inside of my thighs. He stopped briefly, the momentary pause causing me to open my eyes. I watched in anticipation as he slowly sunk his fingers into his mouth and then proceeded to pull the lace to one side. There was no need for that because I was already wet, but I'd let him find out for himself. I gasped as his finger slid effortlessly inside me. Heat coursed through my body; the feeling so intense it caused my back to arch involuntarily off my bed encouraging him to delve in further. His touch had ignited a fire unlike any other I had felt before. I wanted more. "You feel fucking glorious" he moaned, inserting a second finger, twisting and turning them, hitting some magical place deep within that nobody else had ever discovered. Every movement of his hand sent another tantalising wave of electricity shooting through me. I watched in awe as he delighted in the pleasure he was providing, his eyes holding mine, encouraging me to give in to the sensation. He seemed as happy to give as I was to receive. In and out, gently at first, then faster and more assured. He was commanding me with his hand, fucking me with an urgency that could not be controlled. I was completely at his mercy and reacted as he had intended. My body was his and it rewarded his efforts. I could hold on no longer. The feeling that started somewhere deep in my core, spread like wildfire through my body, sending every limb and nerve into spasm, the heat building into a crescendo, until there was no place for it to go and it exploded. It felt like falling. Like diving off the edge of a cliff into the unknown. I could only hope that he would be there to catch me.

"That's it, come for me baby, I've got you" he whispered as my body clenched agonisingly around his fingers. I clawed at the covers as wave after wave of incomparable pleasure burst through me, my head thrashing from side to side as I gave in to the sensation. His mouth replaced his fingers as he eagerly took everything I had to give.

"Jake!" I cried out as I came again almost instantly on his mouth. His hands gripped my hips, holding me in place as his tongue forged on, tasting me, emptying me of my desire, cradling me until my feet touched the ground. Not releasing me until he knew I was spent. *So, it is possible to have more than one orgasm in a night! Who knew?*

"Everything okay there?" he smirked, clearly pleased with himself. I could smell myself on him as he crawled back up to meet me. His mouth glistened with my desire. He looked heavenly. His skin was dewy and flushed, his hair tussled and out of place. Would I ever get enough of him like this?

"I'm more than okay. Jake…I… need you" I implored, stroking his face.

"I need you to be sure" he replied quietly "I don't want you to wake up in the morning and regret this, to regret me." He looked worried. How could he think that I could ever regret him? It was more likely to be the other way round.

"I don't think that's possible" I said, as I took his hand in mine, kissing his fingers, his palm, his wrist. The weight of his body rested over me, anchoring me to the mattress. I felt so safe and protected. I closed my eyes and exhaled, feeling lighter than I had done in forever.

"God Jemma, what are you doing to me?" He pulled himself upright so that he was kneeling at my feet, our eyes locked on to each other as he pulled a condom from his wallet, pulled down his trousers and slowly slid my knickers down past my ankles, discarding both to the floor with effortless ease. From this angle I could see all of him. He was mouthwatering. Huge. Like huge, huge. Smiling at me, he tore open the foil wrapper and slowly unrolled the condom down his shaft. "Are you 100% sure you want to do this?" he asked gently.

"Please" I begged, my arms instinctively reaching out to him to bring him back closer because the distance between us was making my heart ache. His face lit up in relief, and he lowered himself back down towards me, my legs falling naturally to the side to make way for him. His hands rested at the side of my face as his mouth met mine again. It was soft and delicate, and it instantly halted the aching in in my chest.

"You're so fucking beautiful" he whispered. My hands ran through his hair, down his neck and came to rest on his shoulders, binding me to him, melding us together as one. He smiled again, a warm, genuine smile as he slowly pushed his crown inside me, breathing heavily as he did so. The size of him was immense, even just the tip of him stretched me. I adjusted myself beneath him, trying to accommodate more, fearing it would be too much for me to take.

"We'll take it slowly" he whispered again, sensing my anxiety. "You'll get used to me; I promise. There's no rush, we have all the time in the world." The soothing timber of his voice, the sound of his words, the promise of time and the intensity of the feeling was overwhelming. I gasped for air, my eyes filling with emotion, my fingers digging into his skin, spurring him on. He pushed his way in a little further until he filled me again, resting there for a second, savouring the feeling, whilst he studied my face. "How does that feel? I'm not hurting you, am I?"

"No, you feel..." There were no words to describe how incredible he felt. Every bone in my body had been warmed by his touch so that an incredible heat radiated throughout me. It was as if my life until that point had been lived in the shade, and with him inside me, I was finally being exposed to the sun. Heaven.

"You feel amazing, just how I dreamed you would" he breathed, stroking my cheek. "Can you take any more?"

I had never been with such a considerate lover before. "Mmhmm ..." I nodded, as he retreated out of me slightly, only to return a moment later, a little deeper than before. The slow, rhythmic motion of his body entering me caused unspeakable joy, matched in intensity only by the empty feeling that was left behind as he withdrew from me, forcing me to seek him out each time. We moved as one. It was as easy as breathing, and the world stood still. With time, my body accepted more of him, until it not only welcomed every inch of him, but it actively sought him out. Our movements, although still gentle, reached a more feverish tempo, those black, cavernous eyes looming down over me, watching my every look, savouring my every reaction. "Jemma…. I can't…. fuck, you feel so good…. I'm sorry." We were both ready. One last meaningful thrust from him, and his body jerked violently. I followed suit, luxuriating in the thick, throbbing length which pulsed inside me, our mouths locked as we rode out the orgasm, holding each other tightly until the feeling subsided and our bodies lay lifelessly entwined. I wanted to stay like this forever. It seemed incomprehensible that I had only known him for such a brief time. Had he felt the same connection that I had? Was he now consumed with the same fear as me that this might be the first and last time that we lay together like this? The same dull ache from earlier filled my chest. The thought of not being like this with him again was unbearable. As if sensing my anguish, he raised his head to study my face.

"What's wrong? Did I hurt you?" he asked tucking a rogue strand of hair behind my ear.

"No, not at all. Nothing is wrong" I replied unconvincingly, meeting his gaze.

"Come on, you can talk to me" he persisted, his fingers trailing across my shoulder and down my arm.

I hesitated for a moment, trying to put everything I was feeling into some kind of coherent explanation. "I'm scared," I gushed before I even realised what I was saying.

"What are you scared of?" He was visibly concerned.

"I…, we don't really know each other and I'm worried that I shouldn't be feeling as much for you as I am," I said not able to look him in the eye for fear of crying. "What we just did was …"

"Everything" he smiled, holding my chin, and looking at me with soft, kind eyes.

"Yes," I stumbled, not expecting that response. "It was. But I know it doesn't necessarily mean it's going to translate into anything, and I just think I'm going to wind up getting hurt…" I trailed off, feeling stupid. I took a breath and started again. "So… if this is just a one-time thing, you need to tell me so that I don't get my hopes up. I'm fine with just having sex, but I need to know if that's all it is." I was totally not okay with just sex, I wanted everything, but I had already said too much and did not want to scare him.

"Jemma, there's something you need to know."

My heart plummeted. "Oh god, what is it? You're married, aren't you!" I blurted out involuntarily. "Shit, I knew it. When am I going to learn?" I could feel my body start to tremble. I knew he was too good to be true. I knew, things like this did not happen to girls like me. I just did not know it was all going to come crashing down so quickly. And after such mind-blowing sex! Why was life such a bitch?

He smiled kindly and pulled me closer to him. "No, no, I'm not, I promise." He paused. "But I was. My wife passed away five years ago." He re-tucked the strand of hair behind my ear again. His words bounded round my head, and it took a few seconds for me to register what he had said. When it did, I felt physically sick.

"Jake, … I…"

"Shh… it's okay" he whispered soothingly. "I don't make a habit of telling people. I find it kills a conversation off pretty quickly." He smiled, but it was a sad smile.

My heart felt like it was going to explode. What was wrong with me! It was like I was hell bent on cocking things up. "I'm so sorry Jake," I pleaded.

"Jemma, I'm telling you, because I want you to know that I'm just as scared as you are." He continued to stroke my hair. "You are the first woman I have been with since Erica passed away. In the five years since she has been gone, I have found fault with every single woman who has crossed my path. Nobody ever matched up to her, nobody was ever good enough." He paused. "I felt like I would be betraying her if I moved on. But then I met you, and I wanted you in a way that I didn't think was possible. It scared me because I felt like I was cheating on her." My heart stopped dead. "Jemma, I know we haven't known each other long, but I've known from the moment I first met you that you were special, that you were going to change everything. You are the first person in five long years that I can't find fault with, that I don't want to find fault with. I didn't know that I could ever feel like this again." He paused again, this time to look me straight in the eye. "You've made me feel alive." He rolled off me, pulling me with him so that we lay on our sides facing each other. "I won't ever make you promises I can't keep, but please believe me when I say that I will never lie, or cheat or hurt you."

A million questions flew round my head. Every time I thought I had the measure of this man; he surprised me. A part of me had to concede that I did not know him at all. The other part of me, the part governed by my heart, felt like I had known him forever.

"Give me a second to clean up" he said, stroking my cheek.

Whilst he was gone, a million and one thoughts crossed my mind. I wanted to know more, but I did not want to upset him. It was clear he was still grieving. I was pleased he felt he could share this with me, but did it mean he was not ready to move on? He walked back into the room and re-took his place next to me, hooking my leg over his.

"Can I ask what happened?" I said quietly, not knowing whether I was overstepping the mark.

"Of course, you can," he said, pulling me closer so that my head rested against his chest. We lay in silence for a moment before he began. "Erica was diagnosed with stage four breast cancer seven years ago. I watched her fight it with everything she had, and for a while, she held it at bay. But with time, even she was no match for it. I stood by and saw her succumb to its wickedness. I stood by and watched it take everything from her. It stripped her of her vitality, and when she could fight it no more and passed away, it stripped me of mine too."

My heart shattered for him. For the image of the man that I had never known and for the one who lay beside me now. I clung to him a little tighter. "I'm so sorry Jake."

"It's okay. I spent a long being angry with the world, but I've found peace now." He kissed me on the forehead. "I know she wouldn't have wanted me to carry on living like I was. I was passing time, getting through each day trying to avoid everyone and everything. Trying to avoid feeling - pain, happiness, anything. I was numb. She would have hated what I had become. I was no longer the man she fell in love with. She would have wanted me to live my life to the fullest, the way she did. And I know she would want me to be happy. It's why I've spent so much time working, why I haven't been with anyone else. I didn't feel ready." He paused. "But the day you walked into my life, something changed. I didn't understand it at first, I couldn't work out where all these new feelings had come from. I just knew that I was drawn to you, that being near you made me feel alive again. I wanted to tell you, but I didn't know how to."

"I'm glad you did" I whispered, stroking his arm.

He peeled himself from me so that he could look into my eyes. "Are you? I haven't scared you off? It wasn't too much?"

"Jake, I want to know everything, the good and the bad, the happy and the sad. I want to know it all. I don't want any secrets, only the truth. Promise me."

"I promise you."

"That's all I need." It was the truth. Laying there in his arms, all I needed was him.

"Jemma Lucas, you are an incredible woman."

# FRIDAY

Jake gently moved my hair to one side, his lips kissing me softly on the neck. "Good morning, you."

"Mmm…Good morning" I replied, half asleep, still encased in his arms, my body sated and still a little sore from last night. *God this feels good.*

He kissed me tenderly again "I could get used to waking up with you."

"I could get used to waking up with you too" I admitted, alarmed by just how normal waking up next to him felt. Like we had been doing it every day for years, and in no way mortified that this was the first time, and that I had not thought to wake up before him so I could clean my teeth, apply some concealer and plump up my hair before he saw me. "What time is it?"

"6am. I'm guessing you didn't pack a bag for Paris yesterday?"

"Shit! No, I didn't!" I said panicking.

"It's okay, you can do it in a minute," he whispered, his hands running the length of my body under the covers. It reacted to his touch instantly "There's something I need to do first though" he said.

"Oh, what's that?"

"This" he replied, covering my body with his and disappearing beneath the duvet.

"Oh my!" I squealed. "Twice in the space of a few hours!"

"Jemma, I haven't had sex in five years, I've got a lot of time to make up for" he garbled from down below, his lips tracing the curve of my hip. If the reason for the hiatus was not so sad, I would have laughed at his comment.

"Well, you'll be pleased to know that your time away doesn't seem to have impacted your performance in any way!"

"Good to know!" he chuckled. My word he was insatiable. Had he not told me, I would never have known that he had been celibate for so long. His technique was impressive to say the least, and he already had the measure of my body. He knew exactly what it wanted. I was stuck somewhere between consciousness and heaven, his mouth devouring every inch of me like a starved animal, when my bedroom door swung open, and Sarah came bounding in.

"Morning darling. How are you feeling? I thought you could probably do with a cuppa and some breakfast given that you didn't eat last night." She was backing into the room, tea in one hand, a plate of toast in the other, completely oblivious to the scene playing out behind her. "I hope you gave that arsehole what for when you got in!" She put the tea and toast down, having absolutely no clue what I had actually given him last night. "You're too good for him Jem, he's probably got a tiny dick anyway, any man with an ego the size of his is usually lacking in another department. You'll find someone who treats you like a princess ninety-nine per cent of the time and a filthy whore when you want him to, believe me. It's his loss." She finally turned round to face the bed, a mixture of confusion, mortification and realisation spreading across her face.

"Oh fuck! You …err…you really did give him what for!" she said winking. "I'll leave you both to it!" she laughed nervously. "Tea's there when you're umm…. finished! Oh, and Jake, I was only joking about the tiny dick thing, I'm sure you've got no problems whatsoever in that department!" she joked and bolted out the room without so much as a second glance.

Jake appeared from beneath the covers smiling. "Well, my giant ego just took a bit of a bashing that's for sure, and I can only apologise for the size of my dick" he said with a twinkle in his eye. "She's right though. You are too good for me" he said more seriously. "I do have one question though" he continued, a playful edge to his tone. "How will I know when not to treat you like a princess?"

"You'll know!" I said, placing my hands on his head, forcing him back below the covers to where he had just come from.

Considering I hadn't even started my packing until that morning, I managed to pull together several suitable outfits and accessories in under an hour. Jake sat in bed offering advice on what kind of things I might need, although, if I had listened solely to him, my case would have included little more than some underwear and a pair of thigh high patent boots. "Right, that's me done" I said zipping up my case and popping my passport into my bag. "I'm going to have a quick shower and get changed and then we can leave."

"I'll join you" he replied, getting himself out of bed. "If I go into the office smelling like this, they'll be all sorts of rumours flying around."

I chuckled. "None that I haven't heard before!"

"Maybe, but hopefully now you'll know they aren't all true" he said walking over to me, cupping my face in his hands and kissing me.

"I will. Now come on, or you're going to make me late" I joked, heading for the door.

"I'm right behind you, I just need to find my damn joggers."

"You threw them down by the side of the bed last night" I called, remembering in exquisite detail how he had revealed himself to me for the first time. I darted across the landing to the bathroom before anyone could see me, but before I could dive inside, the door opened and out stepped Ben in a towel.

"Jeez, you startled me" I gasped taking a step backwards.

"Sorry." He stared at me with an unusually grave expression on his face. "Jem, I'm so sorry about last night. I didn't want to be the one to tell you, I just couldn't bear to see you being made a fool of. Can you forgive me?"

"Of course, I can. Look, it's fine, it was all a misunderstanding" I said cheerily.

"What do you mean?" He looked confused.

"I'm running late Ben, but I'll explain everything when I get back from Paris."

"Paris?"

With that, I heard footsteps coming across the landing. Jake, dressed solely in his jogging bottoms, stood territorially behind me.

"I see" Ben continued, looking him up and down disapprovingly. "Well, it's all yours" he gestured to the steaming room behind him.

"Thanks mate" Jake replied off-handedly, taking my hand, leading us through the door. Ben side stepped us and made his way back to his room. Did I just imagine it or was there some kind of silent male face-off happening between the two of them?

The shower took a little longer than usual since I was a little distracted by my new shower buddy. It turns out that two pairs of hands are not necessarily better than one when it comes to doing things quicker! Anyway, we were still in the car and on the way to work before 8am and given that it was my boss who had caused the delay, it was unlikely that I was going to get into any serious trouble.

As we pulled up in the underground carpark, and the engine stopped, Jake twisted hesitantly in his seat to look at me. "Thank you."

"For...?"

"For everything." He leaned in and kissed me gently on the

cheek. This man who had been so wild and powerful less than an hour ago was now so sweet and hesitant. He was a complete contradiction.

"No, thank you" I replied, returning his kiss, not wanting to get out of the car.

"So...," he started again reluctantly "Should we go in together or separately?"

"I think separately, don't you? We don't want people to gossip about us just yet."

"So, you genuinely are embarrassed to be seen with me!" he said in amusement.

"No, that's not it at all" I giggled, slapping him on the leg. "I just need to get my head around things first, have time to work out what this is, before having to try and explain it to anyone else that's all. Does that make sense?" The last thing I wanted was to be headline news when I was not even sure what was going on. What if this was just a casual thing? I know what he said to me last night, but things changed. He might not be ready for anything more than sex, which would not be all that bad given that the sex was mind blowing.

"I'm only joking. I get it. But just in case you do have to explain it to anyone, maybe you could say we are seeing each other?'"

I could not hide the delight I felt inside. "Really? That's what you want?"

"Yes ... but only if that's what you want too?" There was that self-doubt again.

I could not keep the smile from spreading across my face. "I'd like that a lot."

"Me too." He planted another kiss on my cheek.

"Right, I'll see you in a minute." I opened the car door and got out. As I snaked my way through the rows of equally as impressive cars, something inside me made me turn round to look at him just one last time. He was sat there motionless, staring back at me, as if he had been watching me the entire time. As our eyes met, he smiled that same heart-warming smile I had been lucky enough to witness these past few days. He had me feeling like a teenage girl in love. *In love? What the fuck?*

When the doors to the lift pinged open for the last time that week, I quite literally floated out on to the office floor. I had not felt that happy in I could not remember how long. I felt just like one of those ridiculously young and beautiful girls in a Marc Jacob's Daisy eau de parfum advert, running barefoot through a field of white and yellow in a billowing summer dress and floral headband. The only difference being that I was old enough to be one of their mothers, I was wearing trousers and a blouse, and the bulldog clip holding my pile of damp hair in place, was not as elegant or delicate as a fresh flower headdress. Safe to say, I may well have felt like one of those girls, but I sure as hell did not look like one of them.

As if I had landed in an alternate universe, Claire was already sitting at her desk typing away and sipping on her first coffee of the day (workday coffee that was, she usually had at least two before leaving the house). How many times had she beaten me in this week? Either she was after a promotion, or I was slipping, or both.

"Good morning!" I sang as I plonked myself down on my chair, exhaling loudly as I did so, verbalising my contentment with the world.

"I'm surprised you can sit down at all, after all the action your arse has seen in the past few hours" she whispered with a wry smile. "Sarah told me she walked in on you and our incredibly attractive boss this morning enjoying a spot of how's your father! I can't keep up with the pair of you. One minute it's on, then it's off, then you're fucking each other's brains out, it's like an episode of Jeremy Kyle but for people with all their own teeth. Next week you'll find out you're long-lost cousins!"

"Stop it!" I laughed in hysterics. "It's not quite that bad!"

"It totally is, but I love it! It's about time you got some action, and the fact that you're boning the boss is just too much! Tell me, what's his dick like? I've tried checking out his bulge before, but it's so hard to gauge the proportions when it's all tucked up in there."

"Morning ladies." Jake passed our desks, stopping momentarily to give me a private smile, and a glance in Claire's direction to let her know that he had heard every word she had just uttered.

"Holy fuck! How long was he standing there? How does he do that? He's like a fucking mother-in-law, popping up everywhere unannounced and uninvited! He heard everything didn't he?" This was the second time in as many days she had been caught out by him. I could not help but giggle.

"You're okay, he's already heard Sarah say that she thinks he's got a small dick, so anything other than that would be an improvement."

"Thank the lord for Sarah's loose lips!"

"Who's got loose lips?" asked Helene as she threw her handbag and a Waitrose carrier bag full of fig rolls down on her desk. I looked inquisitively up at her. "Don't. Richard's mum is coming to stay with us, and they're the only bloody things she eats" she offered by way of an explanation. I do not know what made her more depressed, the fact that her mother-in-law was coming to stay or the fact that she had just spent about twenty pounds on fig rolls. It was times like this that I realised how scared I was of growing old. Fresh figs were bad enough, but at what age did you start to enjoy a fig roll? They looked like dog biscuits for starters, and I remembered my mum saying that if she ever needed to go to the loo, she would eat a fig roll or two to help push things through. At what point did either of those things make a fig roll the biscuit of choice for people who A) did not have dogs or B) were not constipated? I guess life did not always provide you the answers you wanted.

My computer sprung to life and instantly notified me of a new email.

**From: Jake Bales**
**To: Jemma Lucas**
**Subject: Meeting at 9.30am**
**Sent: Today at 8.35am**

Are you free at 9.30am for a quick meeting?

Jake

**From: Jemma Lucas**
**To: Jake Bales**
**Subject: Meeting at 9.30am**
**Sent: Today at 8.36am**

I don't know, I am extremely busy this morning doing important things. I'm not sure I have time to be having secret meetings with my boss - who I am now seeing !

Jemma

**From: Jake Bales**
**To: Jemma Lucas**
**Subject: Meeting at 9.30am**
**Sent: Today at 8.37am**

No problem at all. I'll let Jeff Thompson know that unfortunately, you can't make it. I'll pass on your apologies. Am happy to let him know that we're seeing each other though if he should ask!

Jake

Crap.

From: Jemma Lucas
To: Jake Bales
Subject: Meeting at 9.30am
Sent: Today at 8.38am

Ignore everything I just said. Will be there at 9.30am sharp.

Jemma

From: Jake Bales
To: Jemma Lucas
Subject: Meeting at 9.30am
Sent: Today at 8.39am

Only kidding. He's not really coming in. Just wanted to see you.

Jake

From: Jemma Lucas
To: Jake Bales

Subject: Meeting at 9.30am

Sent: Today at 8.40am

Idiot. Ok, now leave me alone, I really do have important work to be getting on with.

Jemma x

From: Jake Bales

To: Jemma Lucas

Subject: Meeting at 9.30am

Sent: Today at 8.41am

Ok, but only because you asked so nicely!

Jake x

*He put a kiss on the end of his message!*

As had been the case all week, the morning flew by. What with numerous coffees and in-depth conversations with Claire about what exactly had transpired when I got home yesterday evening, the hours just disappeared. She had reacted like a proud mum when I told her I had performed oral sex on Jake, and even prouder when she discovered that I had swallowed. I had often wondered what kind of relationship she might have with her future children, and it scared the living hell out of me to think that this conversation might be an indicator as to ones she might have with her daughter. I would have to ensure I was always on hand to give more sensible advice and to warn her that she should never feel pressured into carrying out such acts. That it was important for a boy or man to like her for who she was, not just because she was prepared to deep throat him. Even though deep down (pardon the pun) we all knew that it was exactly that type of girl who always ended up with the guy. Here's hoping she had sons.

Aside from the gossip and coffee, we also received news from LJT that they loved our presentation and were coming back in on Monday afternoon to go through the finer points. Jake sent out a congratulatory email to the team, thanking them for all their hard work, whilst I got a private text message saying he would show me his appreciation later, followed by a few aubergine and tomato emojis (I hoped he was implying something sexual rather than telling me we were having Moussaka for dinner).

Just before 2pm I downed tools, switched off my computer, said a coded goodbye to Claire (promising to keep her up to date with everything that happened in Paris), and waited impatiently for Jake to come out of his office so we could leave. At precisely 2.03pm (not that I was clock watching), the door opened, and he breezed over to my desk.

"Are you ready to leave Jemma?" he said sounding as professional as possible.

"Yep" I replied politely, trying desperately not to let on how excited I was or that I had in fact been mentally ready for the past six hours. I grabbed my bag, got to my feet and joined him on the other side of the desk.

"I hope the…meeting goes well!" said Claire looking up at both of us with a knowing look.

"Thank you, I'm sure it will" Jake replied with a wry smile, playing her at her own game.

"I'll call you over the weekend" I promised, before we started towards the lift, Jake's hand resting briefly on the small of my back. My skin tingled beneath his touch. Fire and ice.

"I thought today would never end" he said in a whisper as he hit the down button. "Do you have any idea how much I wanted to call you into my office and take you over my desk?" My breath caught in my lungs. The doors opened, and we stepped silently inside the empty lift, turning slowly to face the disappearing office. His hand casually grazed mine, sending a shiver of excitement racing through my body.

I tried to play it cool. "So, Mr Bales, I hope you're ready for a weekend full of croque monsieur's and pain au chocolates."

"I'm sure we can do better than that Miss Lucas" he replied with a glint in his eye, sending my heart rate soaring and causing my cheeks to blush.

I pretended to ignore the inuendo, but inside, I was secretly hoping he meant he was going to be eating me and not much else. "Ah, so you're more of a jambon baguette and frites kinda guy" I mused, refraining from looking at him.

"Are you just naming all the French foods you can pronounce by any chance?" he laughed affectionately.

"Not at all. I'll have you know I know many French delicacies – croissants, tarte au citron, almond croissants, tarte aux pommes…."

"I'm sensing a penchant for pastry! Does that mean you have a sweet tooth then?" he said looking at me intently with his piercing eyes.

"Yes, but mainly because I can pronounce them!" I conceded. His laugh was warm and genuine, and he seemed instantly more relaxed as he took my hand in his and kissed it tenderly. Mr Bales the businessman had left the building (metaphorically, if not yet physically), and the carefree Jake from last night had returned. I was surprised just how quickly he was able to silence that persona. Perhaps this really was the true Jake.

◆ ◆ ◆

I should have known that travelling with him would be a

completely different experience to travelling with the girls. For starters, we arrived at the airport ahead of schedule (as opposed to re-creating the scene from Home Alone, where the McAllister family stampede through the terminal like a herd of angry wildebeest because they are late for their flight). The valet parking attendant at the entrance to the terminal was also a nice touch. I was much more accustomed to jumping on a crowded and musty smelling car park shuttle bus, where you were forced to crouch below an oversized, string vest wearing ogre, who failed to grasp the concept of personal space, on his way to an all inclusive week in Benidorm or Magaluf. And although until this point, I had naively assumed that this was how all people travelled, I had to admit, that my experience thus far with Jake, was far more preferential.

As we sashayed through the busy terminal, we avoided the snaking economy class bag drop queue and instead, walked straight up the Business and First-Class counter, where yet again, we were met by an amiable lady who bent over backwards to be polite and helpful. Some might say she was the antithesis of the stern-faced dragon who lay in wait next door for the masses travelling in economy. I felt slightly sorry for those unsuspecting holiday goers, sure as hell they were not getting let off with their excess baggage (I miscalculated the number of pairs of shoes I would need for the trip, so brought them all and prayed that nobody would mind). As we thanked her for her kindness (and her willingness to turn a blind eye to the extra thirteen kilos I had packed), Jake gathered up the boarding passes.

"Do you want me to keep hold of everything?"

"Yes please!" I sang light-heartedly, feeling grateful that I had been relinquished of all responsibility.

"No problem at all" he said stuffing the paperwork in his laptop case. "Once we're through security, do you want to pop into Duty Free before heading up to the lounge?" The words rolled off his tongue so naturally. Clearly, going to 'the lounge' was a normal occurrence for him. I did not want to confess, that the closest I had been to an airport lounge was one of the comfy seats in the Wetherspoons pub on the ground floor.

"That would be great, thank you. I just want to grab some perfume if that's okay?"

"Of course, it is" he said, taking hold of my hand and leading me towards the fast track security entrance.

Well, what a revelation that was! Who knew that airport security did not need to be akin to cattle herding. On all my travels to date, I had only ever laid witness to hordes of people being shoehorned into various queues whilst being chastised for not taking out the coins from their pockets or the laptops from their cases. Only to then be ambushed by angry members of security with a magic wand aiming to prove that not only had they failed those two simple instructions, they had also failed to declare that there was a metal heel in their shoe, a gold clip in their hair or a new bionic hip joint in their body. *How very dare they!* This 'Fast Track' alternative had clearly fallen foul of the assumption that anyone with money could not possibly be smuggling drugs or weapons, because we were waved through the scanner with nothing more than a jovial "Good afternoon." The man staring blankly at the bag screening monitor could not have given two hoots that I had a host of lip glosses and a small bottle of perfume in my hand luggage. I really would be unable to go back to my old life after this.

Half an hour later, I was sat in a plush leather armchair, glass of champagne in my hand, a Duty Free bag nestled neatly at my feet, listening to Jake lament about how ridiculous it was that people purchased Toblerone's at the airport when they did not buy or eat them at any other time of the year (I had just purchased two for us to eat whilst we were away). I tried to explain that Toblerone's, much like perfume, were an unnecessary expense at any normal time of the year, but that money spent at the airport did not count, in much the same way that calories consumed on your birthday or at Christmas did not really count either. Whether he agreed with my justification or not I could not say, but he smiled, raised his glass, and toasted to the weekend. I had to admit, that in that moment, sitting opposite him, with a couple of glasses of fizz inside me and a mound of chocolate at my feet, there was no place in the world I would rather have been (except maybe in Paris).

We talked and laughed the whole way across the English Channel. With every story or anecdote he told, I gleaned just a little more about the man behind the suit. Whether he was reminiscing about past summers with his sister in Provence (he could not help but mock me for thinking that Charlie was a boy), or tales of Burt, his English sheepdog, who it seemed was the one who really ran the roost at home, but was much loved regardless. It was like piecing together the bits of a jigsaw puzzle to create a picture of who he really was. I liked the picture that was unfolding before my eyes – very much. Although I did not have the exciting tales to tell like he did, he listened avidly whilst I regaled times spent with the girls, or my family, not once letting go of my hand (until he had to pop to the loo that is). In fact, we talked so much, that no sooner had we taken off from London, than the seatbelts signs came on, and the captain informed us that we were beginning our decent into Charles de Gaulles airport. The time had quite literally flown by.

"Welcome to my home away from home" he beamed as we pulled off the runway and taxied to the terminal. "I hope you enjoy yourself."

"How could I not?" I replied kissing him on the cheek.

Paris was just as beautiful and vibrant as I remembered. I felt the same instant connection with it as I had done all those years ago when I spent the summer working there. She was a living, breathing city, and much like her people, she was joyous and utterly breath-taking. I wound down the window in our taxi, but rather than look out to see the beauty beyond, I closed my eyes and inhaled deeply, feeling the warm breeze on my skin, taking in the cacophony of sounds and the rich smells from the passing street side cafes and restaurants. How I had missed her. It felt like a lifetime ago that I was here, and yet, it was all so familiar. The beeping of car horns, the distant chatter of tourists, the faint sound of an accordion, and the almost imperceptible rustle of leaves as the gentle breeze moved carefree through the trees. It was like putting on your favourite old sweatshirt. Comforting. Warming. It felt like home.

"It's something else isn't it" Jake mused, looking out of his own window. "Every time I come back here; I'm blown away. It's one of the few places on earth I've been to where I notice something new each time." He breathed in deeply as if he were physically taking the city in to his body.

"I know what you mean. It's as if she's alive" I said, watching him.

"She?"

"Of course, she's a she!" I exclaimed with mock contempt. There is no way that something this beautiful, this thought provoking, and this capable of invoking such emotion could ever be a he. That and the fact that the architecture screams femineity."

"You can't tell me that the Eiffel tower is feminine!" he argued with a smile "Everything about it screams dick!"

"God, here was me thinking you were cultured!" I giggled. "The very fact that she is referred to as Madame Eiffel Tower and the French noun for tower is feminine (une tour) proves it! But even from a design perspective, you just have to look at the intricate iron work and the five billion lights on her, to know that she was designed to be shown off to the world like a princess in a dazzling gown."

"You are something else, you know that?" he squeezed my hand affectionately. "You see things differently." He said, chuckling.

"Where you see a Disney Princess, I see a cock. Probably speaks volumes about me!" I shook my head, smiling.

As we followed the path carved out by the Seine, the fading light changed the landscape yet again. For a fleeting moment, as day turned into night, Paris took a ten-minute break, a costume change if you like, in readiness for her second act. And what a costume change it was! A gazillion twinkling lights magically appeared, from down on the pavements up to the roofs of the tallest buildings, signalling to the world that the performance was due to re-start, beckoning her people to join her. If she had been beautiful in the daylight, she was nothing short of majestic now. The hum of the cars and the hustle and bustle of the people were still present but seemed ever so slightly muffled now, the darkening sky above acting as a rich blanket, cocooning the streets beneath, absorbing and softening the carnival like atmosphere of earlier. She was now an elegant lady, a keeper of secrets, an intriguing and mysterious hostess. No wonder she was revered for being the city of love, how could anyone fail to fall under her spell? Here, hope was abundant, anything was possible, love reigned supreme, and I was here, right in the heart of it all!

I was momentarily pulled from my trance by the slowing down of the car. "Madame, Monsieur, we have arrived." As the car halted at the side of the pavement, I focused on the imposing building to the side of us.

"You live here?" I asked astonished, unable to hide the mixture of awe and trepidation in my voice.

"Yes." replied Jake looking concerned. "Is everything ok?"

"It's...."

"It's just an apartment, not the whole building" he smiled reassuringly.

"Thank God. If it's just an apartment, at least it means that you're slightly ...normal." I replied in jest.

"Can't guarantee normal I'm afraid" he said, offering me a hand to get out of the cab.

"Merci Monsieur, au revoir" he called to the driver in a flawless French accent as the car pulled away.

"Wow, can you speak to me in French later?" I joked. "French you is even sexier than English you."

He leaned in towards me "Avec plaisir."

And just like that, I was under his sexy French spell.

As he led the way up the marble steps, I could not help but be impressed by the beauty of the building. It radiated French chic and was far grander than many of the other buildings we had passed along our journey. As I balanced on the step with my suitcase waiting for him to open the door, I glanced inquisitively up and down the street. It was abundantly clear that every property in this neighbourhood was just as resplendent. Pristine white facades with iron railing balconies, huge imposing floor to ceiling windows and entrances which would not have been out of place on a stately home graced the tree lined avenue. Safe to say there were no dingy Airbnb's along here. This was a world which I did not belong in, the world of the aristocracy, 16th century or modern day. Had I been with anyone else, I would have felt entirely out of place, but somehow, as I watched him turn the key, and casually open the door, any hint of self-doubt evaporated.

"Were you just checking out my arse?" he joked, turning round, and catching me off guard.

"Absolutely not!" I protested with a guilty grin. Honestly, could he blame me for sneaking a peak? I did not know any woman, or man for that matter, who would not be tempted to feast their eyes on that perfect derriere.

"Let me take that for you" he smiled, coming back down the steps, grabbing my case and carrying it effortlessly inside towards the dainty looking lift in the foyer.

"Thank you." I stood still in the entrance, appreciatively taking in the surroundings. An imposing display of fresh flowers stood prominently on an elegant walnut table in the centre, and the room smelt like expensive fresh linen. Jake hit the button for the fourth floor on the lift and the doors slid tentatively open.

"Are you ok" he asked, taking me in his arms.

"Mmmhmm…." As I stood there, wrapped tightly in his embrace, I was more than ok, I was great.

"I'm so glad you're here" he whispered, his mouth nuzzling my hair.

"Me too" I replied, momentarily incapable of a better response.

After a few moments, the lift doors glided open, and we stepped out onto to a beautiful corridor. Leading the way, Jake pulled the two suitcases along until he reached a front door. Turning the key, he side-barged the door open, holding it ajar for me to enter, unveiling the most incredible room I had ever seen.

My eyes adjusted to the soft lighting inside. "Wow!"

"You like it?" he asked hopefully.

"Like it, Jake, this is incredible!" Leaving him standing at the door, I stepped cautiously over the vast oak floor. Pale dove grey walls adorned with modern works of art, encased the most elegant open plan living room and kitchen, furnished with soft white sofas, and chairs in accented colours. In the corner, an open fireplace stacked high with logs sat within a huge stone surround, and on the far side, much like his office, an almost complete wall of glass, with French doors leading on to a large balcony. It was a successful blend of modern and traditional, a triumph of interior design.

"I had some help with the interior" he offered apologetically. "I'm not that great when it comes to soft furnishings."

"I think you've done amazingly. It's beautiful" I gushed.

"Thank you. I want you to make yourself at home this weekend" he urged, pulling me back towards him and planting a tender kiss on my lips. Just the feel of his hands on my body sent a warmth coursing through me that had not been there five seconds ago. "I've been wanting to get you alone all day."

"I'm very glad you did" I replied, stroking his face. He kissed me again, more fervently this time, my feet leaving the ground as he scooped me up effortlessly in his strong arms and carried me towards one of the white doors on the right.

"Now," he said slightly breathlessly, "We can discuss paint colours in a while, but there is something I've been wanting to do since this morning."

"And what might that be Mr Bales?" I asked, smiling.

"Get you naked" he replied matter-of-factly, giving my bum a squeeze. His eyes burned with desire; his voice was gravelly and ragged. His words lit a fire within me that I had been trying to suppress all day. Any control I had mustered, dissipated quickly into thin air. As his tongue found mine, my fingers darted from his hair to the buttons on his shirt, frantically trying to free him so that my hands could roam hungrily over his beautiful body once again. He lifted me off the ground, and we stumbled through the first door and down a long corridor towards a second, desperately tugging at each other as we bounced off the walls, discarding items of clothing as we went, our bodies needy.

"God, I've wanted to do this all day" he managed, not taking his mouth off mine as he spoke, discarding my bra to the floor. A low groan escaped his mouth as our naked bodies touched for the second time that day.

"Me too" I gasped, pushing myself against his toned, hard chest, gripping onto his hair with both hands. I could hardly breathe, the need for him was so great. He burst through the door to the bedroom and headed straight for the four-poster bed that sat alongside another huge balcony. Our eyes never left each other as he made light work of our remaining clothes.

"Are you on the pill?" he moaned into my mouth

"Yes"

"Can we… I mean, I'm clean, I've been tested."

"Me too." My voice was breathy and desperate. I was not one for unprotected sex, but I trusted him, and truthfully, I wanted to feel him. Just me and him with nothing between us. "Take me Jake, let me feel all of you."

He growled like a wild animal, as if my permission had flicked a switch inside him, a primal instinct to own and conquer taking over. Without hesitation, he entered me in one fluid movement, strong and confident, sinking into me until he was fully seated inside. His immense size coupled with the heightened sensitivity was overwhelming. He felt even more incredible than before. He was physically bare inside me and that had emotional ramifications. There was an additional layer of vulnerability for both of us, an added layer of trust that now existed, a silent message that this was something more than before. I could see it in his eyes, could feel it in the way he moved. The heavenly friction created by our bodies had his name tumbling incoherently from my mouth within seconds. He moved swiftly; our bodies synchronised. As he ploughed deeper, a rush of adrenalin swept through me.

"Jake, harder!" I begged.

"Are you sure?" His eyes were on me, his breathing rapid and his voice gruff. He was caught between wanting to be gentle with me and wanting to let go and give me what I was asking for.

"Yes, I'm sure" I demanded, sinking my nails into his back. "I need this." That was enough to break his resolve. His hips collided with mine, a frenzy of intertwined bodies and slick skin, pain that turned into something exquisite the more he pounded me. I watched on as he moved instinctively, freely, masterfully. It was intoxicating. This was the man from the office, the alpha male, the one who commanded those around him, just as he was in control now. He was brilliant and I wanted more. So much more.

"More!" I urged, feeling my body start to unravel underneath him. Another animalistic growl emanated from him as he propelled himself forward again with yet even more power, his hands resting underneath me, angling my body towards him, so that I took every hard inch of him. Never had I been with somebody so intuitive, so accomplished, and now that I had, I never wanted anyone else. My eyes brimmed in anticipation of what he might do next, I wanted to try everything he offered me. With one effortless move, he flipped me on to my front so that I was facing away from him.

"Hold on to the headboard baby" he instructed, as he pulled me up on to my knees and parted my legs, bringing me to rest gently back against him. I did as he asked. His fingers trailed down my spine, circling the tight hole between my cheeks. Nobody had ever touched me there before. "Now, what do you want Jemma?" he growled as he continued to run his fingers labouredly between that spot and the wetness between my thighs, all whilst his erection pressed impatiently at my opening.

"I want you."

"And what do you want me to do?"

"I want you to fuck me" I begged, slightly taken aback by my request.

"Do you have any idea how much it turns me on hearing you talk like that?" he asked in that melting, buttery tone. "You know," he said, appreciation in his voice, "You look just as beautiful from behind as you do from the front." My body hummed at the compliment. "So….do you want me to treat you like a princess?" he asked, his finger circling my clit. I could barely hear the question over his rapid breathing.

"No. I want you to fuck me… hard" I replied, pushing myself back onto him, the tip of him entering me.

"Shit Jemma, you're going to make me come" he moaned as he used his hands to pull me open further and push himself deeper inside. "But I promise you I'm going to make you come over and over again to make up for it." There was an urgency about his movements, each powerful thrust providing just the right amount of force to impart pleasure through the pain. "You're going to need to come for me right now baby" he ordered after several particularly rapid strokes. My body, sensing the warning in his voice did exactly as he asked, coming undone at his command, sending bolts of unadulterated pleasure coursing through me. My thighs tightened around him, constricting the throbbing mass which thickened inside me, calling his name over and over again as I rode the wave of immeasurable ecstasy.

"Jesue Jemma!" Before I could finish, he unleashed his own desire deep inside, filling me to the brim, his body jerking powerfully, beads of sweat inching down his muscular chest, before he finally stilled. His face rested in the crook of my neck, his lips delicately tracing a line across the top to my shoulder blades.

"Fuck me Jemma. When you talk to me like that, you make me feel like a teenage boy again. I'm surprised I lasted as long as I did. You felt amazing," he said between ragged breaths.

"I was going to say the same about you" I giggled, my face head down in the pillow, basking in the warmth of his body.

"I mean it" he insisted. "You're incredible." Delicate kisses trailed back down my neck, sending shivers down to my toes.

"I could get used to this" I giggled

"I hope so." He pulled his body free of mine and rolled to the side. We lay facing each other, his hands slowly stroking the curves of my hip, watching each other silently for a few moments. Finally, he spoke. "Are you hungry?"

"Starving!" Thank God. As much as I would have loved to have whispered sweet nothings to each other for the next few hours, I was so hungry I was starting to feel faint.

"Great. I provisionally booked us a table at this amazing little bistro just a few minutes from here, but if you fancy just going for a wander and seeing what you fancy, we could do that instead. Whatever you prefer." I was not used to someone being so thoughtful. Most of the idiots I had been out with in the past would never have given me the option. In fact, the point was moot, because I would not be in Paris with them in the first instance.

"I trust your judgement implicitly" I giggled, feeling like a giddy teenager myself. "Let's stick with the place you've booked a table at."

"Ok" he said lifting himself up off me to see the clock next to the bed. "It's 7.10pm now and I've booked the table for 8.30pm. So that's plenty of time to get showered and ready. Would you like something to drink first?"

"That would be lovely, thank you." He got up and walked leisurely out of the bedroom, those pert cheeks of deliciousness swaying gently as he moved. *This must be a dream.* Once he had left, I wrapped myself in a chenille blanket which was laying casually over the arm of a beautiful chair next to the bed and meandered over to the French doors and out on to the balcony. My word, what a view! My sense of direction was atrocious at the best of times, and I was completely oblivious to where we were in relation to the rest of the city. From up here, it felt like the whole of Paris was splayed out beneath us. The Rive Gauche flowed majestically in front, the Champs de Mars was illuminated like a runway leading up to the Eiffel Tower, and the Musee d'Orsay and the Trocadero gardens shimmered in the distance.

"Some view, hey?"

"It's breath-taking" I agreed, turning to acknowledge the even more beautiful sight stood in front of me.

Jake had returned holding a bottle of champagne and two glasses. At some point he had acquired his trousers, so was now disappointingly not naked (although semi-naked was still preferable to being fully clothed). He made his way lazily over to where I was standing, handed me the glasses, then expertly popped the cork of the bottle, and poured out the chilled bubbles, placing it down on a circular metal table. He edged closer, partially unwrapping my blanket so that he could sneak inside. Even with his trousers on, the proximity of his body, caused my own to stir. Would he always have this effect on me?

"Here's to our first weekend in Paris" he said, raising his glass to mine, and pressing his body closer. There was something reassuring in the way he said "first." It sounded more hopeful than presumptuous, a clue perhaps that he wished for something longer term with me. My heart skipped a little beat at the prospect of more time. I was slap-bang in the middle of a Parisian fairy-tale and I was going to embrace every single second of it. In the words of Edith Piaf "Je ne regrette rien" (although I doubt very much that she was referring to a dirty weekend in Paris with her boss when she sang that song).

"To Paris!" I chimed, placing my free arm around him, drawing him in closer still. He was very quickly becoming a drug to me, something I did not want to be without (which was a little unnerving).

"And … to us?" he added a little tentatively, his piercing gaze meeting mine.

"To us."

Now, it may well have been the glass of Dom Perignon talking (which I hasten to add was exquisite), or the idyllic setting we found ourselves in, but I had an overwhelming urge to try and explain to him exactly how I was feeling (a little premature I hear you all say). Unfortunately, due to the distinct lack of sleep in the past twenty four hours, the previous glasses of champagne (of which there were numerous), the fact that I had not eaten since this morning, coupled with the sudden realisation that I was talking to my boss, I fear my romantic decree did not come out quite as I had intended.

"Jake …"

"Yes…"

"I …."

"Yes"

He held my chin gently in his hand, forcing me once again to stare into those tumultuous dark orbs. The look was so intense it was unnerving. I felt my cheeks flush and my confidence disintegrate. "Umm… I really like you." Perfect. Could not have worded that any better if I had tried. Jesus, what an absolute car crash. Who was I, Rain Man?

"I really like you too" he replied, his lips curling up at the edges, clearly bowled over by my poetic declaration. "In fact," he continued, taking my glass from me and placing it down on the table next to his "I really, really like you." I had very quickly discovered that Jake Bales had the extraordinary ability to look at you in a way that made you feel like you were the only person on the planet. In this situation, it was enough to make even the most cynical person go weak at the knees. Hell, I suspect even Helene might have succumbed to his charm. But for me, an inebriated, famished, hopeless romantic, my legs quite literally buckled. No word of a lie, I physically went over on my ankle.

"Ow, shit!" I whined unexpectedly, clawing at his arm like an angry cat, trying to stop myself from falling completely (I knew I should have had one of those toasted sandwiches onboard the plane).

"That wasn't quite the reaction I was hoping for!" he chuckled, grabbing me by the waist and helping me back to my feet. Bloody hell, why was I so incapable of being cool at these pivotal moments in life?

"Right, pretend that didn't just happen! Pretend I'm not a complete buffoon and start again!" I begged, abject mortification washing over me. His grin widened into a full-blown toothy smile. He took my face in both his hands.

"I was saying that I'm glad you like me because I really, REALLY like you. The short time we've spent together has been amazing and there is nobody in the world I would rather be here with than you." As he spoke his voice slowed so that each word became more pronounced. His eyes drilled into my soul, and I found myself staring hopelessly into them, the melodic tone of his voice sending me into a trance (or maybe it was just the starvation kicking in). Either way, I was falling completely and utterly in love with him. No amount of reasoning, common sense or argument from the opposition could quash this feeling which had been ignited. I closed my eyes, and for the first time in forever, prepared to give myself entirely to the person standing before me, however vulnerable that might make me.

It is also worth noting, that not only did I lay myself emotionally bare in front of him, I laid myself physically bare too. Amid our passionate embrace, the blanket which I had been elegantly wrapped in, decided to fall to the floor and expose me before him. What could have been yet another embarrassing moment on my part, in fact turned out to be one of the most liberating experiences of my life. His eyes followed the soft chenille down to its final resting place and then scanned back up my body appreciatively until he met my gaze again.

"I much prefer you like this" he purred, the words lingering on his tongue as he stepped closer. "You're like a drug to me Jemma, I can't see straight when you're around. And when you're like this..." he added, running the back of his hand over my chest, lingering on my nipple, "I don't even know which way is up." His breathing was ragged, and his eyes were completely black.

My nipples hardened at his touch. "You have the same effect on me." A fire raged in the pit of my stomach, and goosebumps erupted across my skin. I longed to have him again.

"I'm suddenly not hungry for food anymore" he whispered dangerously, moving to within an inch of me, so that I could inhale the sweet scent of his skin. His full, soft, lips trailed tender kisses from my ear lobe down to the nape of my neck.

"Me neither" I concurred, instantly forgetting the toasted sandwich I had been hankering after. My eyes closed again, and I allowed by head to drop back and rest in his hand which was wrapped around the back of my neck, helping to expose more of myself to his heavenly touch.

"Let me make love to you Jemma" he beseeched, his hands tracing delicate lines over my naked skin. "Let me show you exactly what you mean to me."

Now, I just need to press pause for a second, and make a confession. As much of a romantic as I am, I have always had a bit of an aversion to the term 'making love'. Do not ask me why, I am not sure there is a plausible explanation. However, the phrase has always invoked an icky kind of feeling deep in my gut akin to the one you get after eating a whole tub of cookie dough ice cream. Do not get me wrong, the act of doing it (or eating it) is always quite pleasurable, but afterwards, I always berate myself for indulging in something that is too sickly sweet, which invariably promises way more than it delivers, and is often over all too soon. I always find myself wondering whether a Mr Whippy '99 could not provide just as much pleasure without the hype or the cost of its more elaborate counterpart. As a result, I have never found myself in a situation where I felt it necessary to utter those words. Fast forward to now, and my dislike of that expression had disappeared as quickly as the aforementioned tub of ice cream. My entire body tingled at the suggestion. Somehow, coming from his mouth, the words sounded different. They made me yearn to know how it would feel to have him make love to me, rather than throw up as had always been the case. I needed to know what it would be like to have more than just a physical connection to him. I needed that emotional connection too. Every fibre of my being longed for him, all of him and it scared the living hell out of me. *You should not be feeling like this already. It's too soon. You're going to end up getting hurt.*

"What is it, too soon?" he asked, tilting my chin so that our eyes met once more. His face conveyed a mixture of longing and concern – a heady combination, and I found myself unable to avoid answering his question.

"I've never felt this way about anyone before" I admitted weakly, averting his penetrating gaze, and lowering my face.

"Good." He took hold of my face again, realigning it with his once more. It was impossible not to be honest with him. "This might be happening quickly Jemma, but there is no doubt in my mind how I feel about you." His penetrating stare stripped me bare, exposing the very depths of my soul.

"Jake, this past week has been surreal. It's felt like a dream, and I'm frightened that any minute I'm going to wake up and realise that none of it was real. If I'm being completely honest, I don't know how I'd cope with that." There was a momentary silence before his face exploded into the most beautiful expression I had ever witnessed.

"You're right, this week has been a dream come true. I can't tell you how long I've waited to find you. I know you're scared, I am too, but I promise you from the bottom of my heart that what I'm feeling for you is one hundred per cent real. I need you to believe that I'm not going anywhere. I will be right here for as long as you will have me." He rested his forehead against mine. The warmth of his body and the heady smell of his aftershave wafted over me like a summer's breeze. "I'm falling in love with you Jemma" he uttered in a hushed tone "Just give me the chance to prove it to you."

The enormity of what he had just confessed washed over me, taking with it any fear and anxiety I had been feeling. I believed him, I could feel it, could see it in his eyes. I had waited a lifetime to feel like this. "Make love to me Jake" I whispered, sliding my hands through the soft waves of his hair. He scooped me up protectively in his arms. My body melted like butter in the warmth of his embrace. So, this is what home felt like. This is how it felt when people said they 'belonged' somewhere, this is how it felt to give yourself completely to someone, hoping that they would protect your heart with every ounce of their being, to boldly step into the unknown. This was what making love was. His touch spoke a thousand words, his eyes conveyed a million truths. Never had so much been said in such complete silence. He made me feel everything, and it was more than I could have ever dreamed.

# SATURDAY

It was the sweet smell of bacon frying which finally brought me to. Whether it was the expensive memory foam mattress, or just sheer exhaustion from the day before, but I can honestly say that I had never slept so well in all my life. I languidly rolled out of the beautiful four poster and followed the scent of deliciousness like a sniffer dog all the way into the kitchen.

"Good morning beautiful." Jake was standing behind the breakfast bar dressed in a tight white t-shirt which was pulled tort across his ample frame, and pyjama bottoms which hung low on his slim waist. He looked like he had stepped straight from a modelling shoot. As I caught a glimpse of myself in the reflection of the window, it was abundantly clear that I had not yet mastered the same effortlessly chic look. My hair resembled a bird's nest, my left-over mascara had trailed dark lines beneath my eyes, and because I had forgotten where I had left my suitcase, I had hurriedly thrown on his shirt from yesterday to cover my modesty. The only way I would be featured in a magazine looking like this, was if they were doing a makeover project and needed before and after photos (currently I was pre-makeover).

He did not seem to see the bedraggled mess that I did. Instead, his eyes roamed over me longingly like I was the most beautiful thing he had ever laid eyes on. "Looks good on you!" he mused, running his eyes over his shirt whilst turning something in the pan.

"Pft.. this old thing?" I Joked. "Just something I threw on." I walked round the bar to stand next to him. "Morning." I had to stand on my tip toes to reach his mouth.

"It is a very good morning indeed! I could get used to you walking into my kitchen half naked everyday" he beamed, returning my kiss.

"Me too, especially if you are planning on cooking bacon every morning!" I giggled, stealing a crispy strip from the pan.

"I thought you'd be hungry this morning. I completely forgot about food after you distracted me last night." He gave me a cheeky smile. "You barely ate anything yesterday though, and we've got a busy day today, so I thought I'd do us a proper breakfast"

"Sounds perfect. What's the plan for today?" I asked excitedly, stealing another bit of bacon from the pan.

Jake smacked me playfully on the bum. "Hey! No tasting the goods before it's served up" he laughed. He flipped the bacon over in the pan again. "I thought we could do a bit of sight seeing this morning, then lunch, and then Jacques wants to show us his new venue this evening."

"Sounds fun! Anything I can do to help?"

"Nope, it's all under control. Go and take a seat outside and I'll bring it out in a minute."

Out on the balcony a table had been laid. A single white rose sat in a tiny glass vase in the centre, surrounded by crisp white side plates, mugs, a cafetière of freshly brewed coffee, tumblers of orange juice, toast and preserves. It reminded me of breakfast in a fancy hotel. On the street below, people were starting to mill about. Locals ambled along with their fresh baguettes, whilst tourists walked with more purpose, loaded with rucksacks and maps tucked tightly under their arms. The contrast between the two seemed even more pronounced from up above. I imagined that Jake would slip seamlessly into the first category. I was not so sure about myself.

"Bon appetite!" He laid down a plate in front of me laden with more of that melt in the mouth crispy bacon, perfectly cooked scrambled eggs (slightly oozing and bright, sunshine yellow), and sweet, red vine tomatoes still on the stalk. The smell that wafted up was divine and caused my stomach to rumble aloud.

"How on earth are you still single?" I joked.

"I didn't think I was" he said in a low raspy voice, bending down to kiss me. My heart did a little flutter.

"This looks incredible Jake, thank you."

"You're very welcome. Dig in before it gets cold."

It was only as my mouth closed around the first mouthful that I realised how ravenous I was.

"Mmm…" I managed appreciatively. "This is delicious!"

"I'm glad you like it" he beamed, buttering a slice of toast. "But I think you would have eaten anything I put in front of you though!" I watched him intently as he tucked into his plate. He seemed genuinely at home here in this environment, relaxed and carefree. We laughed and joked, disagreed over whether jam or marmalade was the better accompaniment to toast, and almost came to blows over the ending of the final episode of Game of Thrones. *I cannot quite believe I sat through eight seasons for it to end like that.* After breakfast he cleared the table, leaving me alone to finish my coffee. The sun warmed the terrace, and I closed my eyes, savouring the feeling of the heat on my face. Life was good. No, life was great!

Once I had drained the last remanence of my cup, I headed inside. My suitcase sat on the end of the bed waiting patiently to be unpacked. Jake was in the shower, so I took the time to pull out the clothes and hang them in the wardrobe. His were already hanging expertly on chunky wooden hangers. What time had he woken up this morning? I left a blue flowery summer dress laid out on the bed along with my white Converse and denim jacket. I was unsure of how much walking he was planning to do, so avoided the less practical wedges that I had brought along, in favour of something that was not going to have me falling over on my ankle again. As I rooted around my toiletry bag, the water stopped, and I heard Jake get out of the shower. Moments later, he was standing behind me, a towel wrapped around his waist, another round his neck, water droplets glistening on his skin. His hands reached underneath the shirt I was wearing and wondered up towards my breasts, which perked up instantly at his touch.

"Jake, I'm all dirty!" I giggled, secretly enjoying his advances.

'All the better, I love it when you're filthy!" he replied in a mischievous tone, the double entendre quite clear.

I span round to face him. "Not now!" I laughed, batting his hands away playfully. "I need to have a shower, and you need to put some clothes on!"

"Spoil sport!" he moaned.

I had not really paid much attention to it last night, but the bathroom was bigger than most people's entire first floor. It was decked out in beautiful pale grey marble tiles, which stretched from the floor up to the ceiling. A free-standing claw foot bath sat alongside another huge window, whilst an imposing rainforest shower took up the entire length of one wall. It was decadent, but not ostentatious. I placed the bottle of body wash and shampoo into the conveniently located holder, turned on the water, undressed and stepped inside. The water was the perfect temperature, the pressure exactly right. Hard enough to invigorate but not harsh enough to cause discomfort. I faced towards the wall, closed my eyes, and allowed the water to wash over me. It was not long before I sensed his presence in the room. I could not see him, but I could feel him near me, feel his eyes on me. Then I felt his body. His lips found my neck whilst his hands rested gently on my shoulders, binding us together.

"Sorry" he whispered between kisses. "I couldn't help myself."

With one hand still on me, he reached out for the shower gel with the other. "I promise to be helpful if you let me stay" he implored.

"Okay, but no funny business!" I scolded, unconvincingly.

"Scouts honour" he chuckled, taking my warning with a pinch of salt. He lathered up the fruity shower gel in his hands before proceeding to move them in circular motions over my skin, starting at my shoulders and running them agonisingly slowly towards my bottom. His thumbs kneaded my cheeks, sending a surge of heat between my legs. "God, you're so beautiful" he groaned into my ear.

My eyelids closed naturally, savouring his touch. "Why do you always say that to me?"

"That you're beautiful?"

"Yes."

"Because I think you're the most beautiful woman on the planet, but I also know that you are the most self-critical, so I plan to tell you every single day how beautiful you are until you believe it. I want you to look at yourself in the mirror and see what I see." His fingertips slipped round to my front, spreading bubbles over my breasts. My nipples pebbled under his touch. The rough, raspy sound of his voice was a stark contrast to his gentle movements, and my mouth shot open, unable to contain the desire which coursed through me.

"I love hearing you moan like that" he whispered in the same gravelly tone, his own excitement pressing hard against my back. His hands inched from my chest, past my navel and lingered between my legs. His touch was like a red-hot poker. I squirmed in his arms, unable to still my body. "Keep still baby" he commanded as he used his foot to part my legs. Slowly, he inserted two thick fingers inside me. The sensation was overwhelming, and a louder, more urgent groan escaped me. My entire body felt like it was on fire, and the heat radiating through me was all consuming. I instinctively pushed back on his hand, forcing it to go deeper, wanting more of him.

"Do you like that?" he asked devilishly, already knowing the answer to his question. "Do you like it when I fuck you with my hand like this?"

I loved his foul mouth. Loved that he saved it for me. Loved that I drove him as crazy as he drove me. "Yes. Don't stop" I begged, tilting my head back to rest on his shoulder, the rest of my body moving in time with the motion of his hand.

"I'm never going to stop" he growled, "I'm going to fuck you over and over again with my hand, with my mouth and with my cock." Picking up the pace, his fingers began to dance rhythmically around me, hitting that magical place deep within, sliding in and out effortlessly, his hand slick with my excitement.

"Jake!" I cried out, my fingernails digging into his thighs. I was not going to last much longer.

"Not yet beautiful, wait for me, I need to be inside you when you come." With that he pressed my body to the cool marble wall, his throbbing erection taking the place of his hand. He felt so big, it took my breath away. "That's it baby, now you can come," he instructed breathlessly as he moved behind me, his length stroking my insides as he did so. "God, you feel amazing Jemma, you're so fucking tight, it's like you were made for me" he groaned, increasing the speed with which he moved. My body, revelled in his touch, and reacted without warning, an intense heat building in my stomach and rushing to the area where he was, clamping down around him, rendering me incapable of anything. The orgasm surged through me with an intensity I had never experienced. Each new climax with him was more intense than the last. Arching my back, I pushed my hips back towards him, allowing him to feel the full extent of my pleasure. He continued to guide himself, one hand clamped to my hip whilst the other stroked the length of my back, encouraging the orgasm out of me until I was completely spent. Once he knew I was sated, he gave into his own body and allowed himself the same pleasure, calling my name as he came, panting and breathless, his hands slamming on the wall either side of me as he thrust one final time. I remained motionless beneath him, basking in the closeness of our entangled bodies.

"You were never a boy scout were you" I giggled breathlessly.

"How did you guess?" he asked, gently peeling me off the wall, turning me round and wrapping me in his strong arms.

"Because boy scouts don't fib, and you Mr, just fibbed!" I laughed reaching my arms round his neck and kissing him.

"Do you wish we hadn't just done that?" He looked at me with a dangerous twinkle in his eyes.

I smiled. "Not at all, I'm very, very glad we did!"

"Me too. We might need another shower now though!" he joked playfully.

"I might wash myself this time if you don't mind, otherwise we won't ever get out today!"

"Fair point" he laughed, running his hands over my wet hair. "I promise to try and keep my hands to myself this time!"

"Thank you very much!" I reached behind him to grab the shower gel for a second time, trying to ignore his presence and concentrate on the task at hand. Thankfully, he kept to his word and allowed me a few uninterrupted minutes under the water. His eyes never strayed from my body. Never had a man looked at me the way he did, as if he were in awe of me. It seemed incomprehensible that someone as beautiful as him could look at me that way. Even as we swapped places, and he took his turn under the cascading water, his eyes watched me with an intensity that I had never witnessed before.

"What is it?" I asked, worried that I might be misinterpreting his gaze.

"I'm just trying to take you all in" he smiled, holding his hand out to mine, gesturing for me to come closer. He pulled me into an embrace, the water washing over both of us as we stood there for a few minutes in complete silence, holding on to each other. "I never thought I would get the chance to be like this with you. I want to make sure I remember every single second of it."

That was it. Game over. I was smitten.

◆ ◆ ◆

After another half an hour, we did venture outside. We walked lazily hand in hand down the tree lined avenue in the direction of the river. A light breeze filtered through the air, taking the edge off the late morning sun. There was something about Paris in the summertime which delighted the senses. The sights, the sounds, the smells, it was truly magical. As we ambled along, he gave a guided tour of the neighbourhood, pointing out things that only a true native would know. Whether it was a story about a famous building, a scandalous love affair between two members of opposing families, or a sad tale of a struggling artist who lived day to day selling his wares to the local wealthy families, whose work now sold for millions of pounds. Whatever subject he talked about, he spoke with such knowledge and emotion, that it was fascinating. I clung to his every word, feeling like he was taking me through a hidden door to the city that not everybody got to enter. He was opening my eyes to a completely new side of this amazing place.

As we neared our destination, it was clear that the whole of Paris had descended upon the Seine, keen to feel the cooler air and take in the sights. Thousands of people mingled in the cafes and restaurants lining the edge of it, whilst others meandered along the paths next to its banks, chatting idly or pointing a camera at something in the distance.

"Have you been to Notre Dame before" he enquired as we passed what looked like a group of Japanese tourists taking selfies.

"No, I haven't. It was one of the few places I never got round to seeing when I was here before."

"If you'd like, I'd love to take you. It's been my favourite place in Paris ever since I was a child. I used to beg my dad to take me every time we were here," he reminisced, a sad expression crossing his face. "He'd always give the most amazing tours. He'd find something new to tell me each time we visited, and we must have been dozens of times. "

"He sounds like an amazing father" I offered, squeezing his hand.

"He was" he smiled. "He would have loved you too."

Before I could respond with something heartfelt, the sound of the Pussycat Dolls singing 'Don't Cha' came blasting out of my handbag, signalling an incoming call from Claire. She had self-assigned that as her ring tone a while ago now, and despite my many attempts begging her to let me change it, she had point-blank refused. Jake, amused by the choice of song, motioned for me to answer it. I scrambled frantically around the bottom of my bag, hoping to reach it before Nicole could belt out the bit about wanting your girlfriend 'to be a freak like me' to all the unsuspecting people nearby sipping on their cappuccinos. Luckily, my hands grasped the handset just in time.

"Hello!" I called out, flustered. I turned my head away from Jake and the innocent public, trying to shield them from whatever profanities were bound to come flooding from her mouth.

"Bonjour bitch!" the familiar voice sang loud and clear. "How's it going? Have you ventured outside yet, or have you spent the whole time munching on his French sausage?" *No, I haven't actually, but I certainly intend to!*

"Claire!" My face burnt with embarrassment, knowing full well that Jake could hear every single word.

"Apologies is it more like a French stick?!" she roared in her trademark filthy laugh, deliberately misinterpreting my words.

Jake chuckled to himself. She really had no filter.

"We are out now as it happens," I replied a little defensively. "And we are surrounded by people, so watch what you are saying and remember to be nice!" I pleaded, turning to Jake, throwing him an apologetic look.

"I'm always nice!" she laughed, pretending to sound wounded. "I'm just checking in to see that you haven't been murdered, and that you're having a nice time. I'm living vicariously through you remember, given that there's fuck all excitement in my life at the moment!"

"I'm sure the dry spell won't last long" I giggled, knowing full well that a lack of excitement really translated to a lack of sex. "You've got your date with Mr IT tonight, haven't you?"

"Well, it's alright for you to be nonchalant about it now that you're getting some good D!, you're not the one who's practically turning back into a virgin!" she barked, sounding genuinely concerned at the prospect. "And Mark fucking cancelled on me. Apparently, he's got to take his cat to the vet! I hope he has to put the bloody thing down" she spat unsympathetically after a pause. The lack of sex was starting to take its toll on her mental state. A sex starved Claire was akin to a hungry lion - irritable, unpredictable, and downright lethal. I was glad I was not at home.

"Claire!" I gasped, shocked at the savageness of her words.

"What?" she cooed.

"Isn't that a good thing though? the becoming a born-again virgin bit, not the being stood up part – obvs" I asked, treading more carefully.

"But I might forget how to do it!" she wailed. "Plus, I don't want to have to wait to find Mr Right to pop my cherry - again. What I need is a meaningless fuck with a non-verbal supermodel who will leave before I wake up so that I don't have to try and remember his name in the morning." That sounded like my worst nightmare.

"I think it will be some time before you forget how to do it, it's only been a couple of weeks after all. Listen, as much as I would love to carry on discussing your sex life, or lack thereof, I really must go. I will call you later, ok?"

"Ok, but I want to know everything. Don't feel like you must spare me any of the juicy bits just because I'm a eunuch."

"Ok, I won't. Right, I'm putting the phone down now" I warned "Bye!"

"Au revoir you sexy minx. Bye boss!" she screamed before the line went dead. I turned round, placing the phone back in my bag.

"I am SO sorry!" I apologised. Jake burst into laughter.

"No need to apologise, she's great, plus she's your best friend. I need her to like me, so I'd better get used to sharing you with her" he said, pulling me back into his arms. "I also don't think I'd stand a chance against her in a fight – not that I would ever willingly fight a lady of course."

"She's no lady!" I scoffed. "But I have witnessed her mean right hook, so for your own sake, it's probably best you do try to get along with her!"

"Noted. Thank you." We paused where we were on the pathway. "How about we find somewhere to eat, I'm starving again for some reason!"

"Me too. I have absolutely no idea why!" I grinned devilishly, recounting all the things we had done in bed over the past day. He threw a strong arm around my shoulder and placed a kiss on my forehead. Wrapped in his arms, I felt safe and protected, and I would have happily stayed like that indefinitely, had the prospect of food not been on the table.

As a teenager, I had briefly coveted the waif, anorexic look of the models who graced the covers of my magazines. That was until I realised that at five foot two, and coming from a family where no carb was a sin, I accepted that that was a look I was never going to achieve, and wholeheartedly embraced the wonder of food. Since then, it had become one of the few pure pleasures in my life (that and binge-watching countless Netflix series in my pyjamas). So, when Jake, led me across the road towards a quintessentially French looking bistro, I was giddy with excitement. Not only because I could have eaten a scabby horse (not literally as I hear that is a very real thing in France), but because the smell of garlic and tarragon which wafted gently through the air towards us, was mouth-watering. As waiters in their crisp white shirts and black café style aprons topped up glasses of water from silver carafes, satisfied customers chatted animatedly whilst tucking into delectable morsels served on elegant, wide rimmed plates. By the time we had traversed the labyrinth of tables and reached the front of house's station, I was confident I had already chosen what I was going to eat based on what I had seen be delivered to two tables.

"Bonjour. Avez vous une table pour deux s'il vous plait?" To hear Jake speak was like listening to an actual Parisian. His accent, and the confidence with which he spoke, made him indistinguishable from the throng of native speakers around us.

"Ah oui, après vous monsieur!" the tall maître d' with jet black hair answered, ushering us over to an empty round table on the edge of the pavement. Before I could take my seat, Jake made his way round to me and pulled out my chair.

Who knew he would be so sweet? "Thank you."

"You're very welcome" he replied, before moving back to the other side of the table.

On establishing that we were not in fact French, the maître d' switched effortlessly to English. "Here are your menus" he said offering us two crimson leatherbound books. "The wine list is at the back, and Crystal will be with you shortly to run through the plats du jour and take your orders."

Moments later, a young blonde girl came gliding over to us, a tablet wedged under her arm and a stylus tucked neatly behind her ear. She had clearly been given a heads up that we were not French as she automatically greeted us in English.

"Good afternoon, my name is Crystal, and I will be your server today. If there is anything I can help you with, please just let me know."

"Thank you, Crystal,' Jake said politely. Her cheeks flushed slightly, and her smile widened in response. Jeez, did he have this effect on the entire female population? She continued with her speech, directing it solely at him.

"May I point out the chef's recommendations for today?" she asked, fluttering her excruciatingly beautiful long eyelashes in his direction.

"Of course, but maybe you could tell them to my girlfriend, as I'm afraid I already know what I am going to have" he offered apologetically. A momentary flash of confusion glanced across her face before she regained her composure and turned her gaze to me, her smile less sincere than before.

"Certainly! So, today the chef has two dishes he would like to recommend. The first is a blue cheese and endive salad with walnuts and a mustard vinaigrette, the second is grilled sardines on a bed of crushed persillade potatoes, tomatoes and capers."

"Thank you, they both sound lovely" I replied in my sweetest voice, trying desperately to get her to like me.

"I'll leave you both for a few moments to decide" she replied, not returning the pleasantries, before turning and making her way over to another table.

"Sorry about that."

"About what?" I replied, feigning oblivion.

"About how she was with you." He had clearly clocked her indifference towards me and looked genuinely upset by it.

"Don't be silly, it's fine! I'm sure you get this all the time, it's not a big thing, don't worry!" I smiled uncomfortably.

"I don't want you to have to get used to it" he said protectively. "I won't have anyone treat you like that." He reached across the table and took my hand.

"You called me your girlfriend" I said turning my knife over in my free hand, trying to change the subject.

"I'm sorry, it just slipped out, I didn't mean to be presumptuous."

"Don't be, I liked it" I replied shyly, avoiding his eyes. "Now, as much as I would love to tell Crystal to shove her endive and sardines where the sun doesn't shine, I have to admit that they do sound yummy" I said sadly, not wanting to take on her suggestions (although I guess technically, they were not hers, they were the chef's).

"They do sound delicious, don't they, but I can't order them now even if I wanted to, seeing as I told her I'd already chosen!" He laughed.

"You mean you haven't chosen?" I asked, surprised.

"Nope. No idea what I'm going to have. I was just fed up with her ignoring you."

"You did that for me?"

He set his menu down on the table. "I'm starting to realise there isn't much I wouldn't do for you Jemma." My heart skipped a beat.

"Even miss out on two delicious chef's recommendations?" I added, unable to stop myself from giggling.

"It would seem so! Now, what the hell am I going to have?" he said, searching hurriedly through the pages.

"I'll make it up to you" I winked suggestively.

"I'm counting on it" he replied, his eyes conveying a hunger that would not be satisfied by food alone. I was momentarily reminded of our time together in the shower. I felt the blood rush to my face and my heartbeat quicken at the very thought of it. As if he could read my mind, he chuckled.

"There, there, Miss Lucas, you aren't blushing, are you?" he teased.

"Maybe a little."

As if by magic, the ever-charming Crystal re-appeared, breaking the frisson of sexual tension.

"Are you ready to order?" she beamed at Jake, her stylus hovering over the tablet.

"Ladies first" he insisted, rebuffing her advances once more.

"Umm… I'll have the endive salad followed by the sardines please" I smiled up at her. She tapped the screen several times in silence before turning her attention back to him.

"And for you sir?" she asked, her eyes wide and her smile full. The charm offensive ongoing.

"Sod it, I'll have exactly the same actually." I could not help but snigger at the change in direction he had taken.

"An excellent choice!" she enthused, hitting the screen with a dramatic flourish of her pen. "And what can I get you to drink?"

He traced his finger over the wine list. "Could we get a bottle of the 2019 Sancerre please?"

"Impeccable taste!" God this was starting to get embarrassing. I felt like a third wheel in some sort of love triangle.

"It's my girlfriend's impeccable taste you should be applauding. This is her favourite. Isn't that right, darling?"

"Er… yes, it is!" I stumbled unconvincingly, not expecting to be drawn into the conversation (needless to say, she did not congratulate me on my impeccable taste).

"I'll be right back with some water for the table and your wine" she sang unperturbed. You had to congratulate her on her shear determinedness and persistence, most people would have given up already, but she was like a dog with a bone.

"No rush" I mumbled to myself when she was out of earshot. Jake chuckled.

Within seconds she was back with a silver carafe and one of those fancy wine buckets with stands. She freely poured the water until the tumblers were half full, then pulled a corkscrew out from the front pocket of her apron. She expertly inserted it into the top of the bottle, applying just the right amount of force to create that 'pop' as it was released.

"Thank you, I can take it from here" Jake said in an authoritative tone, taking the bottle from her and pouring us both a glass, ignoring Crystal who was still lingering beside the table. After a second or two she came to, and scurried away, her dignity still seemingly intact.

"I thought she would never leave" he said, puffing out his cheeks in exhaustion.

"How do you manage it?"

"Manage what?"

"Manage to be so polite to people whilst effectively telling them to fuck off." He adjusted his position in the chair, leaning back slightly and crossing his legs.

"I've learnt over the years that there's always a way to get what you want without being rude. Whether that's getting a client to sign up, or a server to leave you alone. Dad always drummed it into us that manners cost nothing, and with work, I've found it is far more beneficial to be nice to people than it is to go pissing them off left, right and centre."

"Perhaps. Or maybe you're just a big softie at heart?" I suggested.

"I guess you'll just have to find out!" he smiled.

I stared directly into his eyes which were almost dancing in the sunlight. "I guess I will." We settled into a free-flowing conversation about everything and nothing at all. The only silences coming when our food was delivered, and even then, they were momentary. I feared that at some point the chatter would run dry and it might become stunted, but it never happened. It was so easy and natural. I felt an undeniable pull towards him and a feeling that I had known him all my life. It was him that made everything easy.

"If I don't tell you later, I want you to know that I've had an amazing time this weekend" I blurted unexpectedly.

'It's me that should be thanking you for agreeing to come with me" he said, taking my hand again. "It's not over yet though" he added with a glint in his eye.

"I don't think I want it to end" I muttered embarrassed, staring into my wine glass.

"It doesn't have to" he squeezed. "We can have this anywhere" he gestured to the two of us.

"I'd like that." My head had started to feel warm and fuzzy courtesy of the wine – which as it so happens, could be my new favourite! (clever Jake). He gestured to the maître d' for the bill, and within minutes we were leaving, that fuzzy feeling travelling the length of my body to my feet so that it felt like I was walking on air. With his arm wrapped protectively around my waist I felt lighter than a feather. The warm afternoon sun kissed our skin. If this were what heaven felt like, I could understand why people were so keen to go. We walked along the river a little further in comfortable silence, taking in the beauty around us, stopping to stand against the wall which ran beside it.

Jake stood motionlessly for a moment, an air of melancholy descending over him. "You know, when Erica died, everything lost its colour, its magic. Everything except this place. This was the only thing that didn't lose its shine. I remember coming here, just to escape the pain." He paused to look out over the water. "Not even the darkest times could dim the light of this city." I clasped his hand and squeezed it tightly. I yearned to comfort him, to try and take away some of his pain, but I was not sure that I could. He turned to me, grasping my face gently in his hands. "Jemma, you are like my Paris. You are the brightest light. I believe you have come into my life for a reason. I think you've been sent to me, to give me a second chance at happiness." He moved in closer so that our noses touched. Standing this close to him, I could see every tiny detail of his face, every line, every muscle, and his eyes, they were so full of emotion, so full of hope. "You've made me feel alive again, proved to me that I am capable of love, and that it is okay to feel happy. And I promise you, whilst there is air in my lungs, I will spend every day showing you just how grateful I am." His thumb traced a silent tear which fell down the side of my face. "I told you yesterday that I was falling in love with you. I lied. I am already in love with you. When you asked me the other day at work what I wanted and I told you that you would run if you knew the extent of it, I wanted to tell you that. I knew it was ridiculous, too soon, it's still too soon, I know, but I do, I love you. I've loved you from the moment I first saw you." He looked at me hopelessly, as if needing confirmation that I felt the same way. For the first time in my life, I was rendered speechless. More tears coursed down my cheeks. "I don't think I've made a girl cry as much as I have you! I hope these aren't sad tears?" he smiled, wiping them away. All I could manage was a shake of the head as I buried my face into his huge chest and clung onto his body with every ounce of strength that I had. Had I been able to speak, I would have told him that I could never have run, that even if I had taught him how to love again, he had given me so much more. He had opened my eyes to what love was, and to the endless possibilities it brought with it. He had opened the door to a whole new world that I never knew existed, and as terrifying and as overwhelming as that might be, something inside me was telling it me it was a risk worth taking. "Shh…… it's alright" he soothed, stroking my hair. I tightened my grip on him. "For someone so small, you sure are strong" he laughed. "Hey, look at me" he begged, taking hold of my chin, and lifting my head up so that our eyes met again. "I promise you I will look after you. I won't let anyone, or anything hurt you. I will love and protect you with every bone in my body if you let me." I pressed my hands to his chest, his rapid heartbeat reverberated through my fingers, inhaling a deep breath before delivering my next line, needing to calm my own nerves, before exposing my own vulnerability and the strength of my feelings for him.

"Jake…" I started. "I have never been in love before so I cannot comprehend the loss and heartache you've experienced. But I promise you that I will try every day to mend some of the wounds you carry. I promise you that I will hold your heart in my hands and take care of it for as long as you want me to. I love you Jake, with all of me." The sense of relief from making that wedding vow-esque admission was immense. I had never been so open about my feelings, my wants, and desires as I had just then, because in truth, I had never wanted to say those things before. This man standing before me was the only one who had ever made me want those things.

"You really are something else" he whispered, his eyes glistening with the prospect of tears as he scooped me up in his arms. His mouth found mine, and in that moment, Paris stood still. The noise of the people dissipated, the thrum of the traffic halted, and the Seine stopped flowing. It was just him and I. This was that moment in life that people speak of when finding 'the one.' When you see only the person before you, and you know, without hesitation, that they are the one you would burn the world down for if you had to. It did not matter if it were a week or ten years, I knew enough to know that this was real. "Will you take me home?"

"What's wrong? Are you okay?" The look of concern etched on his face was painful to watch.

I trailed my hand over his cheek. "Everything is perfect, I just want to be alone with you that's all" I replied gently, watching the fear dissipate as he planted another lingering kiss, soft and gentle on my lips.

"Of course," he sighed, not letting go of me. "We'll grab a cab back though; I don't think you realise how far we've walked."

"Thank you." My legs felt like jelly, and I was not sure I could move, let alone trek back across the city.

"Come, we can pick one up from just over there" he said pointing to a row of taxis lined up neatly across the road. "Are you okay to walk, you're trembling."

"I'll be fine, just don't run off anywhere!" I grabbed his arm and held on tight.

"Never" he smiled, offering me a hand, and leading me in the direction of the waiting cars.

◆ ◆ ◆

He was right, the journey back home was surprisingly long. I had been so distracted by our conversation, that I had not paid attention to how long we had walked for. As I sat on the black leather seat, a wave of tiredness crept over me. I snuggled up to him, burying my head in his strong chest. Whether it was the walking, the afternoon drinking, or the emotional roller coaster we had been on, I suddenly felt exhausted. I closed my eyes for a moment, comforted by the warmth of his body. When I awoke, I was in his arms, and we were standing at the door to his apartment.

"Hello sleepy head, we're home" he said softly, kissing my head and turning the key in the door.

"Oh god, did I fall asleep? Did you carry me all the way up here?"

"Yes, and yes" he smiled. "You looked so peaceful; I didn't want to wake you."

"I'm so sorry. I don't know what came over me. Please tell me I didn't snore!"

"Don't be silly, you're tired, you needed some rest." The warm timber of his voice calmed me as he carried me in his arms along the corridor to the bedroom. "We don't need to meet Jaques until this evening, so why don't you get into bed for a bit?"

I did not like the thought of being alone. "Will you stay with me?"

"If you would like me to."

"I would" I smiled as he put me down on my feet next to the bed.

I kicked off my shoes and started to unbutton my dress. Jake took a deliberate step back, silently observing me as he had done earlier in the shower. As the last button was released, and the dress fell to the floor, his eyes lingered appreciatively on my body.

"Wow!" he exclaimed. I basked in his adoration. The way his hungry eyes roamed salaciously over me made me feel confident, like I was worthy of his praise, like all my imperfections were insignificant, like I was beautiful as he said, like I was desirable.

I took a step towards him, closing the gap between us, gripping the bottom of his t-shirt and pulling it up slowly over his head, exposing his chiselled body beneath. I yearned to feel the warmth of his skin on mine. "You're perfect" I whispered as my fingers trailed a line from his chest over the row of muscles which lined his stomach, past the V which sat below his hips and over to the buckle on his belt.

"I'm far from perfect" he exhaled shakily.

"You are to me" I insisted looking him dead in the eye as I unfastened his belt and pulled on the zip of his jeans.

"Jemma, if you carry on down this road, I don't think I'm going to be able to just lay down and fall asleep with you" he purred, his eyes dark and yearning.

"Thank you for the warning" I grinned, freeing his legs from his jeans, "but I'm not ready to fall asleep just yet."

I released the clasp on my bra, discarding it to the side, and hooked my thumbs in the waistband of my knickers, slowly inching them down my thighs, all the while watching the expression on his face turn darker. He looked like he wanted to devour me whole. "Like what you see?" I teased, running my tongue over my bottom lip.

"You know I do" he growled, trying desperately to control himself. I inched closer again, my eyes trained on those soft, full lips that were slightly parted. A hand reached out unexpectedly, grabbing the back of my head, pulling me in closer. "Are you trying to drive me insane Miss Lucas?" The words grazed the side of my cheek, sending little bolts of electricity shooting across my skin.

"Is it working?" I whispered in his ear as I tugged the boxer shorts down over his throbbing erection.

"What do you think?" The words were barely audible, a mere murmur against my skin. Short, shallow breaths escaped his open mouth as his eyes closed shut, no doubt trying to keep his composure.

"Uh-uh, eyes open Mr" I commanded quietly, dropping to my knees in front of him so that I was face to face with his impressive length. "I want you to watch me." Reluctantly, he did as he was instructed, his eyelids lifting on those dangerous dark orbs, studying me intently as I ran my tongue painstakingly from his base up to his tip. A moan, feral and raw escaped his mouth. "Do you like that?" I asked in the same devilish tone he had asked me this morning.

"Yes," he said through gritted teeth, as I retraced my steps back to the bottom.

"Do you want more?" I teased, looking up at him coyly.

"Yes." His response was immediate and laced with danger. His eyes pitch black, his fingers intwined in my hair, gripping a handful of loose waves. He looked down at me with a mixture of pride and rampant desire.

I smiled, opening my mouth to take him fully. "My pleasure." With one hand on his base, I pushed my lips slowly over his crown and down his length until I could go no further. He filled me completely. A raft of expletives escaped his mouth. Watching and hearing him come undone at my touch sent my heart rate spiking. Every inch of me swept up in the moment, my skin tingling, heat coursing through my veins. I slowed the speed with which I was tending to him, needing to savour the intimacy, to relish the feeling of him, to remember the look of unashamed desire on his face, and memorise the sound of his voice – gruff and desperate, powerless. The new, languid pace was making his body even more receptive to my movements. I wanted to drive him wild the way he did me, to tease him, to bring him to the edge of ecstasy and have him beg me for release. I wanted to gift him the overwhelming feeling of euphoria that he was always so eager to give me.

"Fuck!" he groaned, grabbing my head with both hands, unable to resist the need to take control, to be the alpha male. Faster, more urgently he delved in, his thick length hitting the back of my throat with each stroke. More garbled words of ecstasy before he moaned "Jemma, you're going to make me come already!" The sound of his desperate confession ignited a primal urge in me to make him do just that. Sensing that he was completely at my mercy, that I was the one who held the control, I surged on, slamming my mouth down around him harder and faster than before. I moaned as I felt the tell-tale signs of him coming apart inside me, the beginning of his ejaculation lingering on the end of my tongue. Two more powerful thrusts and he exploded, yelling as he did so. A mixture of torment and release etched over his heavenly face. I lapped up everything he had to give, licking my lips seductively to show my appreciation. He stood there for a moment, shaking, as he emptied himself fully into me. Those black, dangerous eyes of his boring into me. "Jesus, what are you doing to me?" he grinned admiringly, pulling me to my feet before gently gathering me up in his burly arms, and walking me over to the bed.

He laid me down with such ease and tenderness, it felt as if I were a precious gift, weightless and so small in comparison to his huge physique. In the centre of his bed I lay, my legs parted, my heels digging into the mattress, breathy and expectant, completely exposed, but not the slightest bit embarrassed. The sun streamed in through the windows, highlighting every contour of his impressive body. Every well-defined muscle was amplified ten-fold in the golden blaze surrounding him. He was breathtaking, although that seemed to be too inadequate a description. Yes, he was beautiful, but he was also masculine and powerful, kind, and gentle. He was more than just one thing, he was everything. His sheer size demanded attention but coupled with that disarming smile and those dazzling eyes which sparkled like rough diamonds, it was impossible not to be captivated by him. My whole body tingled in anticipation.

He lowered himself over me, the heady scent of his aftershave filling my nostrils, his warm skin still beaded with tiny pearls of sweat. I breathed him in deeply, closing my eyes, waiting expectantly for his first touch. "Uh-uh, eyes open Miss Lucas. I want you to watch me pleasure you" he whispered commandingly in my ear, sending a jolt of unexpected electricity through my body. There was something about his deep, raspy sounding voice that exuded power and confidence. Even here, in the bedroom, there was no disputing his dominance. I may have been in control momentarily, but he had regained his composure now, he was back in charge, and I succumbed to his request. Slowly, his mouth made his way from the shell of my ear towards the valley in my chest. "I want to get to know every inch of your body" he teased, his tongue languishing over my nipple. "How you taste …, how you feel." His fingers traced a delicate line between my breasts down to the inside of my thigh. "How you sound..." His thumb brushed lightly over my sensitive spot causing me to buck unexpectedly and my hips to grind against his hand, yearning for more. "Jemma, you're so wet already" he noticed appreciatively, kissing me gently where the moisture pooled, his tongue dipping in and out, relishing my body's inability to hide its desire. Fire erupted in my belly. Nothing felt as good as being touched by him. "I want to pleasure you in ways that nobody ever has" he added, a tinge of jealousy in his tone. If only he could feel how my body was burning for him. How every touch was sending scorching flames across my skin. If he could only read my mind, he would know that no man had ever come close to giving me this kind of indescribable joy. He would know that what I felt for him was all consuming, irrational, and terrifying in equal measure, and that the fear of losing him was already beyond comprehension. Could he not see that I was completely his?

His mouth continued to take me, dancing around until fire burned between my legs, threatening to tip me over the edge. "Tell me what you want Jemma" he said, momentarily lifting his head to look at me. I was so consumed with pleasure that my brain and mouth found themselves completely disconnected, and I was rendered incapable of speaking. "Tell me. If you want something, you have to ask for it" he urged again, his tongue sweeping gently back and forth over the same area. "What do you want?"

"I want you...all of you" I managed, finally meeting his gaze, unable to stop the surge of emotions inside me from pulling me under.

"I'm right here baby, I'm always going to be right here" he hummed comfortably into the inside of my thigh, sensing my vulnerability.

"What if you leave?"

"If how you feel for me is anything close to the way I feel about you, you'll know that leaving isn't an option" he said seriously, shifting his weight, making his way back up towards my face.

"Promise? And don't say scouts honour, because then I'll know you're bullshitting me" I joked feebly, trying to stop the torrent of fear currently washing over me.

Taking my face in his hands, he studied me intently for a moment before speaking. "A real man doesn't make idle promises because promises can be broken. A real man will give you his word, and he would rather die than break it. Jemma, I give you my word that I'm not going anywhere. I'm completely yours. Now… you said you wanted all of me… do you mean like this?" he asked, a cheeky smile replacing the previous serious expression on his beautiful face, as he pushed himself slowly inside me, stretching and filling me in the most amazing way. All I could feel was him. In me. Over me. Around me. Consuming me. Claiming me.

"Yes, just like that" I breathed, as all the tension in my body dissipated and it started to move in sync with his.

◆ ◆ ◆

"Well hello sleepyhead!" he said, kissing me on the forehead and pulling me into his muscular chest.

"Mmmm…. What time is it?" I replied sleepily.

"Nearly seven."

"Oh god! we've been asleep for ages!"

"Well… you have," he chortled affectionately. "Has anyone ever told you that you snore like a baby warthog?"

"I do not!" I replied indignantly. "I sleep serenely, like a beautiful Disney princess!"

"Perhaps, if Sleeping Beauty suffered from sleep apnoea and needed a CPAP machine!" he scoffed. I slapped him playfully on the chest, knowing that I did tend to get a little bit snorty when I was particularly tired.

"Luckily, I've always had a penchant for baby warthogs" he

laughed, scooping me up and pulling me on top of him, covering me in featherlike kisses.

A taxi arrived just after eight and whisked us through the darkening streets along the river towards the Latin quarter and its impressive gothic buildings. Even without the light of day, there was no concealing its, vibrant, bohemian, and authentically Parisian vibe. Jake pointed out various buildings, most notably the Pantheon perched on top of Saint Genevieve hilltop, which he said housed the tombs of some of France's most celebrated citizens. It was magnificent.

"You can stop here" he instructed to the driver in French, who dutifully pulled up alongside a beautiful looking patisserie. The shop's pale pink facade was adorned with a sweeping silk flower garland which hung over the window, framing the display behind the glass which was full to the brim of Parisian fare. Pastel-coloured macarons sat proudly next to intricately decorated millefeuilles, which in turn sat next to dark chocolate eclairs, all in neat, uniform rows. It was everything that a French patisserie should be. Abundant, beautiful, classic and pricey.

"Let's come back here tomorrow when they're open!" I announced, practically licking the window.

"We can do whatever you want, you're the boss" he explained.

"Hmm…. are you sure you're comfortable with relinquishing your power?" I teased moving away from the buttery filo pastry begrudgingly.

"Is it too late to change my mind?" he asked, feigning concern.

"Yep!"

As we walked hand in hand, he explained that Jacques had managed to find a disused old monastery within the quarter and was in talks with local officials about the prospect of renovating it and turning it into a contemporary gallery. This area was supposedly synonymous with the world of art, and galleries, museums and examples of exquisite architecture had made their homes here nestled amongst an eclectic mix of cafes, shops, and restaurants, all of which made up the rich tapestry of this part of town. Curious as to why it was known as the Latin quarter, Jake explained that it was due to the language spoken by the early day scholars who studied in the educational institutions here, and not, as I had naively assumed, because of an influx of Latin immigrants. I decided to bank that titbit of information for any future pub quizzes I might attend.

Rounding the corner, the familiar figure of Jacques came into view. Propped up against the side of an unassuming building, dressed in a light linen jacket and jeans, he looked just as I remembered him. His jovial face and warm gait welcomed us from a distance.

"Jemma my dear!" he bellowed in a thick French accent. "Wonderful to see you again!" he beamed, throwing his arms around me as we got closer, enveloping me in a heartfelt embrace.

"And you!" I shrieked, allowing myself to get caught up in his infectious excitement.

"Jake, my boy!" he added, releasing me, and turning his affections to him. "You look…. great!" he smiled. "Happy!" he added, with a parental arm on his shoulder.

"I am." Jake glanced at me and took my hand in his again, a relaxed smile creeping over his face. "So, where's this new gallery then?"

"You're standing right outside it!" he laughed, pointing to the huge but unremarkable barn style door behind him.

"Really?" Jake did not look convinced.

"Don't judge a book by its cover as you English would say! Wait until you see inside!" He pulled an ornate iron key from his pocket and turned it in the lock. "Now, where was the light?" he asked himself as the door creaked open and he disappeared into the pitch black. "Ah, here we go!" A switch was flicked, uncovering a cavernous room with Herculean stones adorning the floor and walls, and towering columns reaching up to the heavens. This was not what I had been expecting. It truly was something to behold.

"Wow!" I gasped. "What an incredible space! Jake said this used to be a monastery?"

"Yes, that's right. It was built in the 17$^{th}$ century. This is the original stonework" he said gesturing around us. "Now, imagine this space with proper lighting. I'm thinking of an industrial set up – exposed metal trunking, huge, commercial strip lighting suspended from wires, juxta pose the old architecture with contemporary fixtures and artwork. What do you think? Could it work?"

Jake had ventured off and was walking around the room by himself, his hands trailing over the cold stone walls, his head locked skywards to the ceiling above. He was lost in thought.

"Jake?"

"Er, sorry" he said turning around and making his way back towards us. "You'd need a decent climate control system to keep the moisture out of the air and maintain an ambient temperature. But yeah, I reckon if you can get that sorted, you've got yourself one hell of a gallery!" He looked genuinely excited. I had seen that face once before on him, when we were at the gallery opening in London. It was like watching a child on Christmas morning witnessing the magic and awe as they saw the tree laden with gifts for the first time. This was his passion, his calling, no doubt about it. "How long until you can open? Any ideas on how long the work will take?"

Jacques held his arms aloft. "Your guess is as good as mine, dear boy! You know what French bureaucracy is like. I might need to grease a few palms to get things moving" he winked. "In an ideal world, we would be up and running this time next year. I've already spoken to a few contractors and have quotes for the work, I just need the bloody local government to pull their fingers out of their lazy, corrupt arses!"

"Well, if anyone can achieve the unachievable, it's you" laughed Jake affectionately.

Jacques threw his arm around him "With you by my side, there is nothing that cannot be achieved!" I had not seen a picture of Jake's father, but as I watched the two men standing in front of me, it was hard to imagine that they were not related. To the untrained eye, they could have been father and son. Both so relaxed in each other's company, there was even a slight physical resemblance.

"Have you had any thoughts about which direction you want to go in for the launch?"

"That's why you're here isn't it?" Jaques laughed, patting him on the back, heading into the centre of the room.

"Same as London? Black tie? Get the usual crowd in, lavish them with French champagne and oysters?"

"Or you could do the complete opposite" I blurted, suddenly feeling like I had spoken out of turn.

"Please, tell me what you think Cherie" Jacques said, beckoning me to come closer.

"Forgive me, but there's something I haven't been able to get out of my head since the moment I saw you standing by the front door to this place." I shifted uncomfortably on my feet, not sure how to continue. Both men gave me an encouraging smile. "Well, what if you didn't do an over the top, lavish opening? What if you played to the strengths of this building instead?"

"I don't understand" Jake said looking perplexed.

"Think about it" I continued. "From the outside, from the unassuming façade, you'd never guess that such a treasure lay hidden inside. What if your launch capitalised on that? What if you did something radical and didn't advertise it at all?" There was a look of abject horror etched on their faces. This would need some more explaining. "Jake, you must know about the early nineties rave scene in London?"

"Woah there!" he laughed, slightly offended. "I'm only thirty-four, I was probably about five years old when that started."

"My bad!" I apologised, making a mental note of his age, realising that I had not thought about how old he was before now. "Anyway, the idea was there were these huge underground raves which were completely illegal, so they were never officially advertised. People never knew where the venue was until right at the last minute to avoid the police showing up and closing them down. However, despite the lack of exposure, hundreds of people always showed up."

"Go on" Jacques said looking intrigued.

"Right, well, I'm not suggesting you do anything illegal, like sell ecstasy to your guests." I chuckled at my own little joke. "But what if you pique people's interest by keeping an air of mystery about the whole proceeding?"

"But how will people know where to turn up? You can't have a gallery opening without anyone to open it to!"

I racked my brain, thinking of how this could work. "You send an initial invite but go light on the details. Invite them to Paris on a certain date, get them to come to a central location at a specific time, and only when they are there do you give them another clue. Make them work for it, lure them here. Let's face it, even if they were standing on top of this place, they wouldn't suspect a thing. People love a mystery; they love the allure and anticipation of the unknown. I'd bet money on the fact that the press would get wind of this far quicker and remain interested far longer than if you went down the usual route. Plus, you'd save a fortune on marketing! Sorry Jake." I pulled a face mimicking regret.

"My dear girl, you are a genius! Do you think it could work?"

"I don't see why not. You'd have to make sure that nobody knew what you were doing here, the less people who know that you are connected to this project the better."

"How many people know about this already?" Jake asked joining us.

"Only the two of you, the mayor and the three contractors."

"Okay, so it's doable in theory" Jake mused, the cogs starting to turn. "What do we do when we get them here? Is there a theme or a plan?"

"I hadn't really thought that far ahead to be honest," but as I said that a thought came to me unexpectedly. "What if there wasn't a dress code or a theme as such? What if it were just a celebration of Paris, of this part in particular? I mean, I don't know the area that well, but from what I've seen this evening, it's a vibrant, eclectic place, why not celebrate that? Don't just invite the usual crowd, invite people from all levels of society – art is for everyone after all isn't it? Bring different communities together – scholars, true art lovers, shop owners mixed in with the usual crowd." I could see them mulling over my ideas. Was it a step too far, a risk not worth taking?

"We'd be breaking all the rules" smiled Jacques devilishly. I wasn't sure if he thought that was a good thing or not. "I love it!" he proclaimed jubilantly. "My dear girl, we'd be the talk of the town!"

"You certainly would! You'd be making art cool again – not that it isn't already" I added, slightly shame faced. "But you'd certainly be opening it up to a whole new demographic which has to be a good thing, right?"

"It's an exceptionally good thing indeed! Let me rack your brains some more over dinner. There's an excellent little place round the corner which does the most fantastic seafood. This really is extremely exciting!" he sang as he headed back towards the door.

"How do you do it?" Jake asked stroking the side of my face with his thumb.

"Do what?"

"Make people fall in love with you" he replied, leaning in to kiss me.

"I don't know" I replied truthfully before his lips connected softly with mine and I was lost to him once again.

"Enough of that already!" called Jacques jovially. "I don't pay you to fornicate on the job."

"I didn't realise you were paying me at all!" Jake quipped cheekily, not taking his eyes off me.

"Come on, we don't want to jeopardise your career" I smiled, taking his hand in mine, and leading him out on to the street.

The rest of the evening whizzed by in a whirl of animated conversation, laugher, and fantastic food, all three of us becoming more excited and convinced by our rapidly developing plan. Something about this risqué approach captivated our imaginations. It was going to be different to every other project I had worked on, and truth be told, I could not wait to make a start.

# SUNDAY

My phone buzzed incessantly on the bedside table next to me. At first, my brain did not register it, but as it continued, I was pulled from my delicious sleep and forced to open my eyes. The room was pitch black, only a shard of light crept in between the curtains from outside, piercing the darkness like a dagger. It was just before 3am and Ben was calling.

"Hello?" I croaked, hitting the green button to silence the buzzing.

"Hey Jem." He sounded drunk.

"Are you ok?" I asked forcing myself to sit up in bed.

"Yeah, I guess." His words were slurred, and his breathing laboured.

"Ben, have you been drinking?" I asked, knowing that the answer was yes.

"Just a bit." Something in his tone concerned me. Usually, he was a happy drunk. If anything, he got funnier the more inebriated he got. But this did not sound like that Ben. He sounded troubled.

"You're worrying me, what's happened?"

"Ah, nothing" he trailed off. "I just wanted to talk to you that's all."

"Ok, talk to me. What's wrong?" There was silence on the other end. "Ben, are you still there?" The silence was perforated by a faint purr. He'd fallen asleep. I put the phone back down on the table and slid under the cover again. Probably best he slept it off. Jake turned over and wrapped me in his arms.

"You ok? Who was that?" he asked half asleep.

"Just Ben" I whispered, snuggling into him.

"What did he want?" His tone was curt even though he was not fully conscious.

"Not sure" I replied, wondering the same thing, closing my eyes again.

As if I had been magically transported through time, the next time my eyes opened, bright sunshine was flooding in through the windows.

"Good morning beautiful!" Jake smiled, placing down a cup of coffee next to me.

"This is becoming a bit of an occupational hazard" I joked. "What time is it?" I asked hoisting myself up onto my elbows.

"Just gone ten" he replied as he sidled up next to me in bed.

"Jeez! I never sleep in this late! What are you doing to me?"

"Maybe you're relaxed… or maybe you're worn out?" he grinned cheekily.

"You might be right on both counts!" I said stretching out and grabbing my cup.

"So, what do you want to do today? You're in charge remember!"

"Hmm…. can we go back to that patisserie from last night?" I asked, remembering the divine tarts and pastries from the window. "And then how about a guided tour of Notre Dame? I want a professional one though, an insider's guide, don't try and palm me off with some cheap-arse 10-euro tourist one." Jakes eyes lit up at the prospect.

"Are you sure, we don't have to go there; we can go anywhere you want."

"I'm sure" I said kissing his hand. "I've always wanted to go, but knowing it's important to you makes it all the more special. I mean it though; I want my money's worth!"

"Do I have to walk round holding an umbrella?"

"Abso-bloody-lutely! It wouldn't be a proper tour without a proper tour guide!" I chided.

"I'll make sure I dig out my brolly then" he chuckled.

A message came through on my phone. It was from Ben.

**Sorry for last night. I had too much to drink. Just pretend it never happened! Hope you're having a wonderful time.**

**Ben xx**

I immediately started texting back, relieved he was feeling better.

**Morning! Don't worry about it, we're all guilty of making a drunken phone call occasionally! Glad you're ok. Paris is AMAZING!!!!! Will tell you all about it when I get back**

**J xx**

"That him again?" Jake asked, trying to sound nonchalant, but failing miserably.

"Yeah, he's just apologising for last night."

"You know he's got a thing for you, right?" he said still trying to sound casual.

I almost burst into fits of laughter. "Ben? Don't be absurd, he's like my brother. I love him to bits, but not in that way. Honestly!"

"You might not, but he might not be on the same page." He looked at me as if what he was saying was abundantly clear and I was failing to see what was right in front of my eyes.

"He is, trust me. We've known each other our whole lives, we're just close that's all."

"So, I've got nothing to be worried about then?"

"Absolutely nothing" I assured him, putting my cup down and rolling back towards him, straddling his body.

"That's good" he smiled, looking relieved. "Because I don't want to do this with anyone but you."

"Do what?"

"This!" he said flipping me back over so that he was now on top of me.

"Oh!" I squealed, delighted. "We're doing this again are we?"

"You forget that I've got a lot of years to make up for," he smiled. "I'm like a kid with a new toy!" he joked. "Of course, if you have any objections …"

"Absolutely no objections here. I'm more than happy to be your plaything!" I giggled.

◆ ◆ ◆

Jake agreed that as the patisserie was en route to Notre Dame, we could stop there first. What he failed to appreciate was how long the slight detour would take given the plethora of delicacies on offer. How was anyone supposed to choose between a tarte au citron or an éclair au caramel? The answer was you were not, hence, the need to buy both, and a couple of millefeuilles for good measure.

"You know these won't make it home in once piece" Jake admonished me jokingly.

"Oh, I know, but they'll be gone by then anyway, they're journey snacks!"

"What the hell are journey snacks?" There was a look of genuine confusion on his face.

"Hold up, please tell me you're joking!" I replied, looking utterly disgusted. "You don't know what a journey snack is?"

"Nope."

"You've heard of car snacks though, right? Please tell me you've heard of car snacks!" A sudden fear that we might not be compatible after all, filled my lungs.

"Of course, I've heard of car snacks! It's what you pack for kids when you're going on a long car journey," he continued, laughing. I ignored the child reference, that was an argument for another day.

"Well, journey snacks could be considered the same thing except that they are usually consumed when taking different modes of transport – otherwise they would just be car snacks" I said, wondering why cars had been given their very own form of snack, and every other form of transport had to share.

"I see…" he replied looking thoughtful and amused in equal measure. "So, we need all of these cakes for our 20-minute walk?" He was clearly trying to rile me.

"Listen buster," I said, feigning agitation. "A good friend of mine once said that when purchasing travelling snacks, it should look as if a five-year-old has been given £100 and let loose in a supermarket. On that basis, our efforts look tame! What would you have done if you fancied an éclair, and I hadn't bought any?"

"Doesn't bear thinking about" he mocked.

"Exactly" I agreed, ignoring his flippancy. "Now, would you care for a journey snack Mr Bales?"

"Do you know what, I could murder a caramel éclair!"

"You're in luck!" I said retrieving one from the pastel pink box and handing it to him.

"Thank you'." He put one end of it in his mouth. "God, this is actually really good!" he exclaimed appreciatively after a couple of seconds. "Here, have a bite."

I sank my mouth around the other end, only considering afterwards that I probably shouldn't have taken such a big bite. "Wow, that is incredible!" The thin and crispy choux was packed full of deliciously sweet and creamy crème patisserie, and the gooey caramel fondant on top was a decadent addition (although I could feel my arteries clogging up even before I had fully digested it). "See, I bet you're glad we got them now aren't you!" I said diving back into the box and pulling out a miniature tarte au citron.

"Oh wow, that éclair has nothing on this!" I declared as I shoved half the tart in my mouth.

"You not planning on offering me any" Jake said looking like a dog waiting to be thrown a scrap.

"Of course. Here!" I pushed the remaining half into his mouth, accidentally spreading lemon curd around his lips. "Let me help you with that" I said chasing the line of curd with my finger and then licking it off seductively.

"You'll get me into trouble doing things like that" he whispered, leaning in closer to steal a lemony kiss.

"I don't know what you mean" I replied coyly.

"Hmm...., of course you don't." His eyes gave me a disbelieving look. "Right, come on, let's get going, it can get pretty busy over there and we want plenty of time to have a proper look" he smiled excitedly.

"Lead the way!" I declared, closing the box, and putting it snugly inside my bag.

As tour guides went, Jake was the absolute best, despite not actually being able to step foot inside the building due to the ongoing renovation works. I imagined him and his father taking the same tour, and my heart broke a little. Even without his brolly and obligatory backpack, he shone brighter than the rest. He was so knowledgeable and animated (something the other guides seemed to be lacking), that he caught the attention of many of the visitors, who I caught eavesdropping and falling behind in their own tours just so they could listen to him.

"I think you should make them aware this is a private tour" I said nodding in the direction of four elderly women who were hanging off his every word. "Is no woman immune to your charms?" I joked.

"They just want me for my knowledge" he laughed, flashing them one of his winning smiles in the process.

"Yes …I'm sure that's all they're after!" I said, noticing that one of the ladies was now looking particularly flushed.

"Now, if you look up at the flying buttresses" he continued.

"The what?"

"The flying buttresses" he repeated. "Those external supports which are constructed around the naive. It's thought that Notre Dame was the first church to ever have them - she was a real trend setter!" he beamed excitedly. "Not only are they architecturally beautiful, but they perform a vital function. The church, because of its size was exceptionally dark, so bigger windows were installed. The problem was, this left the structure unstable due to the thin walls, so these were added afterwards to offer additional support. Other churches followed suit, but she was the one, it is thought, that started the iconic trend in sacred architecture."

As I stood there in the warm sunshine listening to his melodic voice, I realised that I could have listened to him speak all day. He could have been lamenting about gothic architecture or the salt content of an OXO cube, and it would not have mattered. He had the ability to captivate and mesmerise, make you feel that you were the only person in the world who he wanted to talk to. Which may well have been the case, except for the fact that we were being followed again by the gaggle of old women, who seemed to have now permanently left their tour and tacked on to ours instead. Once we found ourselves back at the gift shop, he officially brought the tour to a close, thanking everyone that was now gathered for listening.

"How did I do?" he asked apprehensively.

"I think you're wasted as a hot shot exec" I said truthfully. "So, do you want paying now or later?"

"Depends how you're intending to pay" he said mischievously.

I pulled a guilty face. "I'm fresh out of cash I'm afraid."

"Later would be better then," he added with a glint in his eye. "Now, I don't know about you, but all this walking and talking has made me hungry. But not for another one of your journey snacks!" he added panic stricken as he saw me rummaging in my bag for the box of remaining treats.

"I'm hurt!" I joked, closing the bag. "What do you fancy then?"

"Apart from you?" he teased. "There's a great little café just around the corner from here that does the most amazing croque monsieur" he said practically salivating.

"A cheese and ham toastie! That's a bit basic for someone like you, isn't it?" I mocked.

"You've got me all wrong. I am basic!" he laughed. "M&S suits and cheese toasties, that's the real me I'm afraid. I'm just a basic kinda guy."

"Yeah right! You don't fool me Mr Basic! Spend a week with me and you'll see what basic really looks like!"

"I accept" he said kissing me softly on the cheek. The thought of spending a whole week with him was very appealing. Come to think of it, the thought of spending everyday with him sounded very appealing, although I might leave that suggestion for another day – give it a couple of weeks before suggesting marriage and kids.

The café was jam packed with people, proof of just how good the toasties were according to Jake. We loitered on the periphery of the seating area, waiting for a table to become available, discussing the merits of a croque monsieur verses a croque madame. When a pair of beautiful teenage lovers more intent on eating each other than the food laid before them decided to find somewhere more private to make out, we darted into the centre of the tables to fill their seats, much to the displeasure of several other eagle-eyed couples who also coveted the spot.

Laminated menus stood proudly in a holder on the table, further proof if we needed it, that this was a no-frills establishment. I immediately felt at home amongst the wipe down tablecloths and paper napkins. We had already decided what we were going to eat, having used our standing time wisely. We had reached an impasse in the debate over which was the best sandwich. Him opting for the croque monsieur and me for the madame (he could not be persuaded by my logic that a fried egg on top of anything only helped to elevate it). What he did not need his arm twisting on was ordering fries to accompany them. The only slight issue was that he assumed I meant we order one portion to share rather than one each as I had intended (I made a mental note to be more explicit next time around). Once we had placed our order with the waiter (who thankfully was not a tall, leggy blonde with a penchant for an attractive Englishman), Jake sat forward in his seat, elbows resting on the table, suddenly looking serious.

"I have a confession to make." A million awful possibilities raced through my mind. Had he got Crystal's number from the restaurant the other day? Had he decided that he could not possibly date someone who could eat more carbs than him? Had he just realised he was in fact gay? The more I thought about what he was going to say, the sicker I felt.

"Go on" I said, convinced I did not actually want to hear what he was going to tell me.

"Don't look so worried! I'm not about to admit to being a serial killer, or worse, a fan of true crime dramas" he winced.

"Nowt wrong with a gritty crime drama" I replied, not feeling any more optimistic about what he was about to divulge.

"Well, you know how I said you were going to be in charge today, and that we could do whatever you wanted."

"Yes...."

"Well, I may have already made some plans for this evening" he said tentatively. I had not realised I had been holding my breath the entire time until that point. I exhaled, feeling some of the tension leave my body as I did so.

"I see... so I'm not in charge then, you are? Are you scared of letting a woman make decisions for you?" I said trying to hide the smile which was desperate to come out. Jake's face was a picture, a mixture of fear and incomprehension.

"I didn't mean to upset you" he apologised, "I can cancel them, it's not a problem."

It felt cruel to revel in his agony. "Relax, I'm busting your balls!" I giggled, squeezing his hand.

He looked instantly relieved. "I thought I'd upset you again for a minute!"

"It takes more than that to upset me" I laughed. "So, what's the plan then."

"Well...contrary to all the stories circulating at work about me," my cheeks warmed at the thought of some of them. "Exactly!" he added, as if reading my mind. "Regardless of what people think, I'm pretty old fashioned. I know things have moved quickly, and I know that we have done things out of sequence, but I would like to take you on a proper first date."

"Was the kebab shop after Jacques' gallery opening not a first date?" I chortled, my heart secretly bursting at this basic, old fashioned sex god sat in front of me.

"I want to do things properly" he smiled. "I want us to be able to look back and remember our first date together."

"You don't think I'm going to remember all of this?" I said, waving my hands around me.

"Maybe, but I want to make it special" he said, his deep brown eyes holding mine.

"Jake, all of it has been special, I couldn't have wished for anything more and I wouldn't have changed a thing. Apart from when you blew me off on Wednesday, and when I thought you were having a torrid affair with your sister" I added shame faced.

"See, I've got a lot of making up to do!" he smiled. "I'll drop you back at home after this so you can get ready. I'll go back to Jacques and then I'll pick you up around 7.30pm."

"Am I allowed to ask where we're going?"

"If I tell you, I'll have to kill you!"

"Okay 007, but can you at least give me an idea of what I should wear? The last thing I want to do is rock up to a night at the opera in a pair of crotchless leather chaps!"

"You have crotchless leather chaps?" he said raising an eyebrow more in hope than anything else. "I'd say go with something smart, one of the many dresses you brought along? Perhaps save the chaps for a night in?"

"Hmm... very intriguing" I exclaimed, ignoring the ravaging look in his eyes, and stealing a French fry from the bowl which had just been delivered.

◆ ◆ ◆

After lunch Jake dropped me back before disappearing in a cab to Jacque's. As his car sped down the street and out of sight, a strange feeling of loss and longing crept over me. My sensible hat reminded me that this was not a scene from a Nicholas Sparks novel, and that we were not destined to not see each other for years on end, like so many of his star-crossed lover protagonists. My irrational heart on the other hand could not be consoled or cajoled into feeling any less bereft. It was time to put my big girl pants on (similar in style to those worn by the queen of big girl pants, the mighty Bridget Jones) and get ready for my first date. I hot footed it up the steps to the apartment, let myself in and grabbed a bottle of fizz en route to the bathroom. If I was going to be sad and lonely and blast out an eye watering rendition of Celine Dione's 'All By Myself,' I might as well do it with bubbles!

Not knowing exactly where we were going was causing me all sorts of anxiety. Usually, my outfits were planned meticulously around venue, time of year and other people likely to be in attendance. A general suggestion of 'dress smart' gave little to nothing away. Luckily, as Jake had pointed out, I had brought most of my wardrobe with me. A pretty three-quarter length cerise dress and gold strappy sandals might just do the trick, but then again, it might not. As I stood staring at the plethora of dresses before me, second guessing everything, I feared the nerves might finally get the better of me. Thank God you only had one first date! At least we would not have the awkward moment at the end of the night where we had to decide if we were doing the one cheek, both cheeks, or full blown lip lock kiss. We had already gone way past that stage I thought as I sank down beneath the bubbles in the bath, my lady bits tingling at the sweet recollection.

Despite the constant urge to throw up, there was no denying the little butterflies that were dancing excitedly in my tummy at the prospect of seeing him again. Barely thirty minutes had passed, and I missed him already. How the hell was I going to cope when we got home, and things returned to normal? It would be like asking a crack addict to go cold turkey – an almost certain disaster. Seven thirty-two, and after much coiffing, numerous outfit changes (obviously reverting to my original choice) and a change in heart regarding my eyeliner, the buzzer went.

"Hello?" I answered eagerly, knowing exactly who was on the

other end.

"Hello beautiful, it's me" a silky-smooth voice replied, sending those butterflies into overdrive. "Are you ready?"

"Yep, two seconds and I'll be down!" One last glance in the mirror, one final glug of fizz, and I practically danced downstairs to meet him. As the rackety lift doors parted, my eyes were instantly drawn to the beautiful man standing in the middle of the foyer. Dressed in a dark blue suit which fit snugly in all the right places, and a crisp white shirt unbuttoned at the top, which subtly enhanced his defined body beneath, Jake stood there waiting patiently, eyes down, a single white rose in hand. As he looked up our eyes met. All my nerves disappeared. Home. His enchanting smile made me want to run to him, but there was no need, because he glided effortlessly across the floor towards me.

"You look exquisite" he smiled, taking me in, offering me the rose. "Would it sound too pathetic if I told you I'd missed you?" he said looking a little embarrassed.

"Not at all" I whispered, holding my hand to his cheek. "I've missed you too."

"Are you ready for our first date?" he asked taking my hand, his lips placing a gentle kiss in the back of it. I nodded silently, so overwhelmed that I dare not speak for fear of saying something ridiculous. Opening the front door, he led me outside to a waiting, blacked out Audi Q7. A driver exited from the front to hold the rear door open for us.

"Thank you" I said as I slid over to the other side. "So, can you tell me where we're going now?" I begged.

"You'll see soon enough" he laughed, enjoying the suspense he was creating. His eyes lingered on my face. "I don't think I will ever get used to how beautiful you are" he smiled.

"Oh, I don't know, you might not think that if you saw me straight after a run!" I giggled, uncomfortable from the praise.

"Why do you put yourself down all the time Jemma? You are

beautiful, smart, funny, kind. You are incredible, and I will make sure I tell you every single day just how amazing you are. Besides, I've seen you running remember!" he joked. "How did the new breathing technique go?" The broad smile on his face was a dead giveaway that he had not bought my bullshit excuse the other day.

"Umm..." my cheeks flamed with mortification. "I can't believe I told you that!" I burst out laughing. "To be honest, I hadn't brushed my teeth that morning and didn't want you to notice in case you thought I was some kind of Save The Planet, soap dodging degenerate." I cringed now at how I must have looked.

"Kudos to you for the imagination, that was one hell of a story!"

"You just made me so nervous. Once I started, I couldn't stop. And then it went too far, and I had to keep going because I was in too deep!"

Jake laughed heartily. "Thank God it's not just me that felt like that!"

"What do you mean? Why would you get nervous?" I could not imagine someone like him being affected by nerves.

"Are you kidding me? I'm always nervous around you!"

"But why? Why would someone like you be nervous around someone like me?" There went the self-doubt again.

He stopped for a second to mull over his response. "Because I never believed in love at first site until I met you." There was a prolonged moment of silence as we both took in what had been said.

"What?" I replied meekly, my heart pounding faster and harder than I thought was physically possible.

"Jemma" he said turning fully towards me. His face was tormented, his eyes burned, and the vein in his neck was pulsing frantically. "You have no idea how much it has killed me the past few months seeing you every day and not being able to tell you how I felt. Every time I heard you laugh, I wanted to know who was making you happy, when you seemed stressed, I wanted to be the one to hold you. So many times, I wanted to get you alone and talk to you, but I could never pluck up the courage. You consumed my every thought." He took my hand. "Jemma, you make me want things I never knew I wanted, you have made me happier than I ever thought possible, and it scares the shit out of me because I didn't see it coming, I wasn't expecting to ever feel like this. I'm not used to not being in control. It feels like I've jumped out of plane without a parachute. It's exhilarating, but I also know it's going to kill me if it goes wrong. You make me vulnerable, and I'm trying desperately to learn how to deal with that." He smiled weakly. "So yes, in answer to your question, you make me very, very nervous!"

"I had no idea." We had obviously had numerous conversations these past few days, but I had not appreciated that he might be feeling just as scared and vulnerable as me. Nothing I could say could equal what he had just told me, so I stuck with the truth. "Jake, you mean everything to me." I muttered, trying to stifle a trickle of silent tears from streaking down my cheek.

"Please don't cry" he said, pulling a hanky from his pocket and handing it to me. "Tonight's meant to be a happy night."

"Oh, it is happy! These are happy tears!" I sobbed, praying to God I was not ugly crying, and that my mascara was still in its rightful place.

"Mr Bales, we're here" the driver said over his shoulder.

As we got out of the car, I noticed that it had pulled up alongside a jetty on the river. At the end of it sat the most beautiful walnut clad motorboat I had ever seen. It reminded me of the ones you saw bobbing lazily around exclusive marinas in Monte Carlo or floating leisurely down the canals of Venice.

"Is this for us?"

"It is!" he replied, pleased by my obvious delight. "Miss Lucas," he said offering me his hand to help me aboard.

"Thank you" I beamed. "Wow, you've really pulled out all the stops, haven't you!"

"I told you I wanted to make tonight special for you, and what better way to see Paris than by water at night?"

"This is just perfect!"

"I'm glad you like it. Champagne?" he asked gesturing to a bottle sat casually waiting in a cooler.

"I'd love to, thank you!" As he popped the cork, a typically Parisian looking gentleman in a navy polo shirt and white chinos made his way confidently down the pontoon.

"Mr Bales!" he said extending his hand to Jake. "I trust you are well. Welcome back!"

"I'm good Phillippe, great to see you again."

"Miss Lucas," he said offering me his hand next. "Welcome aboard La Mariana."

"Thank you for having me" I smiled. I got the distinct impression that the two men knew each other well, although their relationship seemed quite formal. Had Jake brought other women to Paris with him? Was this his go to 'first date'? Is that how they knew each other? The thought made me feel sick, and I shifted uncomfortably on the plush white leather seat. Sensing my change in mood, he placed his hand gently on my leg.

"Phillippe works for my family" he said by way of explanation.

Relief flooded through me. "Oh. Wait, is this your boat?" I asked, putting two and two together.

"My family's" he replied, trying to distance himself from the vessel. Although it was obvious that he came from a wealthy family, I had noticed that he did not like to talk about money. Infact, I would say he was almost embarrassed by it sometimes. Talking about his family was something we had not done too much of, and I was interested to know more.

"Tell me about your parents" I asked gently as we took our seat at the rear of the boat.

"What would you like to know?"

"I don't know, how they met, what they were like when they were younger. I want to get a picture of where you come from" I smiled, resting my hand on his thigh.

"I might have to give you a condensed version" he chuckled warmly, settling back in the chair. "Mum was studying art here in the sixties. She was working part time in one of the restaurants. My dad was a trainee architectural surveyor and had come over to Paris for work. His company was working alongside a French one to build a new commercial building in the business district. Anyhow, he went for lunch one day at the restaurant mum was working at, she ended up accidentally throwing his bouillabaisse in his lap, and that's how it all started."

"Love at first sight!" I beamed. "Sounds like something out of a romance novel. The perfect meet-cute!"

"I have no idea what a meet-cute is, but yes, dad always said it was love at first sight, for him, anyway."

"Then what happened? Did your dad quit his job, stay here in Paris and the two of them spent all day making beautiful babies?" I asked wistfully.

"Not quite" he chuckled. "My mum's parents weren't particularly keen on dad, he didn't come from money, and they thought he was only with her for that reason. Which he wasn't" he added protectively. "He adored her. Anyway, he stayed here for a few months until she finished college, and then they went back to England so that they could be together – and practice making babies! As the years passed, my grandparents realised that they were truly in love, and when Charlie and I were born it helped to bring the family back together. By then, dad owned his own company, he'd proved that he was not after their money and that he could more than provide for his own family, and that's when we started splitting our time between here and Hampshire."

"So, your grandparents lived here in Paris or down in Provence back then?"

"They had the apartment here, but they obviously had the vineyard and chateau down in Provence, so they spent most of their time down there and then visited once every month or so. My grandparents come from old money, everything they have has been passed down from generation to generation. There's a snobbery about it which I don't agree with. They can't help it, it's how they were raised, and I guess they are just trying to protect what they believe in. I love them dearly, but I can't forgive them for how they treated my dad in the early years. He spent his whole life trying to prove that he was good enough for their daughter."

"Is that why you're so driven and don't like talking about money?"

"I just don't think money is important. Don't get me wrong, I know I have the luxury of being able to say that because I have it, many people aren't fortunate enough to be able to say it doesn't matter. But I have seen the damage and the hurt it can cause. It really doesn't make you happy. I'm driven because I want to do well, because I believe that you can do anything if you put your mind to it, I like the sense of achievement I get from being good at something. I don't do it to get rich." He paused and took a sip from his glass. "Anyway, I think that's enough back story for one date," he said smiling, topping up my champagne.

Phillippe started the engine and the boat purred into life, pulling away from its mooring and heading out into the open channel.

Jake turned towards me, holding his glass up. "Here's to the first of many, many dates."

"To jumping out of a plane without a parachute" I added cheerily, and chinked glasses.

The sun was only now just disappearing below the horizon, and the water reflected the light from the surrounding buildings like tiny sparkling Christmas fairy lights. Only the sound of our voices and the gentle hum of the engine interrupted the silence surrounding us, making it feel like we were a million miles from anyone, cocooned in our own little romantic bubble.

"Hands down, best first date I've ever been on."

"Really?" he said "But it's only just started. It might all go downhill from here" he smiled confidently, knowing that it was not going to.

"When you consider that my last few first dates have included a midweek Nando's, a night at the dogs where I was fed an undercooked hotdog and a warm beer, and dinner at my dates mum's house, this rates pretty highly" I giggled.

"You obviously weren't going on dates with the right men" he said seriously, holding my gaze intently.

"That's a given" I joked, trying to steady my racing heart.

"I want to give you everything you deserve Jemma, and you deserve so much more than what they gave you" he said sounding almost angry on my behalf.

"I'd be happy just to have you" I whispered squeezing his hand.

As the awesome sight of the Eiffel Tower came closer into view, I instinctively sat forward to get a better look. For a moment, I felt like I was slap-bang in the middle of a scene from Emily in Paris. Hot guy – check, champagne – check, iconic French landmark in the foreground – check! The only thing missing was a fantastically camp sidekick and a pair of exquisite Chanel boots. Alas, Phillipe, did not hit the necessary mark on the campometer, and my footwear, although lovely was not Chanel.

"What are you thinking?" Jake asked, placing his hand softly on the small of my back.

"Just how unbelievably happy I am" I replied honestly. "And it's because of you." I said, turning to look at him. His features were lit up. That chiselled jawline and model-like bone structure of his were dazzling, but it was his eyes which sparkled like two polished jewels that took my breath away. If it were possible, he looked as happy as I felt. For the first time in my life, someone was looking at me in a way that implied they were not only happy to accept me for who I was but love me unconditionally for it – faults and all. "Nobody has ever looked at me the way you do" I admitted, embarrassed by my honesty.

"Then nobody has ever looked at you the way you deserve to be looked at." He said, closing the gap between us, his thumb making gentle circles on my cheek.

"I think you are possibly the sweetest man I have ever met" I murmured, losing myself in his penetrating stare.

"Don't go telling everyone that, I'd hate to ruin my reputation for being a philandering arsehole" he winked, reminding me of what I had accused him of being just a few short nights ago. Holding my chin, he pulled me gently towards him, his lips taking mine in the most delicious kiss, his arms encircling me in a blanket of warmth. His mouth was tender and attentive, the taste of champagne lingering on his tongue as it flitted softly around mine, transporting me to a place that only he could. And in that moment, I was both utterly lost and finally found – a contradiction that was not entirely lost on me. "Now I know dinner is a bit formal for a first date" he said smiling, pulling away ever so slightly. "But I was hoping you could make an exception given it's our last night here."

"I'm sure I can make an exception just this once" I replied, catching my breath. "Don't tell me, you know a great place to grab a kebab?" I joked.

"I do as it happens," he laughed. "But we can save that for another time. Tonight, I want to take you to a restaurant that I've not been to before. A first for both of us - for our first date."

"Ooh, where?" I asked intrigued and excited.

"There!" he said turning me back to face the front, pointing up at the Eiffel Tower.

"Are you being serious?" My eyes were wide and unblinking at the prospect. "Jeez, how on earth are you going to follow up on a first date like this?" I teased.

"Pizza and a film at mine when we get home?"

"Ooh, are you inviting me back to yours Mr Bales?" I said fingering the lapel on his jacket.

"Yep, but I warn you, I might not ever let you leave."

"I'm sure you'll get sick of me soon enough" I chuckled in a hollow voice.

"After everything I've told you, everything we've done together over the past few days, why do you still doubt how I feel about you?"

"I don't doubt you; I doubt my ability to cope afterwards if things don't work out. I've gone through life with the mantra that if you expect the worst, hopefully it won't hurt as much when the inevitable happens."

"What happened to no parachutes and taking risks?" he smiled gently, stroking my arm.

"I'm afraid of heights" I admitted.

"Life is scary" he said running his fingers through my hair. "But sometimes we just have to take a risk. We can't play it safe all the time or we'll never know what could have been. Take a chance on me Jemma, please. I promise I'll catch you." His eyes were pleading.

"Just don't drop me" I begged. "Or Claire will chase you to the corners of the earth, and your life as you know it will be over!" I smiled.

"Shit. That's enough of a deterrent to put even the most roguish of men off. Thankfully, I have no intention of leaving your side. Jemma, I want a future together. I'm getting too old to waste time on things that aren't important. I know what I want, and I want you. And if you think there's even a chance that you might want the same, then we must at least try to make it work."

"Jake, I do. I want that, and I want it with you."

"Then take my hand and jump" he begged.

"Okay."

I read something once which said that those who have known flight and felt the exhilaration and the freedom of hurtling towards the ground unchecked, spend the rest of their lives looking skyward, longing to recreate that feeling, often unsuccessfully. It made me think. What if they were talking about love? What if they made that jump with someone, and then they lost them? What if you could only truly make that jump once? Was it worth trying and failing or was it better not to jump at all and never experience the rush, instead, protecting yourself from experiencing profound loss and hurt? As I looked into Jake's eyes, I knew deep down that I would have followed him out that plane time and time again. In years to come, I wanted to look up and remember how it felt. Even if I lost it, I'd rather look up and be sad that it had happened and ended, but joyous that it had happened at all, than look up and have to try to imagine how amazing it would have been because I was too scared. And so, I decided to jump. Who could have known that jumping out of a plane to your death could make you feel so alive?

# MONDAY

Last night had been truly magical. Not only would I remember the boat trip and dinner for the rest of my life, but I would also remember the way he opened up to me, the way he let me see parts of himself that no one else had seen, the way he made himself vulnerable to make me feel safe. I had fallen for him before that, but last night made me realise that a life without Jake would only be half a life, he could make me whole. As we lay in bed in each other's arms in comfortable silence, neither of us wanting to move, I contemplated how easy it would be to not go back. To stay here and create a new life together.

"Shall we stay here forever?" he said stroking my arm.

"You read my mind" I replied, manoeuvring myself in his arms so that I could see his face properly. "I can't thank you enough for this weekend Jake. It has been the most wonderful few days of my life."

"There is no need to thank me baby."

"Yes, there is" I insisted.

"Then I should thank you for making me the happiest guy alive" he beamed.

"This is my new happy place" I giggled, tucking myself under his arm again.

"Paris?"

"Nope, right here, next to you, silly!"

"Not under me?" He joked, rolling on top of me, stroking my face with the palm of his hand.

"Under you, over you, I don't mind, so long as you are between my legs!" I chuckled.

"There's nowhere else I'd rather be" he added, pushing himself against my stomach so that I could feel his morning excitement.

"One more time for the road?" I chortled.

"I thought you'd never ask."

Reluctantly we packed up our bags and tidied the apartment. Our flight back was in a couple of hours, getting us home for about 1pm which gave us just enough time to get back to the office and the real world before LJT came in to finalise the deal at 3pm.

"Have you got room for these in your bag?" I said chucking the duty-free bag with the two uneaten Toblerones in them on the bed.

"I told you they were a waste of money" he laughed, grabbing them, and stuffing them in his case.

"I'll give them to the girls; they love a duty-free gift!"

Twenty minutes later and we were in the back of the cab heading off to the airport. I could not help but feel a little sad to be saying goodbye.

"Fancy coming back next month with me?" he asked, noticing me staring wistfully out of the window.

"Really? We could do that?"

"Of course, this is my home Jemma, it could be yours too if you wanted" he said sounding hopeful.

I watched him for a second, unable to speak. How on earth did I get so lucky? I reached out to take his hand. "Thank you, I'd love that."

"Stop thanking me" he said gently. "If we're going to do this, we are going to be partners, what's mine is yours and I don't want you to thank me every time we do something, okay?"

"Okay. But you do realise I can't offer you anything like this in return, right?" I said feeling guilty.

"You've already given me more than I could ever offer you" he smiled.

"I don't think that's strictly true" I smiled back.

"It is Jemma, it is," he replied stroking my hand.

The plane landed into Heathrow five minutes ahead of schedule, much to the delight of the flight crew who proudly announced their achievement over the PA system, as if they had singlehandedly brought a newborn baby into the world. Jake had already turned his phone back on and was answering emails as we taxied to our gate. Part of me did not want him to slip back into work mode just yet, wanting to cling instead to the memory of how we had been the past couple of days.

"Sorry" he said apologetically, as he looked up from his phone, noticing me staring at him.

"Don't be silly, we can't avoid reality forever" I smiled weakly.

"Stay with me tonight" he asked, "Give me something to look forward to?"

"I'd love to" I replied. "Now go and take over the world Mr Bales" I smiled, pointing back at his phone.

"I love you."

"I love you too Jake."

❖ ❖ ❖

Had I known what was going to happen, I would have taken more time to tell him how much I loved him, I would not have thrown those four words out into the universe without giving them an accompanying explanation. But hindsight is a wonderful thing. Grabbing my bag from under the seat, I took my phone out and switched it on. As it sprang to life, countless messages came flooding through, the buzzing sounding angrier with each new one.

"Jeez!"

"Someone's popular" Jake mused, looking over.

"It's the girls" I answered, starting to open them up.

"What do they want?"

"I don't know, they just said to call them."

"Perhaps they're just making sure I haven't murdered you" he smiled.

"More than likely" I replied, but something inside me was telling me that was not what they were trying to get hold of me for. Each message I opened sounded slightly more frantic than the last, and although there was no bad news in any of them, I got the distinct impression that bad news was indeed the reason behind them. As soon as we got inside the terminal building, I called Claire.

"Where the fuck are you?" she cried inconsolably. The sound of her voice made me instantly panic. It was so unlike her to be overly emotional. Jake looked at me concerned; hearing her on the other end of the line.

"I've just landed. What's wrong darling?" I tried soothing her.

"I thought you were coming back this morning; I've been calling and calling you!" she wailed uncontrollably, sounding manic.

"Claire, ... breathe, ... tell me what's happened?" I begged, my phone shaking in my hand. Jake put his arm around me, trying to steady me.

"There's been an accident" she howled like a child in pain.

"What accident, are you hurt? Claire, you need to breathe darling, I can't understand what you're saying" I pleaded, my heartbeat racing, resisting the urge to cry myself.

"It's Ben, he's been in an accident Jemma, and I don't know if he's going to make it" she sobbed, trying hard to slow down her speech.

My brain could not comprehend what she was telling me. "What do you mean he might not make it?" I was now the one shouting, blind panic sweeping over me in waves. "Claire, what the hell has happened?" Other passengers in the queue for passport control looked on with curiosity.

"I don't really know. I can't get the doctors to tell me anything" she wept. She sounded petrified.

"Where's Sarah? Is she with you?" I asked as I stormed through security towards the baggage hall, hoping she was with her.

"She's on her way. She was in a meeting; I couldn't get hold of her either. I couldn't get hold of anyone" she added "I don't know what to do Jemma. It's bad. Really bad."

"Stay where you are, I'm on my way" I reassured her. I turned to Jake, fear in my voice. "How long will it take us to get back home."

"About an hour" he said, hurriedly grabbing our bags from the conveyor belt and lifting them on to a trolley.

"I'll be back in an hour" I said relaying the message to Claire. "Whereabouts are you darling?"

"St. Mary's" she whimpered.

"Okay, stay where you are, I'll get there as soon as I can."

"Okay. Please hurry" she begged.

"I will. I'm so sorry Claire. I should have been there with you." Wracked with guilt, I put the phone down and stared at Jake, broken, scared, and incapable of doing anything other than allowing tears to free flow down my face. So, this is where the Turkish Delight had been lurking. Fuck.

Jake took me straight to the hospital, driving through the streets of London like a man possessed. I could not tell you how we got there or how long it took, everything was a blur, like watching an action scene from a movie in slow motion. All I could think about was what if he did not make it? What if I never saw him alive again? What if I never got the chance to hear his voice again? What if I never found out what he wanted to speak to me about the other night? Over and over, the thoughts rampaged through my head until I was exhausted. A couple of hours ago I had been happier than I had ever been, and now my world was falling apart before my very eyes.

"Jemma, we're here" Jake said softly. "I'll go and park the car up and follow you up in a minute."

I turned to look at him, snapping out of the trance I had been in. "Thank you" I whispered.

"He's going to be okay Jemma" he added reassuringly, holding my face in his hands.

"Yeah" I agreed half-heartedly.

"I'll be back in a minute" he said as I opened the door.

"God, no!" I exclaimed, my brain suddenly coming back into focus. "You've got Geoff Thompson coming in at 3pm! What time is it?"

"Don't worry about that, I'll cancel it."

"No, you can't! Head back to the office now, call Erin on the way and tell her to let them know you'll be half an hour late. Say the flight was delayed or something."

"I don't want to leave you, not like this, you're upset."

"I'll be okay, there's not going to be much any of us can do" I said trying to convince him. "You need to be there for this meeting Jake, it's important" I smiled.

"You're more important to me than any meeting."

"I know, but I'll be okay. Maybe you could pick me up from mine later?"

"Are you sure, you don't want me to stay?"

"I'm sure, you go. We'll see each other later."

"Okay but call me if you need me. I'll have my phone on me. I can leave whenever."

"Okay." As his car left I turned to the entrance of the hospital and stumbled inside feeling afraid. Having him by my side had obviously kept me calmer than I realised. I scouted the board in the foyer for directions to the ICU and walked absentmindedly, following the yellow circle symbols which lead the way. When I reached the entrance to the ward, I rang the bell hesitantly and waited for someone to let me in. A kind, elderly looking woman in a dark blue nurse's uniform opened the door.

"Hi, I'm here to see Ben Angolino" I said in a tiny voice.

"Are you family dear?" she asked.

"Er, yes, I'm his sister" I replied, the lie coming out easier than it should have.

"Of course, come in my love. Your other sister is already here" she smiled. Her softly spoken words and her caring manner caused a tear to fall down my cheek. It must be bad if they put the nice nurses on this ward, I thought to myself.

"We've had to put him an in induced coma" she said gently, placing a tubby hand on my shoulder "Don't be alarmed by all of the tubes, they are there to help him." As we rounded the corner, she pointed me in the direction of a room leaving me to walk the last few yards alone. I could see Claire sitting in a chair by the side of his bed, her head in her hands. As soon as she saw me, she came bounding over.

"Oh, thank God!" she sobbed, her chest heaving in and out at a rate of knots. She was struggling to catch her breath.

"It's going to be alright" I said, calmly, my words belying the fear I felt inside. "Let me get you a cuppa" I added, "You're shaking darling." I sat her back in the chair, and without so much as glancing in Ben's direction, left again to find a coffee machine. Perhaps if I did not look at him, I could convince myself for a bit longer that this was not really happening. I returned with two cups of tea, handing one to her and placing one down on the side table in the room. She had pulled over another chair so that we could both sit next to him. I did not know how to tell her that I could not sit down, that if I did, I might throw up, that it might cause me to breakdown and that if I started crying, I might not be able to stop, that what I really wanted to do was run out of this place and get as far away from here as I could. But then I inadvertently looked at Ben, at his lifeless body laying silently in the bed next to us, an army of machines and tubes around him, their beeping a reminder that he was here, but utterly broken. And suddenly the only thing I felt was overwhelming love, and a need to be by his side. How could I leave him now? I took up the chair next to Claire, resting my hand on Ben's, trying to avoid the canula protruding from it.

"Hello, my angel" I said softly, my thumb stroking his pallid skin. "You look like you've been in the wars" I added as the tears streaked down my face. "You couldn't have waited til I got back to do something stupid?" I smiled weakly. "I guess you always were one for a big gesture, but you didn't have to go this far to get me back home" I joked. "I was on my way back anyway, so you could have saved yourself the trouble." The last few words were punctuated with silent tears. Claire put her arm around me, as the flood gates opened, and I sobbed into her chest.

"It's okay" she said, "You're here now, that's all that matters."

"Where's his mum and dad? Do they know?" I asked panicking, lifting my head from her now soggy jumper.

"Shh, yes, yes, they know" she soothed. "They were the ones who called me. They've been on holiday in Cyprus. The police called them first thing this morning. They've managed to get on a flight later today but probably won't be here until the tomorrow. Jemma, I only saw him this morning, how can he have been okay just a few hours ago and now be laying there like this?" she said bewildered.

"I don't know darling; I just don't know. All we can do is be here for him. He's going to need our help more than ever when he wakes up."

"He is going to wake up Jemma, isn't he?" The sound of uncertainty in her voice was palpable.

"Course he is, he's a fighter. He'll be up and running again in no time." But as I looked at his shattered body, part of me questioned whether that would be the case. He seemed so much smaller laying there, and so very fragile. His usual olive skin looked abnormally pale and clammy. It was as if the life had already left his body. I shuddered at the very thought of it. He could not leave us. We had not had enough time. I had not had a chance to say everything I needed to say.

"Good afternoon." A tall, middle-aged doctor entered the room with a clipboard.

"Good afternoon doctor."

"Your brother has been very lucky" he smiled gently, walking over to the set of machines on the other side of the bed to check them.

"What happened to him?" I asked.

"He's been involved in a road traffic accident. I believe, he was hit by a van whilst crossing the road" he added.

"What injuries has he suffered?" There were a million things I wanted to know but there was only a few that he could help me with.

"He's suffering from substantial internal bleeding, both his lungs were punctured, his spleen was ruptured, and there is evidence of swelling on his brain which is why we took the decision to put him in the induced coma. We need to reduce the swelling first before we can think about bringing him back round."

"He doesn't sound very lucky to me" I said, not really intending for anyone to hear.

"Most people wouldn't have made it this far" he smiled, as if that should make us feel any better.

"How long will it take for the swelling to go down?" Claire asked.

"It's too early to say at this stage. He's been in a big accident. We need to monitor him for a while before we know any more."

"Doctor, what are his chances?" she asked again.

"The next twenty-four hours are critical" he said, clearly reticent to put a figure on things.

"Okay, thank you."

Half an hour later Sarah rushed in through the door.

"Oh, dear God!" she gasped, taking one look at Ben, before skirting round the bed and throwing her arms around us.

"Were they okay letting you in?" Claire asked. "I thought it was a maximum of two visitors at a time?"

"I told them I was his sister" she smiled, already knowing that we had said the same thing. The three of us burst into fits of uncontrollable laughter, welcoming the momentary distraction. "He would have done the same had it been one of us laying here" she added, still laughing, none of us feeling guilty about the lie we had all told. "We might need to give his mum and dad a heads up that they've gained three extra kids though" she chortled.

It was so good to have her here. With the four of us altogether again, things did not seem quite so scary. We grabbed a third chair from a room next door and sat there talking for the next four hours. Filling each other in on what had happened over the past few days. It was comforting to think that even though he was not participating in the conversation, he might be listening in, mentally raising an eyebrow, or shaking his head in the way he usually did when we had our girlie chats. At 7pm the nurses changed shifts. Sue, the sweet nurse who let me in came in to say goodbye. "I'm off now ladies but I'll be back in the morning. Why don't you head home too and try and get some rest? Nothing much will happen this evening, and you can leave your numbers with the girls on the desk in case they need to get hold of you. It has been a long day, you need to pace yourselves, he might be here for some time" she said solemnly.

"Thank you, maybe we will. We can grab some things for him from home to bring back tomorrow" Sarah smiled.

"That's a good idea. See you tomorrow" she called as she left the room.

"I'm not sure I can leave him. I don't want him to be alone if he wakes up." Tears trickled down my face again. "I wasn't here" I trailed off. Guilt returned to me in waves. The truth of it, battering me from the inside out. I was not there when he needed me the most. This man would have stood beside me through everything, and I was not there for him.

"Darling, he's not going to wake up, not yet anyway, you heard the doctor. We have to take solace in the fact that he is in the best place, and that they are doing all they can for him. We will come back first thing. We will be no good to him if we don't get any sleep. He won't even know that you're not here." Sarah placed her hand around my shoulders and pulled me into her.

"Okay." The word barely made it out my mouth.

Claire joined the hug too "Sarah's right Hun. There's nothing we can do. Let's go home, get some of his things together, get a shower and a few hours kip and then come back. We're no good to anyone if we're exhausted."

I leant over the bed and kissed his forehead. His skin was warm to the touch, but his body was lifeless. "Sleep well my darling, I'll be back in the morning. Don't go doing anything daft while I'm gone."

Claire had moved to the other side of the bed and was stroking his face, her eyes full of yet more unshed tears "See you later bro."

"Yeah, see you tomorrow honey" added Sarah.

None of us could face getting on the tube or being surrounded by people, so we hailed a cab from outside the entrance and sat in silence as it crawled painstakingly through the stagnant evening traffic. When we finally made it back, we trudged inside discarding our coats and bags in the hallway and headed straight for the kitchen. Claire grabbed three clean wine glasses (a miracle, given that nobody had washed the dishes in what looked like days), and free poured a bottle of white wine equally between them.

"What a fucking day" she exclaimed, sliding onto a bar stool, and placing them in front of us.

"You can say that again. I just don't get it. How the hell did he get run over? It just doesn't make sense, he's the most safety conscious one out of all of us. If you were to put money on anyone getting hit by a car it would be you Claire, not him" I smiled weakly.

Completely unoffended by my comment she smiled. "Tell me about it! What's worse, is that his mum said the police told her that the guy who hit him is accusing Ben of walking straight out in front of him. He's denying all responsibility!"

Rage boiled inside of me. "Seriously, what the hell? I hope they lock him up and throw away the key" I said seething, taking a gulp of my wine.

"Apparently, they're not going to charge him with anything until they can speak to Ben."

"And what if he doesn't fucking wake up?" I screamed, unable to contain my fury. "Then what, he gets off fucking free?"

The girls flinched. "He's going to wake up Jem" Sarah said teary eyed, wrapping her arms around me. "You wait and see. He just needs a bit of time."

"But what if he doesn't?" I asked meekly, needing more reassurance.

Claire took a long slug from her glass, then moved in to join the hug. "We will deal with whatever happens the way we always do – together."

"But it won't be the same without him." I could not even imagine a life without Ben, he had always been there, constant, present, unfaltering. How could I live without him?

"We can't think like that, we've got to stay strong for him, he's going to need us" she insisted.

In times of trouble, she was always the one to take on the role of mother, to keep the group together, reminding us that we were stronger together than we were apart. But the responsibility of doing so this time, looked like a dead weight around her shoulders. She may have been preaching about staying positive, but the fight seemed to have disappeared from her eyes. She looked as lost and as scared as we did.

"Right, now come on, I thought you were seeing Jake again this evening? He can't see you looking like this!" she said, in a forced cheery voice.

"It's okay, I text him on the way home asking if we could cancel. I'm going to go and get a bag of stuff together to take back to the hospital in the morning and then I'm heading straight to bed" I said sliding off my stool whilst knocking back the last of my wine.

"I'm going to head up too" Sarah yawned.

Claire did not move. "What about you, you coming up yet?"

"Not yet, I'm too wired to sleep. I'm gonna have another glass or six of wine and put the TV on for a bit. I'll be up soon though, don't worry about me."

"Okay, but don't be too late, you've been through a lot today" I reminded her.

"I know, I'm fine though" she smiled hesitantly. If she had heard how she sounded on the phone earlier, she would know that she had not sounded fine at all, on the contrary, she sounded like a woman on the edge, but I could tell she did not want to be pressed on the matter, so I headed upstairs.

◆ ◆ ◆

Ben's room was as it always was, a vision of organised chaos. How he managed to find anything in there was beyond me. Piles of clean clothes sat next to mounds of dirty ones, paperwork covered the entire surface of his desk, apart from a tiny, uncluttered area on which stood a picture of the four of us. It looked as if he had thrown a grenade in and quickly shut the door on the aftermath. It felt like he should be walking back in any minute to clean up the debris. And then the realisation that he might not walk back in at all hit me like a tsunami. I sat on the edge of his bed, my legs suddenly unable to take my weight, buckling beneath me. He had to come back, he just had to. How could I carry on without him? I hated myself for being so selfish, but in that moment, I was consumed by my own pain and fear. My chest ached; my arms felt like lead weights and my head was pounding. All I wanted to do was get under the covers and wrap myself in his duvet. To feel close to him.

"Pull yourself together!" I told myself tersely. "This isn't helping anyone." I reminded myself of what mum used to say, "The best thing to do in a crisis is keep busy." The thought of doing anything other than just trying to cope seemed mind blowing, but I was prepared to test her theory. If Ben woke up tomorrow, the first thing he would want to do is have a shave because he hated having a 5 o'clock shadow. He would also want to have a wash and brush his teeth, so I went to the bathroom to grab his shaving gear, shower gel, toothbrush, and toothpaste. I would grab a fresh towel and flannel from the airing cupboard at the end. As much as he was a bit of a slob when it came to his room, he was fastidious about his personal hygiene. He would need clean underwear, some fresh pyjamas, hairbrush and most importantly, his earbuds (he was currently going through a bit of a rock phase and was listening to Oasis on repeat). I pulled his sports holdall from the wardrobe and started putting in the things I had collected. All I needed now were some clean pants and socks. I sifted through the top drawer, wondering whether white or black boxers would be more appropriate, eventually deciding that he would not give a shit which colour I brought, then rooted around for some socks. And that is when I found it. The letter. Hidden under a pile of black ankle socks.

I have always believed that life is punctuated by a series of pivotal moments. Moments which cause you to question or challenge everything you know. Moments which can alter the trajectory you are travelling in. Moments so powerful, that they change the way you view the world forever. As I ran my fingers over the crisp, white envelope addressed to me in Ben's hand, I genuinely had no idea that this was one of those moments. Had I known, I would have made the decision not to open it and chosen instead, to live in blissful ignorance of what was written inside. But without the benefit of hindsight, or x-ray vision, I cautiously peeled back the flap of the envelope. Nothing could have prepared me for what was inside.

*My Dearest Jem,*

*If you are reading this, then I am gone. Know that my heart is breaking as I sit here writing these words. I will forever regret not having had the courage to say this in person, instead, choosing to hide behind a pen and paper to express what truly lies within my heart. My only hope is that one day, you find it in within yours to forgive me. If not, maybe you can at least learn to understand why it had to be this way. The thought of you hating me tears me apart, so much so, that I would rather leave you than witness it. I wish I had been braver; I wish desperately that I'd had the courage to tell you how I felt, but the truth is, I was scared. So scared that if I did, and you pushed me away, there would be no way back for us. Deep down, I guess I always knew that I would end up telling you like this.*

*The truth is Jemma, I am in love with you. Always have been, always will be. I have loved you from the moment we first met, and I will love you until the sun stops shining and there are no more tomorrows. You have and always will hold my heart. There has only ever been you.*

*It has been my privilege to watch you grow and blossom from a shy and inquisitive girl, into the amazing woman you are today, and I will cherish every moment we have shared and every memory we have made together. My life has been blessed because you were a part of it.*

*I have only ever wanted the best for you, to care for you and protect you. After all, you are the most precious thing in my life. These past few days I have seen a side to you that I have not witnessed before. You have come alive, radiated light, your heart has blossomed, and I know why that it is. You love him. Love him the way that I love you. Love him in a way that now I know, you can never love me back. And that's okay, things are as they should be, I know that now. Love is not selfish, it's patient and kind, and I want you to know a love like that. But as much as I want that for you, I can't carry on pretending that it doesn't kill me every time you say his name or stop myself from wishing that it was me you spoke about the way you do him. I'm not a jealous man, but I can't watch you give your heart to someone else. I would give everything to be the one to hold you at night, the one to make love to you, the one you look at as if I am the only person in the room, the one you plan a life with, a family with. But I think you've found that guy, and he isn't me.*

*If being with Jake makes you as happy as I believe it does, then that gives me great comfort. You deserve a life full of joy and happiness, to have someone treat you the way you deserve to be treated, to love you unconditionally the way you deserve to be loved. You deserve the world Jemma, make sure he gives it to you!*

*Please don't think of this as goodbye, think of it more as farewell. I go knowing that you are left in safe hands and that you will thrive in his care. But know this, you will always hold my heart, and whatever happens, I will always love you. Until we meet again…*

*Yours forever, Ben xx*

A river of tears ran down my cheeks, my eyes so full of unshed ones I could barely see. "What have you done?" I whispered. I held the letter to my chest, hugging it so tightly, hoping that I might physically be able to make it disappear. It was all too much; I was gradually losing my grip on things. The ground was crumbling beneath my feet, threatening to take me under. This did not make sense. None of it made any sense. A maniacal howl escaped my lips, the sound wild and terrifying. He would not do this, would he? He would not do this… to me? Claire burst in through the door; a look of shear panic plastered across her weary face.

"Jem, what's wrong?" Her eyes stumbled across the letter. "What's that?" she asked coming towards me.

My hands were trembling. "It's from him" I whimpered, using the cuff of my sleeve to mop up the tears which showed no sign of abating. I handed the note to her as she took a seat next to me on the bed, watching intently as she read and re-read the contents of Ben's letter. A tear trickled down the side of her face, as the realisation of what she was reading hit her.

"Jem," she said reluctantly, not taking her eyes of the piece of paper, "Was it an accident?"

I nodded. "I don't think so, and it's all my fault" I wailed, my chest heaving in and out, trying desperately to catch a breath. She held me in her arms tightly. Every time a fresh wave of terror crashed over me, she held me steady, wiping the tears away like a parent consoling a child. All night she tried reassuring me that none of this was my fault, that there must be some mistake, but in my heart, I knew that she was wrong. Ben was laying in hospital and had tried to kill himself because of me. If Claire was honest, she would think that too.

# TUESDAY

Morning came around all too quickly, neither of us getting more than thirty minutes of sleep. The bed smelt of him. Every time I rolled over or pulled the cover up to my face, I could see him as clear as day, hear him like he was right beside me. And then I remembered that he was not, and I remembered the letter, was reminded of what he had told me, saw him laying lifelessly in that hospital bed, and the tears would start again.

"Here you go darling, drink this." Sarah had only just found out about Ben's letter, having slept through our discovery last night. I stared at her mutely as she handed me the cup of coffee, a look of abject pity etched on her pretty face. If I looked half as deathly as I felt, the look was undoubtedly warranted, but it was unwelcomed none the less. I did not deserve anyone's pity. I cupped the mug in my hands, the burn from the hot liquid inside penetrating my pale skin, the pain a welcome relief from the nothingness which was all consuming. It was as if I had woken to a world shrouded in a suffocating grey fog. There seemed to be no respite from the emptiness I felt. My tears all dried up; my body left exhausted.

I sat numbly under the duvet, silently repeating the same questions in my head. Why? How? How did I not know how he was feeling? Why did he feel he could not talk to me? And then the gut-wrenching realisation that he had tried to talk to me. Saturday night. The drunken phone call. Had he been attempting to tell me how he was feeling then, and all I had done was send him away knowing that I was having the time of my life. Had I acted differently, could I have stopped this from happening? Deep, deep down, did I know that he was in love with me? Everyone else around me seemed to. Myriad questions raced through my mind, but not one solitary answer presented itself. All I knew was that it was all my fault, and if Ben did not pull through, I would have to live with that for the rest of my life. I shifted in the bed, the burning sensation on my hands suddenly too uncomfortable to bear. How could I have let this happen?

"Bathroom's free." Claire popped her head round the door. A silent exchange of words between her and Sarah ensued, both looking pointedly at each other and then over at me, the same pitiful expression on their faces. "I'm going to quickly dry my hair and get dressed and then thought we could get a cab to the hospital about 9am. I've called work and told them we won't be in today."

"Huh?" I asked through glazed eyes. It was all too much to take in.

She ventured further into the room. "I said I've called work and told them we won't be in today. We can get a cab to see Ben in a bit if you want? Jemma... are you okay?" She looked concerned.

"Er... yeah okay" I replied absentmindedly. It felt as if the world was still spinning but I was stuck still. Surely, everything had stopped? How could the world carry on as normal when our lives had fallen apart?

"Oh, and Jake's been trying to get hold of you. He asked if you would call him back." Jake. I had completely forgotten about him. Claire must have seen and understood the look on my face because she added "It's okay, he knows you've had a lot going on, he just wanted to know you were alright." Yet more guilt ripped through me. How could I have forgotten all about him. After we had spent the past week together declaring our love for each other. What kind of person was I? I slumped back against the pillow. I did not deserve either of them. I rolled over and picked up my phone from the bedside table.

"Hi" I managed as the line connected and Jake's voice sounded at the other end.

"Hey, you" he said cautiously. "How are you doing?"

My voice was hoarse from all the crying. "I'm okay. I'm so sorry I haven't called you."

"Don't apologise, I knew you were going to be busy. How is he?" He sounded genuinely concerned.

"We don't know yet. We're heading back to the hospital in a bit, so hopefully we'll know more shortly."

"How about you? How are you really?" His voice sounded strained. This wasn't like the easy, free-flowing conversations we were used to having. "You don't sound okay Jemma" he added, sounding worried.

I could not bring myself to tell him about the note, to say that Ben's apparent accident was looking suspiciously less accident like now, and that it was all because of me. That he had been right about how Ben felt about me. Instead, I opted for the safer option.

"Honestly, I'm fine, I'm just tired."

"Jemma, please, let me help you. You don't have to do this alone" he implored. The concern in his voice only amplified my resolve to save him further pain. I would only hurt him at some point, better to get it out the way now. What if I did the same to him as I had done to Ben? What if I hurt him so badly that he could not see a way back and did something stupid too? I could not do that to him. He had been through so much already. He needed to be free of me, and right now, I needed to be here for Ben.

"I'm not alone, I have the girls." I knew I had wounded him as soon as the words left my mouth, and I felt terrible. I wanted nothing more than to rewind the clock forty-eight hours, to go back to laying in his arms where I had felt safe and loved. But if

I had learnt anything in life, it was that you could not turn back time, you just had to roll with the punches, take whatever the day had to throw at you. The fact that the last couple of days had thrown more at me than I knew how to cope with, was neither here nor there, I had to do the right thing, even if every fibre of my being was telling me it was the exact opposite. I had to do what was best for him.

"Jake, I can't do this."

"Do what?" his voice sounded suddenly panicked.

I pulled my hand through my matted hair. "This. Us. I can't do us."

"Jemma, slow down, what do you mean you can't 'do' us?"

I could feel my heart pounding against my chest, the panic was setting in again. "I can't be with you."

"What's happened? What's changed since yesterday?" He sounded confused. He was not listening to me. Could he not see that I was just trying to do the right thing? I guess not, given that I had given him no warning and no explanation for my decision.

"Jemma stop for a second, for fucks sake, tell me what's going on!" His confusion was tinged with agitation now.

"It's just best if we keep things as they were. I... I can't be with anyone right now. I'm sorry." The words stung like a fresh cut against my skin. I did not believe what I was telling him, how could I when my heart ached for him? All I wanted was for him to hold me, to wrap me in his arms and tell me everything was going to be okay. But it was not going to be okay, was it? It was never going to be okay, and I could not drag him into the mess I had created.

"Jemma, please" he begged. "Don't do this, you don't mean what you're saying. You're upset and I get that, you're close to Ben, you have every right to be worried, but don't do this, don't give up on us before it's even started. Let me come over and we can talk about this." He was pleading with me, sounding like a frightened child, and it was ripping me in two knowing that I was the one causing his pain. If only he knew the truth of what I had done. It felt like a knife was being twisted in my chest. I could not breathe. I had to stay strong though. If I broke now, I would not have the strength to see this through.

"No. I'm going to the hospital. Please, just do as I ask" I said in a voice devoid of all emotion. "Just accept my decision, Jake… I'm doing this for you." I added unexpectedly, hoping he would see that I really was thinking only of him.

"Like fuck you are!" he bellowed. "You're not doing this for me, you're doing it for you, because you're scared, and you're hurting. I love you Jemma, and I'm begging you, if you feel anything for me, please, please, don't do this."

"I can't. I'm so sorry Jake." I put the phone down, the last ounce of strength fleeing me as the line went dead. I had nothing left to give. To Ben, to him, to anyone.

"He's right you know; you don't have to go through this on your own" Claire said, taking up a seat next to me. "We're all here to help. Do you think shutting him out was the right decision?" Her tone was caring rather than accusatory.

"It's for his own good" I whispered; my eyes full of tears. "He'd only end up getting hurt like Ben. I'm bad news, he'll see that and realise he's had a lucky escape."

"He's a grown man, I think he knows what he's getting himself into. I just don't want you to do something you'll regret later down the line. You seemed so happy together." Her face crumpled and a tear made its way slowly down her cheek. "What has happened is nobody's fault Jemma, and if Ben were awake now, he would hate to see you like this. He never would have wanted to see you this way. You can't throw your own happiness away because of it."

"How can I think about my own happiness when Ben might die?"

She took my hands in hers. 'Jemma… there is every chance that he won't die, and if he doesn't, you will have thrown everything away for no reason. His letter said it gave him comfort to know that you were with someone who loved you. You have to believe that. There is enough pain and suffering in this world as it is, you have to grab love and happiness wherever you can find it. And I know that you found it with Jake, I saw it in the way you looked at each other. That kind of feeling comes around once in a lifetime if you're lucky. Cherish it, embrace it, run towards it, not away from it. I know you're scared darling, but not feeling anything is not going to protect you from pain. It will only hurt you more, and I'm quite sure he feels the same way. He would walk over burning coals for you, you aren't protecting him by keeping the truth from him, you're hurting him. He will want to be with you regardless."

She did not understand. "But if Ben wakes up, it will look like I chose Jake over him. I've known him my whole life, Claire. How do you choose between two people who mean everything to you? It's an impossible choice to make."

Her eyes softened in pity. "But if he wakes up and you've chosen him, he'll know you're only there because of what happened. He wouldn't want that either. He would want you to choose him because you felt the same way about him as you do about Jake. And you don't darling, and there's nothing wrong with that." She wrapped me tightly in her arms. "Life is full of impossible choices. Listen to your heart and let that guide you rather than your head. Trust me, no good decisions were ever made with the head.

"Perhaps not" I mused. "But I don't think he will ever talk to me again, after what I just did."

"Don't bet on it. He's crazy about you. Give him some time. He'll be back."

I crumpled at the thought of not seeing him again, of not hearing his voice, of not feeling his body against mine. How had he become so vital to me in such a short space of time? "I can't do this Claire, I'm not strong enough."

She squeezed me tighter. "You are, you're stronger than you realise, Jemma. You might feel like you're breaking right now, but you'll come out the other side of this, I promise you."

"I don't feel strong at the moment" I smiled.

"I know, but you'll get through this, and so will Ben, you'll see" she said, leaving the room.

◆ ◆ ◆

Sue the lovely nurse from yesterday was back on the ward when we arrived. "Morning Girls!" she sang. "Your parents are in with your brother, head straight in" she said closing the door to the ward behind her. Claire and I looked at each other and smiled.

"We'd best go say hi to mum and dad!" she winked.

"How was he last night, Sue?" I asked.

"The girls on the night shift said he was peaceful" she said leading us down the corridor. "He's a fighter your brother that's for sure! We'll be taking him for a scan later this morning to see if the swelling on his brain has started to go down, but for now it's a case of keeping him comfortable and giving his body time to heal. He's not out of the woods yet, but the fact that he's hanging on in there is a good sign!" she added cheerily.

She was a gem. It was times like this that you really appreciated what the NHS did. How she could manage a smile and an encouraging word for patients' families, whilst dealing with what she did on a daily basis was beyond my comprehension.

Ben's parents were sitting by the side of his bed. His mum was holding his hand, her eyes red from crying and looking completely broken. His dad had his arm around her and was trying to console her, but he looked equally as distraught. What did I expect, they looked like two people wracked with pain and fear at the thought of losing their child. I froze. I should not be here. I had put him in that bed.

"Girls! come in" she called when she saw us in the doorway. Claire ventured in but I stood rooted to the floor, unable to move. Ben's mum misinterpreted my lack of movement. "I know it's scary seeing him like this Jemma, but it's okay, the doctors say he seems to be responding well" she said suddenly cheery, trying to be overly positive for my benefit. The problem was, I had witnessed how bereft she had been just moments before, she did not really believe that everything was going to be fine. If she knew the truth, if she knew that it was not an accident that had put her son in hospital, she would not want me anywhere near here. Claire looked at me concerned, reading my mind.

"Come on Jem, come and sit next to me" she said motioning to bring a chair over from the other corner of the room. I looked from the chair to the three of them and suddenly had the urge to run. I could not do this.

"I'm sorry, I can't" I whispered, turning on my heels and running from the room. Bile gathered at the back of my throat and tears streamed down my face as I bolted off the ward and out into the hospital corridor, ignoring calls from Claire behind me to come back. I could not stay there; I could not watch his poor parents prepare themselves to lose their only child. No parent should have to do that. And so, I did what I do best, I ran. Out of the hospital, down the road, I did not know where to, I only knew that I had to get far away. I ran until my lungs felt like they were going to burst, eventually collapsing on a park bench when my feet would take me no further. I deserved the pain which radiated through my body. I wanted to feel like this, to feel like I was on fire because I should not go unpunished. I had to pay. Could I not just love him back the way he wanted me to? It was not that I did not love him, I had loved him my whole damn life; if I had known, could we have made things work?

A squat, elderly lady walking with her dog approached the bench, looking at me peculiarly. "My dear, are you ok?"

"Pardon?" I asked, looking up at her from where I was sitting.

"Are you ok dear? Only that was a terrible noise you just made."

I blinked, bewildered. "What noise?" I said staring off into the distance, looking for its real source.

"Do you mind if I have a seat" she asked, gesturing to the spot beside me on the bench, slowly positioning herself, before I could answer.

"Not at all."

She lowered her elderly body gingerly onto the seat, her dog plonking himself down by her feet. "Old age is a wonderful thing and a blessing not everyone gets to experience, but I'll be damned if I can get used to these bloody aches and pains!" she said, smiling, not sounding the least bit moany. "Now," she sighed, wiggling about on the seat to get comfortable. "I don't know much my dear, but I know what pain looks like, and you look like you're riddled with it."

"It's okay," I said vacantly. "I'll be alright in a minute; I just need to catch my breath."

"I'm not talking about physical pain my dear, I'm talking about emotional pain - the pain of the heart."

"Sorry?"

She looked at me for a moment, her kind, pale blue eyes sparkling in the sunlight. "You look like you're suffering dear, and in times of trouble, I always find it's best to talk to someone, a problem shared is a problem halved and all that. Do you have someone you can talk to?"

"I did" I admitted, thinking about Ben and Jake. "But I think I've lost them both."

"Oh, how so?"

Something about her made me want to open up. Was it her sweet face or her caring demeanor, or was it something else? I could not put my finger on it, but whatever it was, it had me wanting to talk. "I've pushed them both away. I wasn't there for them when I should have been, and I said things I shouldn't have said." It was a simplified version of events and did not come close to what had really happened, but she looked at me with such understanding, that I thought she might have seen straight through my sketchy explanation to the truth beneath.

"My dear girl, nobody is lost forever. If you pushed them away, can't you bring them back? Maybe you could start by explaining to them why you did what you did. People are forgiving by their very nature. There is nothing that can't be resolved with a little talking, you'll see" she smiled, bumping my shoulder with hers.

"I don't know. I've hurt them both in different ways, I don't know if there is a way back from that."

She squeezed my leg gently. "That may be the case, but you won't know unless you try. They should at least be given the chance to know why you did what you did, and be given the opportunity to decide if they want to forgive you, no? They're obviously important to you if you are this upset over it, and I'd hazard a guess that you are just as important to them."

"They are important to me" I smiled. "I love them with all my heart."

"Then my dear …" she said slowly getting to her feet. "You should go to them. But think hard about who you go to first. The world needs more love. If he loves you half as much as you love him, he won't push you away. The other one will understand. There's no shame in coming second."

I watched her blue eyes twinkle in the sunlight. "How did you know?"

She smiled brightly. "Our hearts are capable of loving more than one person my dear, but only one person can own it. Avoiding the call of the heart is futile" she chuckled knowingly as she ambled away without saying goodbye, her little companion trotting behind her to keep up, her white hair swaying in the breeze. A gust of wind blew through the park, disturbing the leaves in the trees, and as quickly as she appeared she was gone. Vanished into thin air as if she had never been there at all. Had I imagined the whole thing? Was I going mad? She had seemed so real.

◆ ◆ ◆

It was just gone twelve when I exited the cab and hurried into the building. Only a few stragglers loitered in the foyer, the majority of people still safely locked away in their offices, waiting for the release of lunchtime. I pressed for the lift and was relieved when the doors instantly opened and nobody else was inside. I quickly hit the button for the twenty second floor, knowing that if I thought too much about what I was about to do, I might never be able to go through with it. The journey up through the floors seemed to take an age, and I wondered if perhaps the lift was offering me an opportunity to back out. The thought now seemed quite appealing. But before I could nip out at a lower level, the little green light illuminated, and the doors sprung open. Too late. I calculated that if I kept my head down and walked with purpose rather than dawdling, I could make it to my destination unseen and unscathed. The less people that knew I was here the better. I pulled myself up tall and practically darted out of the lift in the direction of his office.

"Oh, Hi Jemma! I didn't think you and Claire were going to be in today?" called Effie as I rushed past her desk, trying to avoid eye contact. Helene looked up from her computer, alerted to my presence.

"What are you doing here? Jake said there'd been an accident." Nope, no accident Helene, just a complete emotional breakdown, two relationships in tatters and a failed suicide attempt, I replied in my head as I passed by her desk, ignoring her too. His office was mere feet away.

"Jemma, he's with…" she called from her seat, but I was not

listening. I banged on the door and entered before he could respond, scared that he might not let me in if he knew who it was. As I barged in through the door, a mixture of panic, fear and relief swept over me. My knees knocked, and my well-rehearsed speech neglected me.

"Jake!" I blurted in a crazed, demonic sounding voice. He stared at me in disbelief, his eyes round like saucers. For a second, all I saw was him, but then I sensed someone move off to the right of me. That is when I started to take in the bigger picture. Jake at his desk, Geoff Thomspon, Andrea, and a few of the guys from the other day sitting opposite him on the sofa and chairs. All of them gawping at me in fascination.

"Jemma?" Jake looked just as shocked by my presence as I did about gate crashing his meeting.

"I'm so sorry! Please accept my apologies" I said in Mr Thompson's direction and quickly retreated.

"Jemma, wait!" Jake called as I abruptly pulled the door to and headed back towards the lift flustered, my mind racing, my plan in tatters. Why is it that when you need to make a quick escape, lifts suddenly decide to stop at each floor? *Perhaps, that's why burglars always take the stairs?*

"Come on, come on!" I begged. Seventeen, eighteen, nineteen. "Oh, sweet baby Jesus, will you hurry the fuck up!" I said more desperately, my hands repeatedly hitting the button to call the lift. I heard a door behind me open and close.

"Jemma!" *Oh shit, oh shit, oh shit. Someone kill me now.* Still no lift. Twenty, twenty-one. "Jemma!" This time he shouted my name across the floor so loudly that I could not pretend that I had not heard him. I turned slowly on the spot, tens of pairs of eyes peaked over the office dividers to witness what was unfolding. Jake strode purposefully towards me, ignoring the interest we were receiving. My heart was lodged somewhere in my throat. He looked beautiful (and slightly menacing). I doubted that I had looked so enigmatic when I had tried to do the same thing just minutes before. "For God's sake stop running from me!" he barked, clearly not concerned that anyone was listening. As he got closer, I could see the features of his face more clearly. His beautiful dark eyes looked sunken and tired, his tanned skin was unshaven, a shadow cast over his jaw, and I was pretty certain that he was in the same clothes he had worn yesterday. And yet there was no anger in his eyes.

"Hi." It was barely audible.

"Hi" he smiled, his voice warm and comforting. It was my undoing. I wanted to hold him and be held by him. I had missed him. The little old lady from the park was right. My heart was calling for him. I could no longer pretend that I did not want him, did not need him. I needed him more than air.

He stepped closer, seemingly able to read my thoughts. "It's all my fault!" I whimpered as he gathered me up in his arms, his touch a soothing balm, dampening the flames of fear which were threatening to take me over.

"Shh…" he whispered, his face in my hair. "Shh… It's all right, everything's going to be all right."

"No, it's not" I mumbled into his chest.

"It is Jemma, I promise you it is. I love you and I will do everything I can to make things right for you" he breathed, stroking my hair.

"You don't understand Jake…" I paused not sure if I was able to continue.

"Then make me understand" he said looking me directly in the eyes, pleading with me. I was silent, wanting to take in exactly how he looked in case he left me after I explained and I never got another opportunity to look into those beautiful eyes again. "Please, Jemma" he begged. "Make me understand."

I buried my head back into his chest, unable to look at him whilst I made my confession.

"You were right" I sighed. "You were right about everything."

"What do you mean I was right?"

"About Ben being in love with me." I expected some kind of reaction. A fist pump, an "I fucking knew it" even, but he remained silent, encouraging me to continue. "When we got back from the hospital yesterday, I found a note...." I could feel my heart racing. This was harder than I expected. Saying the words aloud made them real, impossible to ignore.

"Go on..."

"It said...." the words would not come out.

"What? What did it say?"

"I... I don't think it was an... accident." There, I said it. It was strangely liberating, although my heart broke at the sound of the words. "He said he couldn't watch me be in love with you..." I sobbed. "That's why I told you I couldn't be with you. It's all my fault. He tried to kill himself because of me!"

"Oh, my angel. This is not your fault. This is one hundred per cent not your fault. Are you sure it wasn't an accident?"

"As sure as I can be. The note was pretty clear."

"Listen to me, whatever the reasoning behind it, he made a choice Jemma. You can't be responsible for other people's choices."

I knew what he was saying was right, but it did not make it any easier. This was Ben, it was not a random stranger. I sobbed again. "I couldn't love him the way he wanted me to Jake, I hurt him, hurt him so badly, he couldn't see another way out. What if I hurt you in the same way. I'm bad news Jake. Good people suffer because of me."

"Now listen to me Jemma Lucas!" he said raising my chin so that I was looking again into those dark, penetrating eyes of his. "I am completely and utterly in love with you, nothing you could do could hurt me more than the thought of losing you. I can't comprehend a life without you in it. I won't. And I will fight anyone and anything that tries to take you away from me. If that means going down to the hospital and punching Ben's lights out when he wakes up, so be it!" His words might have seemed menacing but the boyish grin on his face proved there was no real intent behind them.

"That might not be the best idea given that he's already got a brain injury" I smiled, feeling guilty that we were joking about him whilst he was laying lifeless in a hospital bed. "But I appreciate the sentiment."

"It might not feel like it now, but together we can get through anything. I asked you before if you thought you could trust me...."

"I do!" I interrupted.

"Then let me in. Talk to me. I can't help if I don't know what's going on."

"I thought I was doing the right thing" I answered feebly.

"Did it feel like the right thing?"

"No."

"Promise me something, Jemma."

"What?"

"That you'll listen to your heart sometimes rather than your head."

"You sound just like Claire!" I sniffled.

"Oh? What did she say?"

"That I should run towards love rather than away from it."

"A sensible suggestion. Is that the reason for you kicking my office door off its hinges and scaring Geoff half to death?"

"Yep" I grinned. "What's he doing here? I thought you saw him yesterday."

"I love it when you smile" he said, running his thumb over the corner of my mouth. "I cancelled the appointment yesterday just in case you needed me to come back and get you. So, tell me" he continued, "What else did Claire say? I'm intrigued."

"She also said that life is full of impossible choices."

"She is a very insightful woman."

I cupped his face in my hands. "Jake, I panicked earlier, and I am so, so sorry. I thought that if I chose you, it meant that I couldn't love Ben, and that is not the case. I can't change the fact that I don't feel for him the way I do about you, even after all these years. I love him deeply, but I am not in love with him. I am in love with you. The thought of losing him terrifies me, but the thought of living without you is incomprehensible. If Ben comes round, I will do everything in my power to make things right. But Jake, if I must make a choice, I choose you. I will always choose you, because I don't want to live without you. I can't." I stared tearfully into his eyes, silently pleading with him to forgive me.

His voice was soft, his eyes holding mine with an intensity that was spellbinding. He held me tightly in his arms, "Jemma, I will never ask you to choose between me and him because I know how important he is to you. All I ask is that you love me." I squeezed him harder. That would be an easy promise to make. "There is nothing I would not do for you Jemma," he continued "No mountain I would not climb. You will be my first choice, my last, and each one in between because I am madly in love you."

"I love you too."

Loud clapping erupted around us. The whole office was on its feet.

"Do you think anyone saw us" Jake whispered before kissing me again.

◆ ◆ ◆

The thing with life, is that time is not infinite. Ben was proof that it could be extinguished in an instant. And whilst we walked the earth naively believing that there would always be a tomorrow and another opportunity to tell someone how much they meant to us, invariably, that was not always the case. When faced with the unenviable task of choosing between him and Jake, I realised, that given the option, I would have chosen not to have lived without either of them. I loved them both equally, if not in different ways. The truth was, I was praying with every fibre of my being that Ben would pull through, so that selfishly, I might be able to have both of them in my life again. If I could have one more day with him, I would tell him how sorry I was that I had failed him. That though I could not be with him in the way he wanted me to be, I would always be by his side as his friend, as part of his family. That just because I had found Jake, it did not diminish the love I had for him, that nothing could do that. Just a chance, that is all I needed. To make him see that there was still every reason to be alive.

But I did not know whether he would survive. I did not know if by being with Jake, I would lose him regardless, or whether if he pulled through, he would even want to be a part of my life again. I knew things could never go back to how they were and that made me sad, but if I listened to my heart, I knew that I had made the right choice. The rest I would just have to figure out along the way.

Forest Gump was right; life really was a box of chocolates, and only God knew what it had in store for me. I sincerely hoped it was a six-foot two sex god and multiple orgasms, but I also knew that I could not live in fear of the unknown. I could not miss out on delicious soft centred caramels because I feared stumbling across something less palatable. As with life, I just had to suck it up, swallow it down, take the good with the bad, and just pray there were not too many Turkish Delights hiding in amongst the good stuff!

THE END